SHRAPNEL™

ISSUE #20   **THE OFFICIAL BATTLETECH MAGAZINE**

SHRAPNEL.

THE OFFICIAL BATTLETECH MAGAZINE

Loren L. Coleman, Publisher
John Helfers, Executive Editor
Philip A. Lee, Managing Editor
David A. Kerber, Layout and Graphic Design

Cover art by Eldon Cowgur
Interior art by Pablo Asche, Jared Blando, Jason Cheesmann-Meyer, Liam Curtner, Mark Hayden, David A. Kerber, Natán Meléndez, Marco Pennacchietti, Matt Plog

Published by Pulse Publishing, under licensing by Catalyst Game Labs
5003 Main St. #110 ▪ Tacoma, WA 98407

Shrapnel: The Official BattleTech Magazine is published four times a year, in Spring, Summer, Fall, and Winter.

Available through your favorite online store (Amazon.com, BN.com, Kobo, iBooks, GooglePlay, etc.).

ISBN: 978-1-63861-208-7

COMMANDER'S CALL

FROM THE EDITOR'S DESK

Sound the alarm and get to your muster station, because there's a British invasion incoming!

As I was putting this issue together, it occurred to me that a few of the new authors in this issue are from the British Isles. I already knew one of my repeat authors on the gaming side of things, Lorcan Nagle, hails from Ireland, but I started counting, and there's a total of *five* authors from Ireland and the UK in this issue! In fact, by a stroke of kismet, I was informed that three of these five are close friends who've been playing *BattleTech* for more than twenty years, and it was only by some quirk of fate that their first *Shrapnel* publications all ended up in the same issue. There's always been a strong legacy of *BattleTech* writers from the British Isles, and I am happy to report that the tradition continues. Must be something in the water over there...

For fiction, let's get the big guns out of the way first: This issue marks the blistering conclusion of Russell Zimmerman's four-part serial novel, *Violent Inception*, and as you can see in that gorgeous cover from Eldon Cowgur, things are about to get dangerous... From our returning authors, we kick off with "Ride a Black Horse," by D. G. P. Rector, whose last turn in the cockpit was the much-lauded story "The Plowshare" from issue #11 (which was featured in the cover art, if you recall); this story sends a Goliath Scorpion Seeker to a Deep Periphery planet with a dangerous secret. Then we head off to the Free Worlds League planet of Paradise, where infamous mercenary commander Ace Darwin takes a much deserved break in James Bixby's "Ace Darwin in Paradise." In "Not Without Sacrifice," Giles Gammage gives us a naval training exercise gone horribly wrong in orbit above the Draconis Combine's temporary capital of New Samarkand. In "Second Exodus," Alayna M. Weathers continues her poetry series with the rise of the Clans from the ashes of the Pentagon Civil War, and finally, Michael A. Stackpole himself brings us another entertaining misadventure of the Death Kangaroos in "A Night to Forget," a gripping look at what it *really* means to be a mercenary. (This is a stand-alone story, but if you'd like to see what the Death Kangaroos are all about and catch up on their previous exploits before you dive into this story, be sure to check out the first two stories, "A Night at the Lake" and "A Night in the Woods," available at your favorite ebook retailers.)

Foremost among the stories for our first-time fiction authors this issue is "Deeper into the Machine," by Lorcan Nagle. Lorcan has been writing *Shrapnel* articles for a while now—issue #12 featured his first—and this story marks his triumphant transition to short fiction. In it, a Republic of the Sphere team shows off a proof-of-concept program for remote-controlled 'Mechs, but the results are not quite what the operators expected… Other first-time authors this issue include Lukasz Furmaniak with "In the End," which follows the pilot of the sole *Rifleman III* prototype during the Star League Defense Force's liberation of Terra; O. J. S. Goodman, with "Hard Targets," where a Hell's Horses Elemental defies the stigma of her Mark of Hell; Bryan Carter, whose "Market Ready" sends us on a roller coaster of a prototype-development disaster involving a short timeline and impossible promises; and finally, Brian F. Kenny's "The Promise," in which a team from the Marik Protectors must follow through on their vow to find and rescue a compatriot lost to the clutches of the Marian Hegemony.

For articles, we have a Voices of the Sphere discussion of how total warfare applies to the modern-day 3150s battlefield; a closer look at hyperpulse generators, the lifeblood of interstellar communications; an after-action report of the Federated Suns' military efforts to mitigate the Palmyra Disaster of 3144; and an investigation of the "free zones" on some Lyran Commonwealth planets where laws are not strictly enforced. Game features include a planet digest for Hean, a world notorious for its poisonous flora and fauna; a unit digest for the Sharpe Redemption, the Special Operations company of the Capellan Confederation's Fifth Sian Dragoons; a technical readout for the Royal *Orion*, the ON1-Kb often piloted by Commanding General Aleksandr Kerensky; an RPG adventure in the aftermath of the Rasalhague Dominion's vote to join the Star League; and a Chaos Campaign scenario set in 3148, where the Wolves-in-Exile seek to exact revenge against the Jade Falcons for the fall of Arc-Royal.

No matter which side of the pond you're from, we'd love to hear from you. If you think you've got what it takes to join the corps of *BattleTech* authors, show us what you got! We're always looking for fresh new voices to feature in the pages of *Shrapnel*!

—PHILIP A. LEE, MANAGING EDITOR

RIDE A BLACK HORSE

D. G. P. RECTOR

MOTE
THE EYES IN THE DARK
ANTI-SPINWARD DEEP PERIPHERY
17 MAY 3110

Beneath red suns in a black sky, the Seeker fought.

It had taken most of a year to reach this place, months of trials before that to secure warriors and equipment for the journey. It had been a long, lonely flight through the half-forgotten stars of the Deep Periphery, hunting what the sacred necrosia had shown him.

The vision was powerful. He had seen a great black horse, eyes blazing red, charging across the sky. Wherever its hooves struck, cities melted to nothingness, like fruit rotting upon the vine. Stony fractal patterns spread in its wake, and on its back was a figure robed in shadow.

Feverish research into the captured archives of the Eridani Light Horse illuminated his vision. Before their conquest by the Goliath Scorpions, they had been revered as one of the greatest fighting forces to descend from the Star League. Their symbol was a black horse, their blood flowed in him, and the Seeker knew that made them the key.

Centuries ago, at the height of the Amaris Civil War, the Eridani had received a secret order to depart for the Deep Periphery. Whatever was here had been something Star League Intelligence trusted only to them; yet, in the chaos of civil war, they had rejected their duty. Now the Seeker would find it, and fulfill the task the Eridani had failed.

He was Suero of the Goliath Scorpions, his BattleMech the mighty *Warhawk*. Together with his Yeomen—Malia in her *Mist Lynx*, Zane in his *Phantom*, and a group of Elementals under Star Commander Norizuchi—they had touched down on this unrecorded world. The

Eyes in the Dark, a binary system never thoroughly scouted, had no recorded exoplanets. The presence of this near-miraculous world had been the first vindication of Suero's visions. They named it "Mote" at Norizuchi's sarcastic suggestion.

The second vindication had come from sighting the strange complex they now fought within. The rest of the world was desolate and lifeless, covered in a constant storm of black ash. Only this cluster of brutalist ziggurats showed signs of human artifice. Megalithic spikes protruded from the roofs and walls, recalling a great thicket of stony thorns. The architecture itself seemed hostile, provoking a sense of unease in Suero as he and his column descended into the complex.

The final vindication came when they were fired on. Infantry in ash-stained cloaks and enviro-suits had ambushed Norizuchi's Elementals as they cleared the rooftops, while the 'Mechs took up positions in the central plaza. Malia moved her *Mist Lynx* to support the Elementals, shredding the ambushers with her machine guns and sending the survivors fleeing for cover. It was then that the enemy 'Mechs emerged, and the true battle began.

They were of a make he had seen only in intelligence reports. A trio—medium, heavy, and assault class—flitting ghost-like in and out of the darkness. All sharp edges and bristling weapons, there was something terribly beautiful in these machines. Like metallic birds of prey, they moved with a grace that made Suero's *Warhawk* seem clumsy and brutish.

There was only one force in the galaxy that used these 'Mechs, dubbed the Celestial class: the Word of Blake.

Those techno-animist fanatics had plunged the Inner Sphere into an orgy of bloodshed. The Scorpion Watch's reports said they had been destroyed decades ago, around the time of the Clan's own exile. *How fitting,* Suero thought, *to find them alive on this world of ghosts.*

"Engage the *Preta*," he said, locking the medium 'Mech in his sights and firing a salvo of PPC shots.

Blue bolts streaked through the darkness, joined by a full volley from Zane's *Phantom*. A hail of missiles was shot down by the defensive systems on the nimble *Preta*, but its pilot was neither swift nor skilled enough to avoid Suero's fire. A bolt took it in the shoulder, another in the lower torso, blasting away hunks of armor.

More shots came from the Blakist 'Mechs, this time a barrage of plasma fire that coruscated up and down Suero's *Warhawk*. Warning lights flared to life, informing him armor was critically low in a dozen places. The *Warhawk* was a formidable machine, but it was old, and the Celestial 'Mechs had been manufactured with the highest technology the Inner Sphere could produce.

Suero took cover behind one of the buildings, letting his quad PPCs recharge. Zane followed suit, harassing and distracting the Blakists with his missiles. The fanatics fell for the bait, moving to flank the two of them on either side. Wordlessly, Suero and Zane engaged the *Preta* as it darted around their right. It loosed a burst of laser blasts, battering Zane's *Phantom* before retreating under their combined fire.

They had left themselves exposed in the rear, and now Suero felt the full fury of the lone assault 'Mech, the *Archangel*. It fired a fusillade of plasma and PPC bolts, ripping into the back of his *Warhawk* and sending his targeting computer into a cascading failure.

"Pull back," he snarled. "Norizuchi, prep for reembark."

Suero and Zane sprinted their 'Mechs across the plaza, away from the Blakist's raking fire. As they approached the rooftop firefight between the Blakist infantry and Norizuchi's Elementals, Suero targeted the center of the roof and charged his PPCs.

"Norizuchi! Embark on my mark! Three...two...one! MARK!"

In perfect synchronicity, the Elementals leaped through the air just as Suero fired his weapons. They soared above his salvo, landing with practiced precision on the back of his *Warhawk* and securing themselves to the handholds. Blue energy enveloped the Blakist infantry, and for a brief moment every 'Mech and Elemental under Suero's command fired on them. Robed figures pitched and fell, roasting and liquefying under the unrelenting salvo. In seconds, the black robed Blakists were all dead, dying, or fleeing, using grapnels to scramble down the sides of the building.

"Malia, form up on me. Everyone, prepare for close assault. Target the *Preta*," Suero said.

His troops responded with a chorus of *aff*s, but there was no enthusiasm among them, only grim determination.

It was a crude tactic. Once, it would even have been called un-Clanlike. But Suero had been born after the Scorpions' fall from grace, after the devastation of the Wars of Reaving. *Batchall*s and honorable trials, the elegant skills of MechWarriors of old: those were things of the past. Now they were only to be done among the Scorpions themselves. The rules of war created by Kerensky were tradition, no more. To survive, they had to ensure victory first.

As one, the trio of 'Mechs charged toward the loose line of Celestials. They fired their weapons, punishing the badly damaged *Preta* even further. At the last moment, Norizuchi and the Elementals riding on Zane's *Phantom* triggered their jump packs, swarming the Celestial 'Mech like mad hornets. Now their battle claws did their work, wreaking havoc on the *Preta*'s remaining armor.

As Suero strafed to the right, drawing the *Archangel*'s fire, he saw Norizuchi leap onto the *Preta*'s cockpit and begin hammering its canopy with laser fire. It was the glory of the Elementals to remind MechWarriors that they, too, were mortal. Once that canopy was peeled open, he would rip the pilot out and cast them to the ground below.

Suddenly, a torrent of missiles streaked toward him from the third 'Mech, a *Grigori*, its boxy right arm letting loose with unerring aim. Missiles tore into the *Warhawk's* carapace, penetrating deep within and damaging one of his actuators. Limping now, Suero returned fire, blasting the *Grigori's* left arm apart.

He saw on his scanner a burst of comm chatter from their foes, encrypted and indecipherable. The *Archangel* turned, swiping its blade arm at the *Preta* as it passed, clearly trying to pick off the Elementals. The *Preta* also began to reverse, feebly swinging its arms back and forth, trying to pry the Elementals from its armored body like parasites from a great beast.

"Disengage, Norizuchi! Disengage now!" Suero commanded.

"*Neg*, Seeker, we almost have them—"

"By the blood of Kerensky, DISENGAGE OR YOU WILL DIE!"

"*Aff*, Seeker," Norizuchi said sullenly.

The Elementals vaulted away from the *Preta*, and it broke into a run after a cursory shot in their direction. The Blakists disappeared into the darkness in full retreat.

Suero scanned his cockpit displays, taking stock of his troops. The Elementals had suffered a few casualties, and Zane's *Phantom* was badly mauled. His own *Warhawk* was in dire need of repairs, but its weapon systems were still functioning. Only Malia's *Mist Lynx*, small and swift, had avoided the worst of the beating.

"Malia," Suero said. "Take Second Elemental and pursue at distance, keep us apprised of their movements, but do not engage. I will summon support personnel from our DropShip. We make camp here and begin repairs. Norizuchi, resupply. Your warriors and I are going to find out just what the Blakists were guarding..."

The interior of the complex had the stale air of a tomb. Suero walked down one of its dusty corridors, flanked by a pair of Elementals. They had found and disarmed a few traps the Blakists left behind: crude things, swiftly improvised once they caught sight of Suero's DropShip descending.

Sage Pilara walked behind him, careful to shelter in the massive shadow of the Elementals.

"There are two points of interest, Seeker," she said, flicking through her noteputer. "First, we've found what we think is the central mainframe. There's a reactor buried hundreds of meters below us, but most of its power is going directly to a massive computer system. It's some of the most sophisticated Star League technology I've ever seen."

Suero grimaced beneath his litham. She was of Castilian extraction, a freeborn, and as a consequence her mastery of Star League English was informal. Still, as a member of the scientist caste, she was both wise and indispensable.

"Good," he said. "I wish to examine this mainframe personally. It may be connected to my vision."

"There is a second point of interest as well, Seeker. We discovered the Blakists' dormitory, abandoned, of course, but of particular interest was a…'greenhouse' nearby."

"A greenhouse?"

"More a hydroponic garden. It's quite sophisticated."

"That is how the Blakists were feeding themselves on this barren planet, *quiaff*?"

"*Aff*, Seeker. But there is something strange. It also seems to have been used as a burial chamber. We found evidence of several fresh graves, and a body in an adjoining room looks like it was being prepared for burial."

"They used the corpses as fertilizer. Efficient. Admirable."

"Indeed. But what troubles me, Seeker, is that the body appears to have died of starvation."

Suero turned to her, arching an eyebrow.

"The greenhouse is full of vegetation that looks edible: meat trees for protein, every kind of nutrient you might need grows here," she explained. "So how did that Blakist starve?"

"Curious," Suero said. "The entire complex is built around the computer system you spoke of. Let us see if it can reveal the truth to us."

The mainframe was a black obelisk, surrounded on all sides by snaking cables that ran into the surrounding walls. Lights winked on and off across its surface, and a solitary screen and keypad stared out at him like a glowing eye above dozens of tiny white teeth.

And there, above that screen, was a pair of icons. Chess pieces, knights, facing each other. One a white horse's head with green eyes, the other…a black horse, lidless eyes glowing red.

For more than an hour, Suero worked alongside Pilara, probing the depths of the computer system. The interface was simplistic, designed for efficiency and security. Everything was displayed as plain green text with the occasional low-resolution image or graph. Alongside the program files themselves, there were patch notes and the personal logs of the system's prior operators.

"It's an adversarial AI network," Pilara said finally. "Connected to something called Project Cornucopia. This facility was a Star League black site."

"An intelligent machine? You mean it *thinks*?" Suero asked incredulously.

"In a manner of speaking," Pilara continued. "The mainframe hosts a pair of highly complex algorithms. One is called White Horse, the other is Black Horse. Just as warriors test one another in combat trials, the two systems constantly probe each other for weaknesses, and by doing so, improve their performance."

"Fascinating," Suero whispered. "A forebear to the wisdom of Kerensky himself. But what do these machines do, precisely?"

"They..." Pilara hesitated before continuing. "Well, the White Horse program was intended to assist in agricultural production. It's connected to a massive catalog of seed strains, forms of edible vegetation that can be cross-bred to produce virtually any kind of foodstuff imaginable. I'm seeing data on crops that could be grown under almost any conditions. It would be a blessing to the Scorpion Empire's agricultural centers."

"And the Black Horse?"

"It...it designs blights. It contains a similar catalog of viruses, parasites, things any basic bio-chemical lab could produce. Everything the White Horse can make, the Black Horse can kill. One could use this program to induce famine on every world in the Inner Sphere.

"From what I understand of the original facility's logs, the two systems were supposed to work in tandem, but over the years, the Black Horse became vastly superior. During the Amaris Civil War, the scientists abandoned this place. I believe, Seeker, the Eridani's mission was to force them back to work, or recover this system for use against Amaris."

"I have Eridani blood," Suero said quietly, staring hard at the machine before him. "Perhaps...that is the reason this vision was granted to me. To fulfill the task they failed."

"I could not say, Seeker. The visions of necrosia are beyond my understanding. But there is more."

She tapped in a command, calling up another series of logs. These were from centuries later, the 3080s.

"The Word of Blake fled here after the Jihad," Pilara explained. "Their JumpShip was crippled, their DropShip almost destroyed on landing. It seems they were led by someone called Nakir..."

Pilara selected a log and read aloud.

"August 7, 3081. Bertolli, Programmer First Class. Buried in Blake's name. November 3, 3081. Ada. Three thousand grams. Buried in Blake's name. November 17, 3081...

"It goes on, Seeker. He records dozens of deaths. Adults he marks with rank and duty. Children he marks with...with weight at time of death. He also has a record of caloric rationing over decades. These people were starving themselves."

"Why? He had the White Horse. He could have used that hydroponic garden to produce a surplus—"

"He is a Blakist, Seeker. The garden is part of this facility's automated experiments, and most of it is turned over to the Black Horse's productions. Half the food produced here would be inedible, or poisonous. But as a weapon of vengeance, the Black Horse is indispensable. Nakir had a choice between turning this place into a true home for his people, or holding on to the hope that someday they might have a chance to release the Black Horse's creations on the Inner Sphere. He chose the latter."

"So this Nakir let his people starve..."

"He did," Pilara said. "And, from what I can tell, loathed himself for it."

There was a moment of silence as they stared at the computer screen. The last log entry was from this morning, recording the sighting of Suero's JumpShip, and the Blakists' preparations for defense. Nakir had refused a suggestion that the reactor be prepared for overload. The Black Horse was now his reason for being; he could not condone its destruction.

Their forces were meager, their 'Mechs patchwork. Yet still they intended to fight.

The last line of the entry read simply: *Hope is a poison.*

"The mainframe can be disconnected for transport," Pilara said. "Our portable memory cores could retain ninety percent of the archive here. In conjunction with the mainframe, we can effectively transport the entire project to the Empire. If...if that is the Seeker's will."

Suero looked down. His visions had led him here, seeking weapons and technology of the past. The Black Horse was undeniably a weapon. Indeed, one so powerful it might prove decisive in the Empire's coming campaigns. He was a warrior; why should any weapon fill him with such revulsion?

He thought of his vision, of cities rotting away. A rampaging stallion. Had he seen himself upon its back? And he had seen graves. Very small graves.

"Seeker." Norizuchi's voice cut in over his personal comms. "MechWarrior Malia reports sighting the Blakist force. They are active; speculated route is directly for our DropShip."

"Is Second Elemental still with her?"

"*Aff*, Seeker."

"Take your Point and mount the *Phantom* with Zane. You and Foot Point One are to take all transport vehicles and return to the DropShip immediately. Take up defensive positions, and make no effort at stealth, am I understood?"

"I will do as you ask, Seeker. What of Third Elemental?"

"They will remain here with me and the scientists," Suero explained. "You are to hold the DropShip against all assault. You have permission to evacuate if the situation becomes critical, but do not disengage under any other circumstances. Call on the opponents to surrender on first contact."

"Understood, Seeker, though I doubt the Blakists will agree to terms."

"You have your orders, carry them out."

"*Aff,*" Norizuchi grunted, then the line went silent.

Suero turned away from the console and headed briskly for the external airlock.

"What am I to do with all this, Seeker?" Pilara called after him. "Should it be...destro—"

"No," Suero said firmly. "Secure it. That is our duty."

And, he thought, *our shame.*

Suero's *Warhawk* had no hope of keeping speed with the *Phantom* and the various transport vehicles he'd sent to protect the DropShip. It did not matter. His technicians had done excellent field repairs, and though it was nowhere near pristine, the inside of the cockpit hummed with life.

In the central plaza, Suero waited. Black wind whipped around him; endless, boiling columns of ash. He kept an eye on the long range readout, and on reports coming from the DropShip. Not long after Zane and Malia reported contact with the Blakists, he saw the heat signature of a single BattleMech approaching his position. Just as he'd expected.

On the edge of the complex, invisible to the naked eye but burning bright on his heat scanners, the other 'Mech halted. *Archangel.* Assault class. Damaged, but still formidable.

Like the warriors of old, Suero turned on a wide comm-band and spoke. "I am Seeker Suero, of the Goliath Scorpions. I claim this place for my Clan, and for the Scorpion Empire. Who challenges me for this right?"

"Demi-Precentor Nakir," a voice with a metallic quality replied. "Of the Word of Blake. Somehow I knew you'd stay behind, Seeker. You've discovered the Black Horse, and now you can't wait to loot it, can you?"

"It belonged to the Star League," Suero replied. "It is the duty of every Scorpion to recover that which was lost. The necrosia visions brought me to this place, to take the Black Horse and keep it safe—"

"To use it for your own conquests," Nakir spat. "Clanners! Degenerates stealing symbols you cannot comprehend. May Terra be ever kept safe from your kind."

"The day will come when Terra is under the protection of the Clans," Suero said. "The ilClan will rise, and they will unite humankind under one will, as it was in the days of the Star League."

Nakir laughed mirthlessly.

"Look at us," he said. "Both sworn to hold Terra, and now a thousand light years from it. Crusaders, lost on our way to Jerusalem."

"I am not lost. I have come here with purpose, the visions—"

"You're a hallucinating savage," Nakir spat. "You think our forebears wanted something like *you* to come of their great work? The Star League was meant to protect humanity, not deface it."

"The great Kerensky molded us to be the perfect warriors! We will be the saviors of the Inner Sphere, its protectors—"

"You are plunderers," Nakir said. "You raid and pillage, and call it your sacred quest."

"And you burn entire worlds," Suero said. "We know of the Jihad, Nakir. We know what the Word of Blake inflicted on the Inner Sphere."

Nakir was silent for a moment. When he spoke, his voice was less certain.

"There is always a cost. Always. It was our holy duty, and we tried, may Blake forgive us, we tried so hard to fulfill it. If only those fools had listened, if only the House Lords had put aside their petty bickering for *once*. We could have had it! The Star League reborn! Humanity united as one, an age of peace and prosperity...but the flesh is weak, and men's souls are frail."

"Surrender, Nakir. No blood stains your hands that cannot be washed away. Come with me, see the Empire. See what my kin and I are building together."

"I would rather die than bow to a savage."

"We call you barbarians, too," Suero said. "But I see now that you are a man, like me. I know your dreams, Nakir. I know your sacrifice. You are right, we are both crusaders. But our Jerusalem is a long way from here. Come with me. Please. Or the people you have shepherded these years will all die."

"You think your warriors will keep the DropShip from mine?"

"I know it," Suero said. "Desperation cannot make up for a lack of ammunition and training. I have seen your troops, Nakir. They are brave, but they are sick. How long have they starved here? You cannot ask them to fight any more. All you are doing is sending them to their deaths."

"They are already dead!" Nakir snarled. "They have been dead for *decades*! We died with the Jihad. All we sacrificed for...it came to nothing. Nothing. But if I take this weapon, if we find a way to unleash what the Black Horse has created on the Inner Sphere, then we will have a *measure* of vindication!"

"Starving a thousand worlds will give you no peace. The Black Horse should never have been made, and it shall not be used while I breathe."

"You truly are a hypocrite," Nakir replied. "You say it's your mission to recover the relics of the Star League, yet you revile the sacred technology of our ancestors."

"I seek the wisdom of the Star League. We must learn from their triumphs...and from their mistakes. Look around you. This place was never meant to be found. The Star League knew it could only bring misery. The Eridani refused to retake it. We are no wiser than them."

There was a long silence. Suero thought he saw the *Archangel* turn its cockpit slightly, as if Nakir was looking around the cursed ruins.

"How old are you?" Nakir asked.

"Twenty-six."

"You sound older," Nakir said. "Blessed Blake, what your people must have done to you... How old were you when you took a life for the first time?"

"Sixteen," Suero said. "A training accident. I struck my sparring partner too hard. She fell and broke her neck."

He could see her: Amina. Alive, laughing. Always driving him harder, to be the best of their peers. Always mocking him for his self-serious attitude, his bookishness. His *sibkin*. His friend.

Amina, dead on the training ground, surprise in her glassy eyes.

His instructors had been so proud of him that day.

"Nineteen," Nakir said. "Mine was on purpose. Lyran boy, recon, about my age. Cut his throat. Blood all over that stupid blue uniform. I remember seeing that blue cloth go red, and all I could think was: what a damned waste."

There was another long silence, the only sound the wind whipping ash between their two 'Mechs. They had both been out in the elements so long they were coated in it. Everything on Mote turned black eventually.

"Who did this to us?" Nakir asked.

"Kerensky teaches that...war is a natural part of humankind. Like breathing."

"You think he was right?"

"I...have to. Otherwise..."

"Otherwise you're a monster. Just like me. Come, Clanner. We've no more time for philosophy. Let's finish this."

Suero breathed out. He primed his weapons.

"Aff," he said, and the battle began.

For an eternity, they dueled. Nakir was as skilled as any warrior Suero had faced. He could make his *Archangel* dodge and weave in ways that should have been impossible, taking Suero's fire and returning in kind. Warning lights blazed, armor melted, circuits fused. Yet on they fought.

Suero found himself in the battle trance, his mind fading into his body, his body fading into the 'Mech. Left arm, fire, recharge. Right arm, fire, recharge. Left. Right. Left. Right.

Sweat drenched him even beneath his cooling suit—circling and firing, circling and firing, blue bolts illuminating the dark as they exchanged blow after blow. Twice his *Warhawk* surged past the critical heat threshold, and twice Suero overrode his 'Mech's safety systems. It was becoming sluggish, its backup targeting systems erratic, but he had given wounds to Nakir's *Archangel* just as savage as those he received.

Suero lurched his 'Mech backward, pulling it deeper and deeper into the narrow streets of the complex. He targeted the *Archangel*'s damaged right arm, and fired a last volley. The mangled heavy PPC was finally sheared clean off the enemy 'Mech. Now Nakir was at a disadvantage. He had only two choices: retreat, or charge.

There was no more talk between them, no threats or calls for quarter. Their 'Mechs spoke a language of their own, and the thunder of the *Archangel*'s clawed feet as it rushed toward Suero's *Warhawk* was more furious than any battle cry uttered by a man.

It sprinted forward, deadly blade in its left arm raised high, the plasma rifle beneath the cockpit burning like the maw of a dragon. A plasma blast took Suero's *Warhawk* full in the torso, melting the last shred of armor to slag. Warning lights screamed that he had suffered a minor reactor breach. Rad counters crackled, their dirge deafening.

"Third Elemental! Now!"

On gouts of blue flame, the Elementals soared out of the darkness. Just as he had planned, they had kept still and silent as the battle raged, and now the trap was sprung. They fired a salvo as they shrieked through the air, missiles erupting on the *Archangel*'s damaged surface. Then they struck the side of the 'Mech, clinging with their metal claws, ripping, tearing, and shooting into every exposed gap.

They were gnats felling a giant. The *Archangel* teetered and whirled, clawing at the Elementals as they crawled about its surface, wreaking havoc. Suero fired a volley from his *Warhawk*, blasting apart one of the *Archangel*'s legs. With what sounded terribly like a human moan, the *Archangel* pitched backward onto the ground.

Its arms spasmed, and a last bright bolt streaked up from its plasma rifle, the last breath of a dying dragon. Then one of the Elementals crawled to the cockpit and ripped out the weapon's moorings. In moments, the *Archangel* was still.

In the days of old, it would have been shameful to win a duel this way. But Suero's fight with Nakir was not a duel, and those days were long gone. The Elementals swarmed about the fallen 'Mech's cockpit.

"Let us finish him," Point Commander Rath of the Elementals hissed, the bloodlust clear in his voice.

"Neg," Suero said.

"Seeker, we—"

"Negative. It is done," Suero said.

He gazed down at the *Archangel*, cold and still.

"*He* is done."

The battle for the DropShip ended as Suero had expected. The Blakists were fearsome, but against the combined firepower of the DropShip and its defenders, they had no hope of victory. Fewer than a dozen survived the assault, looking more like ghosts than people when they were finally captured.

The Word's 'Mechs were both badly mangled in the fighting, their pilots choosing death over capture. Dutiful as ever, Suero's technicians salvaged what they could of their chassis. The *Archangel*, though crippled, was a great prize as well. Yet standing in the 'Mech bay, watching as his technicians did what they could to repair it before the DropShip took off, Suero felt a terrible sense of grief.

He remembered what the Elementals had pulled from its cockpit. What was left of Nakir's flesh was an ashy, wrinkled gray, most of his body replaced by cybernetics to better interface with the 'Mech. Outside of it, he was little more than a head, a torso, and a single shriveled arm. Suero had looked upon the dead old man after their battle, and felt nothing but pity.

Suero returned to the bridge, and gave the signal for takeoff. The Elementals and the MechWarriors were loudly toasting their victory, shouts of celebration echoing through the ship's decks. Suero glanced over at Pilara, strapped in not far from him. She smiled at him, and nodded.

An hour after takeoff, the complex's reactor went critical, as he had ordered. A single spike of radiation registered on their scanners, then nothing. Mote was a dead and empty world again.

In the end, Suero took a third path. He had the central mainframe brought aboard the DropShip, but ordered its archives and data wiped.

The central AI network remained, but it no longer had access to the centuries of information it had built up. The Black Horse was hobbled.

In time, the program could be restarted. Suero had already decided he would advise the Clan Council against it.

As the DropShip burned away from Mote, and his people prepared for the long journey home, Suero allowed himself a brief smile. There were many things he had done that brought him no joy, and many more he was sure to do in the future.

Perhaps someday, one of his kin would be both wise enough and strong enough to use what he had found here today.

But not him.

Suero would never ride the Black Horse.

VOICES OF THE SPHERE: TOTAL WARFARE?

STEPHEN TOROPOV

To those keeping a close eye on the goings on around Terra, the ilClan trial and its aftermath can seem a cataclysmic turning point, appearing to usher in a new world of war between the reborn Star League and those who oppose it. Yet the Inner Sphere is vast, and the ongoing Blackout has already fostered decades of war and instability. We asked sources with military knowledge from across the Inner Sphere to gauge how much has changed and how much has remained the same in the shape of warfare after the proclamation of the ilClan.

—*INN Report*, 4 August 3152

Dobroslav Chinedu, IrTech Supply Sales Officer, Irian: Funny thing about reunification. You see a lot of planetary bigwigs praising the Captain-General for bringing about an age of peace and security. Thing is, I've got the sales numbers to prove we're fighting as much as we ever have, maybe more. But to the average League citizen, well, you aren't worried that freebooters or the neighboring duchy will be burning in from orbit any day now to kick down the city gates. That counts for a lot, and it means a lot more locals are willing to support their sons and daughters donning a uniform and keeping the fighting happening *over there*.

Colonel Jason Anthony, Commanding Officer, Fifth McCarron's Armored Cavalry, in Transit through Draconis Combine Space: Say what you will about the Combine. There's a lot to say. But we've been transiting their space for nearly two months now, moving from one border at war to another border at war. And yet every planet we pass, life is going on as it was. Might be a few more *ashigaru* recruiting broadcasts than normal, but even the old Republic worlds are shouldering their burdens and going on with normal business. After two decades of Mask propaganda exhorting every citizen to full war footing for the survival of Greater Humanity, seeing wars limited to the soldiers and the leaders is a bit of a trip.

Leftenant Tomasin la Verte, Third Davion Irregulars, Le Blanc: We're fighting for our homes. In a fight like that, everything is on the table. The yoke of occupation was damn heavy, and there is no person on this planet the war didn't reach. The Dragon wanted Le Blanc for our mineral riches, but they forgot our other export has always been hired guns. We did a lot of ugly things to get our homes back, and I don't regret any of them. Now that our home is secure, we're gonna have to send out a lot of mercs to go do a lot more ugly things to get our neighbors their homes back too.

Star Captain Nando Chand, Fifth Raven Stoop Cluster, Epsilon Eridani: When we heard about the New Earth Atrocity, the whole Cluster went into a silent, seething shock. Fort Noruff was where final plans to destroy the vile Usurper were laid. The last act when our ancestors and theirs stood on the same side. A history all humanity should have cherished. And the Capellans scoured that sacred space to glass, rendering it toxic for generations. It went beyond defiance; it was sacrilege against the very dream and heritage of the Star League. The first measure of justice has been meted out by our fleet, but I doubt they will be cowed so easily given the depths to which they have already sunk. For the First Lord to rule over all humanity as is his right, we will likely need to endure many more horrors like this.

Yì-sì-bān-bīng Konyashev Yelisey Leonidovich, First Kurnath Liao Memorial Naval Base Service Battalion, Liao: Our world is no stranger to the scars of war. For over a hundred years, we've been hit by the Davions, the Blakists, Stone and his so-called Republic, and even our own people, over and over. Yet even Blake's fanatics didn't match this. Chang-An is gone, burned to cinders. I personally broadcast maps of the city in the clear to the ships in orbit, hoping they'd avoid civilians. They showed no mercy. We've been digging innocents out of the rubble for weeks. In a hundred years, only the Clanners have been such barbarians. And over what? A pile of moldering ferrocrete. The future their supposed Star League stands for is soaked in blood.

Lieutenant Aiko Hatakeyama, Henshin Tigers, Almotacen: There's a perception that the Hinterlands is chaos and violence everywhere you look. And sure, there's no shortage of contracts for us mercenaries. But a lot of contracts doesn't have to mean a lot of destruction. Mercs play fair around here—you have to if you want to keep working out of Almotacen. That means no marauding, no kicking 'em when they're down, and ransoming back salvage for a fair price. You break those rules around here, and all you're gonna do is get some other merc a payday hunting you down. Ain't like the employers want to rule over rubble, either, so a reputation for working clean can work in your favor.

Captain Salvatore Kogan, First Unity Dragoons, Graham IV: Sure, I'm marching under a new flag. I marched for the Republic when the Republic meant Terra. Now I'm marching for the Star League, because the Star League means Terra. The fight itself hasn't changed. I've fought Capellans for a decade. My parents before me fought Capellans in the Crusade. I'm fighting Capellans now. It's always been a brutal fight. Folks talk about some seismic shift, but from where I'm standing, I'm fighting the same war the same way—only we're winning now.

Planetary Councilwoman Eloise Hayden, Lackland: Chaos around New Avalon or Terra always means trouble for us out here on the frontier, no matter how we wish it didn't. Somehow or other, the Filtvelt Coalition will get drawn in, and even if we don't, all it means is the pirates out here get bolder. With Firebeard out at Tortuga running wild and the Concordat and Protectorate getting their acts together, we're gonna have our hands full, even if we're on good terms with the Marsins. And they say life on a Periphery backwater world is dull...

IN THE END

LUKASZ FURMANIAK

ESSEN
GERMANY ADMINISTRATIVE DISTRICT
TERRA
1 JANUARY 2777

Clad in her dress uniform, Maria Escarra battled the urge to sneer at the cheering drunks surrounding her. While such behavior was hardly frowned on per se, what with her being a lauded MechWarrior and the civilians around her being little better than parasites, it would not do to aggravate them in their inebriated state while on her own. The utilitarian gray of her clothing was a stark contrast to the lavish colors displayed on both the men and women celebrating having made it to another year. It made her seem like a shark among shoals of tropical fish.

Fitting.

Her lips quirked into a momentary smirk before dying a swift death as she spied the only other individual at this little shindig not wearing some ridiculous outfit. Hannah Priwitzer was one of those necessary evils when it came to BattleMechs—Krupp's very own test pilot, charged with making sure any design that emerged from their foundries was worth time and investment before it was shipped off to true MechWarriors. She had chosen to come dressed in the simple dress uniform granted to all MechWarrior graduates, bereft of any accolades and accomplishments. Still, she was by far the most tolerable company Maria had met in her two weeks at the company campus.

"Cadet," Maria greeted as she approached, just barely tilting her head.

"Captain," Priwitzer replied, her jaw tensing.

It warmed Maria's heart to see such unabashed jealousy—after all, while being a test pilot came with several benefits (the pay being the least of them), it did leave one forever shackled to their benefactors. Hannah Priwitzer would never truly be a MechWarrior. Not in any way that counted. Still, Maria supposed going the corporate route was the only viable path left for anyone wishing to sit behind the controls of a BattleMech that had not come to Terra from the Periphery.

"Happy New Year," Maria said, raising the small flute of champagne, as if in salute.

The lesser MechWarrior bit back what was surely a grimace and offered a tight-lipped smile as she raised her glass. "Happy New Year," she echoed, her eyes drifting to the emblem on Maria's uniform before snapping back to her face. Her naked envy had done much to improve Maria's mood whilst she oversaw the final preparations.

There was a polite pause. "Any plans?" Maria asked, sipping her drink. Sweet and bubbly, nothing like the wine she preferred.

Priwitzer's polite facade slipped for a moment, revealing utter disgust before it reasserted itself. "No," she replied tersely, taking a sip of her own.

Maria laughed at that. A wonderfully honest reaction to an insipid question that had been posed to her by the various businessmen and women gathered in the hall, desperately acting like everything was fine and the world beyond, with an incensed Russian upstart bearing down on them, did not exist at all. "What, no more wonderful toys to test out?" she offered. "I am sorry to be taking yours, but it is the Emperor's will."

"And his investment," Priwitzer muttered, scowling at the reminder of the machine that she had been granted mere weeks to pilot before it was taken away from her. However, she once again regained her composure and bowed her head. "Still, I hear he is pleased with what the team here managed to achieve."

As if. Emperor Amaris had far more important things to deal with than keeping track of one prototype, no matter how much it had cost him. Still, Maria had been instructed to play nice during her trip to Essen—after all, they could hardly liquidate one of the more influential companies on Terra itself in the current situation. "Oh, certainly. I made sure to cover all the promises Krupp had delivered on in my report—and to downplay the rather unfortunate compromise you had to make."

"The ammunition limitations are well within the specified parameters," interjected Maximillian Grunder, stepping up to the two women as Priwitzer opened her mouth to respond to the bait. "Besides, it is my understanding that the Fourth is well supplied. Or do you have word of some developments that may make this new assault 'Mech... unsuitable for the Emperor's needs?" the scrawny man asked. He was practically swimming in his suit, and his belt was cinched as tight as it would go. As the head of a Krupp subsidiary, he had been unable to share in the grace extended to the company, and had been hit hard by the rationing.

"Not at all. Just common sense dictates a BattleMech should be capable of partaking in an extended engagement before needing to resupply," Maria pointed out, shifting her focus onto the civilian. The man's question wasn't unwarranted, at least for a rat in his position. Of course, if there was a hint of a new contract he would want to be the first to stake a claim, but there was also a chance he was fishing for more nefarious reasons.

Priwitzer took the opportunity to slip away, though Maria paid her no mind as the short man in front of her chuckled. "Ah, but such is the nature of prototypes, no? I've heard some promising things regarding mounting PPCs instead to resolve that particular problem—"

"—but that just creates another one," Maria finished in sync with him, having had this talk several times already. "I suppose we shall see how it fares in the field first."

Maximillian paled momentarily at the sudden reminder of how close the war was to Terra, swiftly downing his drink and plastering on a broad, appeasing smile. "Of course, and I hope in the end you'll agree, the *Rifleman III* is well worth the cost!"

GENEVA
SWITZERLAND ADMINISTRATIVE DISTRICT
TERRA
2 FEBRUARY 2777

"Captain Escarra," Colonel Trask grunted in greeting. He sounded far more haggard over the phone than Maria could ever recall. Ever since Dague's assassination and his promotion to command, something had seemed to die in the man, month by month.

"Sorry for the timing of this call, Colonel," she replied. "However, I wished to verify the last communication—"

"Dammit, Escarra, the SLDF is dropping all over the continent—there's a division touching down near Madrid right now," the man snapped. "Unless that new machine of yours is a Land-Air 'Mech, I don't think it's going to make it in time before we have to evacuate Lisbon."

Maria bristled, but reined in the first words she wanted to say in response. "But sir, if we depart now and keep off the major roads—" she said instead, voice tight.

"No. You are to hold your position and repel the SLDF. Consider that a direct order from the Emperor himself," Trask spat. "Don't even think about leaving Geneva until he comes and fetches you, understood?"

The woman gritted her teeth and nodded. "Understood, sir."

"Good." And with that, the current commander of the Fourth Amaris Dragoons cut the connection, leaving Escarra to stew in her thoughts and anger.

Bloody drones! They had all been assured the *Caspar*s would keep General Kerensky occupied for at least several days—instead, the Star League Defense Force had swept through them in a single day and made all speed for Terra. Now she was stuck half a planet away from her unit, forced to go into battle alongside the bloody Republican Guard!

Imperial Guard, she mentally corrected herself, even as she stood up and glared at the monitor. The desire to punch it was strong—no, it was to punch Trask in his stressed, unshaven face. Even before Colonel Dague's assassination two years ago and Trask's promotion to the command slot, the man had irked her. He carried himself with an unearned swagger and surety. Sure, he had proven himself worthy of joining the Fourth, but he had not been there, at Gorst Flats. He had not been truly blooded the way she had. And yet Emperor Amaris saw fit to grant him command of the Fourth?!

Maria took a deep breath as her outrage gave way to a familiar anger. No, it would not do to lose herself here and now. She was a captain of the legendary Fourth. She was head and shoulders above any other MechWarrior—hell, any other soldier—here. Another breath and she centered herself, forcing the instinct to break something back to the dark corner of her mind. No matter. This little...setback would just let her stand out all the more. Ensure that after this entire debacle, she would be remembered as the finest MechWarrior of the age.

Striding out of the hastily repurposed foreman's office onto the walkways circling the upper stories of the warehouse, she glanced at the wonder machine Krupp had managed to cobble together, partially shrouded under a tarp the technicians still had not gotten around to removing. A sneer touched her lips at the sloppiness on display, the dirty and dejected men and women huddled around a table, drinking coffee out of mugs and cups. The spokesperson for the sorry lot seemed to sense her attention and glanced up, catching her eye.

Edward Hayes was exactly what one thought of when told to imagine a BattleMech technician—portly, always dirty, dressed in heavy overalls and an apron with pockets stuffed with tools. His hair may have been blond once, but the shaggy, partially burned mess was black from God knew what, and kept out of his face by the goggles he had left on his forehead. His shoulders seemed to slump as he read her expression and looked away, saying something to his team that had them reluctantly break apart and get back to work as Maria headed down to the factory floor.

Of course, it hadn't been a factory for a while—Maria didn't know the details and neither did she care. For the moment, it was her domain, her little BattleMech hangar on the northern outskirts of Geneva. She could have claimed one deeper in the city, but that would have involved sharing space with the soldiers of the Repub—*Imperial* Guard. And she had foregone that option when Geneva was just a stop along her route back to the palace, reasoning there was no point in traveling across the rapidly fortifying city, through all the checkpoints, just to do it all again the next day.

That was before the general order had come through activating all units and ordering them to standby for invasion. So now she was stuck on what was soon to become the front line, with only footsloggers, tankers, and Mechjocks with more zeal than sense to back her up. Fortunately, she had the new *Rifleman*. More than a match for anything the SLDF could throw at her.

"Any luck?" Edward asked as she approached, stepping between her and his crew.

"No. We are to hold here and engage the enemy as they approach," Maria replied, staring down at the man as she crossed her arms. "So get it unpacked and set up."

"All right," sighed the technician, who waved to his people and turned away to join them in getting the fresh new BattleMech ready for its first true deployment. At least Krupp had seen fit to provide it with several tons of ammunition—who knows where else they would have been able to find enough Gauss slugs for multiple volleys.

"Reports say SLDF forces have landed all over the continent, so I want it ready to roll out within the hour. Is that understood?" Maria added, glancing at the machine as the tarp was pulled off to reveal it on the back of the cargo mover, kneeling as if in prayer.

"Crystal," the scruffy man grunted.

"Good. I'll be in the cockpit," she said, walking past him.

They had their orders. In the end, that was all that mattered.

GENEVA
SWITZERLAND ADMINISTRATIVE DISTRICT
TERRA
4 FEBRUARY 2777

The SLDF's 209th Mechanized Infantry Division asked for no quarter when they came. Captain Escarra respected that. Breaking such determination and pride would be an achievement worth her time.

Kerensky's lackeys marched on Geneva in good order, only breaking apart once it became clear the artillery hidden throughout the city had pre-sighted coordinates on all major approaches. Meanwhile, the minor roads leading into the city had all been blocked off or mined, forcing the enemy to pick between slowing their advance to clear safe routes or daring to rush along the highways among the respectable barrage the Re—*Imperial* Guard were delivering.

Maria Escarra could feel the tremors from the constant shelling even in her *Rifleman III*, the once-pristine A1 that would have carried her and her 'Mech onward to France and then Spain undoubtedly nothing but a cratered nightmare by now. She wished she could take a look for herself, but discipline reasserted itself and she settled back in her seat, looking over her instruments and screens.

She knew that for many, before a battle came the nerves. She had seen that in her fellow Dragoons, but she had never understood it. Her breath was calm, her gaze steady. The enemy was coming, and they would die. It was as simple as that. And thanks to the null-signature system installed on her *Rifleman*, they wouldn't even know what killed them.

That was a shame. There was something in the foe knowing it was you who slew them, who prevailed despite their finest efforts. It was a heady feeling, undoubtedly the same the Emperor had relished when he had slain the accursed Camerons. *But no, that isn't the way to approach this*, Maria reprimanded herself with a shake of her head. Not until she forced the 209th to acknowledge her first.

But it was only a matter of time. Her *Rifleman's* sensors were already picking up several fast-moving blips turning off the highway and cutting across the suburbs toward her position. A scout lance, judging by the speed—one with jump jets, too, judging by the bounding movement of two of the contacts.

Perfect prey.

A cold smile graced Maria's lips as she shifted her 'Mech, half-twisting its torso to the right to align its guns with the enemy's path. One hand danced over the console, freeing each Gauss rifle from the primary reticle. Crouched among old shipping containers piled up outside the old factory, the *Rifleman III* could only be spotted by the naked eye—which was why she'd had Hayes and his crew cover the machine with that tarp it had come in.

A gentle ping alerted her to the scout lance finally entering visual range. She could make out a *Spider* and a *Wasp*, jumping like insects to keep up with what she realized was a pair of *Locusts* sprinting through back yards, no doubt seeking alternate approaches into the heart of the city. They were moving at an angle, undoubtedly wary of stumbling

across any entrenched infantry or armored vehicles. None of them moved in any way to make it seem they had detected her presence.

Maria moved the targeting reticle over the *Spider* and tagged it. The reticle turned red and continued to track the small BattleMech as another appeared, which she moved over to the *Wasp*, assigning its demise to her second arm-mounted Gauss rifle. That just left her torso guns—harder to aim, but definitely best suited for the *Locust*s, which would be limited in the directions they could scatter the moment they passed between any two houses. Her third Gauss rifle locked on and tracked the trailing bug 'Mech, leaving her staring at the lead *Locust*, painted in the drab green of the SLDF. She licked her lips, waited for the jumping BattleMechs to land, and pulled the trigger.

Three of the scouts died instantly. Her Gauss rifles screeched in unison, placing hypersonic slugs through the cockpit of the leading *Locust*, shearing off the *Wasp*'s leg, and detonating the short-range missiles of the *Locust*. The fourth shot, however, just clipped the *Spider*, as it came down on a patch of soft ground and slipped due to its momentum.

Maria clucked her tongue in displeasure, even as the *Wasp* crashed into the ground and the remains of the *Locust*s slid to a stop. The *Rifleman III* only carried enough ammo for four volleys per gun before needing to resupply. But sixteen Gauss shots were more than enough for her to achieve her goals. She watched the *Spider* pause in shock, the MechWarrior inside probably trying to figure out just what had happened.

Stupid mistake.

She let loose another shot from the *Rifleman*'s arm. The slug burrowed deep into the light 'Mech's torso, blowing out its back with gouts of steam before the *Spider* toppled over.

A good start.

But now the real test of her skill would begin. Eleven shots left, and the 209th knew she was in the area. Bad odds—so Maria shifted the variables. With a groan and the sound of tearing fabric, the *Rifleman III* stood from its crouch and began to move away from the warehouse.

Either another scout lance would be dispatched to the area, or something heavier she wouldn't be able to kill as easily. Either way, best to relocate and retain the element of surprise. Which is why she advanced, closing in on the downed SLDF machines. Her lumbering assault 'Mech took a tense minute to cross the neighborhoods between her sniping spot and the street the scouts had fallen in.

The nearby artillery barrage continued, thundering explosions reverberating in Maria's ears. Then a single alarm blared before she was rocked by a sudden impact. Swearing, she glanced at her readouts even as she corrected the *Rifleman*'s path to take it behind some housing units as she scanned for her foe.

No new contacts—then what—the Wasp*!*

The small BattleMech had managed to push itself up with one arm, launching SRMs from its other in grim defiance of the monster looming over it. Most would have admired the tenacity of the MechWarrior piloting it, but Maria only felt disgusted at herself for forgetting to check that the scout 'Mech was dead. The disgust only lasted as long as it took to march her *Rifleman III* up to the downed machine and drive a heavy foot through its cockpit.

She checked her readouts again, noting how the SRM salvo had barely scratched her front armor—fortunate. Not that a scout 'Mech could threaten an assault, but there was always that chance of blind luck seeing a missile land in just the right spot to dislodge some critical piece of machinery—especially in a prototype like the *Rifleman III.*

But her status was still green. No breaches or faults were detected. Maria allowed herself a moment to relax from the shock as she maneuvered her 'Mech next to a parking garage. It lay just halfway between the warehouse she had used as her initial sniping position and the highway, which had finally crumbled in places as the Republican—*Imperial*, dammit! —Guard's artillery fell silent. She could see the smoke rising from the detonated *Locust* as she sank her *Rifleman* on its haunches, bringing the arm-mounted Gauss rifles level with the top floor of the garage.

The building's open sides made it ideal for shooting through, though it did limit her field of fire vertically. But hopefully it would mask the flare from her guns long enough to allow her to move and fire with the torso guns before falling back.

Maria settled back to wait, already beginning to plan her speech to the SLDF when they broadcast their demands. In the end, it was inevitable.

**GENEVA
SWITZERLAND ADMINISTRATIVE DISTRICT
TERRA
5 FEBRUARY 2777**

The 209th had responded to one of their lances vanishing by sending another *Spider* to check the area. The MechWarrior at its controls had been good, refusing to use jump jets on their approach, so Maria failed to notice them until they were almost on top of her. But they had lingered too long, confirming the identity of the wrecked BattleMechs, and Maria had been more than happy to plant a Gauss slug in their cockpit before they could radio back.

After that, Captain Escarra made good her retreat. Her *Rifleman III* made it to the factory when explosions blossomed throughout the neighborhood she had just left. The SLDF was nothing if not predictable—with the loss of several machines in the area, they elected to bombard it to flush out the supposedly entrenched defenders. Which meant they would soon come again.

Hayes and his crew had worked quickly, repairing and reloading her 'Mech in just under an hour. A passable performance, she had grudgingly noted before executing them. It was better that way. No chance they would be granted the pardon she was about to earn, after all.

Now her *Rifleman III* stood on the edge of the blasted landscape the SLDF had made as dawn came. Four new contacts were inbound. Coming in directly from the countryside, on a steady heading to cut straight through the suburb and into the city beyond. Bold. Or running out of time. Either was fine with her.

Her heart beat steadily in her chest as she toggled the Gauss rifles for individual shots once more. Better to bloody the noses of whoever was coming than overkill, especially now that she had no chance for further reloads. But...maybe it would be more effective to annihilate a single 'Mech in an overwhelming display of force before surrendering—no. No point wasting time considering alternatives. MechWarriors had to be bold, and decisive. Those of the Amaris Dragoons even more so.

Then her targeting computer beeped that the enemy was in range and all distraction was banished from her mind. The computer chirped as it confirmed the two 'Mechs in her arm Gauss rifle's sights—a pair of *Commando*s. Huh. Seemed like the 209th had some Lyrans in its ranks.

The targeting reticles slid over the head of the first *Commando*, weaving between low buildings, going red as the lock was confirmed. Her second reticle moved on, fixing on the other splitting off—to search for the wreckage of their comrades? Or to confirm any enemy presence lingering in the area?

Well, she was happy to confirm their suspicions. Maria's arm-mounted Gauss rifles barked, and the cockpits of the two *Commando*s disintegrated. That certainly got the attention of the two following contacts, who increased their speed—and another lance materialized on her sensors, moving in support.

Captain Escarra swore as she realized she'd been baited. Her *Rifleman* straightened, bringing the torso guns to firing position as she tried to acquire the other two contacts. Judging by the speed of the new arrivals, they were in a heavier tonnage than her current prey.

One of the blocks next to her exploded.

They knew she was here.

She scanned what little her guns could see—until a glint of neon light from a flickering advertisement reflected off a cockpit betrayed the presence of a *Mercury* hunkered down behind what had been a shopping mall. She didn't waste time on any theatrics as she pulled the triggers simultaneously.

One shot slammed into the 'Mech's shoulder, making its torso twist as the second went into the building it was using for cover and plowed through with enough force to still slam into the war machine, sending it crashing to the ground.

She moved around an office block, taking cover just in time. Something hit the front of the old building and detonated, spraying her machine with smoke and rubble. Instinctively Maria threw the *Rifleman* into reverse, striding backward as her cover shuddered and began to fall apart. The fourth contact was still mobile, having chosen to rely on speed over armor, and was moving to flank her—but then what was shooting at her front—

Maria looked away from her targeting screens, out of the cockpit, and swore as she saw the trails of long-range missiles raining down on the garage. Of course. That last bloody light 'Mech had done what it was meant to and radioed her estimated coordinates to its closing support. Rather than bully their way through, the SLDF had decided to run scouts through the defenses of Geneva to locate key targets and guide in their battery fire.

And when they'd stumbled across her, they had chosen to apply that same tactic. Well, that suited Maria just fine—first, she would get the targeting 'Mech, and then tear apart the missile boats.

And then something rocked against her 'Mech, throwing her in her seat with a curse. An alarm chimed as a chunk of her right torso armor dented under a stream of autocannon shells. She snarled as she spun her torso, bringing her guns to bear on her attacker—and saw a loping *Sentinel* accelerate to match her turning speed.

Sneaky little bastard. Unfortunately for them, her Gauss rifles weren't fixed-facing. Her right arm moved out as well and brought the medium 'Mech into her sight. With a squeeze of the trigger, it was the *Sentinel*'s turn to stagger as its front armor shattered. That momentary slowing of its movement was enough to bring her left arm around and follow up, smashing apart the remains of its armor plating and gouging a deep sparking hole in its internals. But it kept its footing.

Maria snarled in frustration as her computer beeped, resolving the identities of the other 'Mechs silhouetted against the morning light. A *Catapult*, *Crusader*, *Dervish*, and *Trebuchet*.

What the hell are they closing in for? Maria thought as she pulled the trigger again, sending another Gauss rifle shot into the *Sentinel*. This one finally made it fall to the ground in a shower of sparks and a spray of coolant. With that threat dealt with, she turned the *Rifleman* to face the incoming machines and began to walk backward. Her torso armor had taken some hits, but was still good.

"Pilot of the *Rifleman*! You are facing the 209th! Stand down," a voice crackled over the radio.

Finally.

"This is Captain Maria Escarra, of the Fourth Amaris Dragoons. Will comply once guarantee of safety and fair treatment under the SLDF Code of Conduct and Justice is assured," she transmitted back, keeping her guns ready but elevated.

There was a pregnant pause. "...Fourth Dragoons, you say," said the voice, which her sensors identified as the MechWarrior in the *Crusader*.

"Aye," Maria answered, a faint smile gracing her lips. Oh, yes, she would be quite the valuable prisoner, and as long as she cooperated, the oh-so-noble SLDF would play her game.

There was another pause, no doubt as the pilot conferred with his superiors. "The offer is rescinded. Light her up!"

"Wait, wha—"

An autocannon shell slammed into her *Rifleman*'s knee as lasers stabbed out and began to carve into her armor.

"We know what you've done. No Dragoon leaves Terra alive. General's orders."

That was—no, it wasn't meant to be like this! Maria snarled as she dropped her guns, focusing on the *Crusader*. "Watch me!" she spat, squeezing the triggers, watching four Gauss slugs slam with pinpoint accuracy into her target's torso. She remembered *Crusaders* had heavier armor on their legs than other BattleMechs. It swayed as if drunk from the blow, taking a step back to brace itself as Maria squeezed the triggers again. An LRM launcher on the *Crusader*'s left arm went flying, but more importantly its torso practically caved in.

A warning blared out.

No no no no no!

The lance in front of her opened fire, rocking her with explosions. The *Rifleman* refused to fall. Common sense held that she would fall back, keep her guns at optimal range. So Maria rammed the throttle forward, throwing her 'Mech in a thundering charge that slammed into the *Trebuchet* as the smoking husk of the *Crusader* fell.

Metal screamed as she smashed her BattleMech into her opponent in a crude approximation of a body slam. Lights flashed and alarms sang as her armor was slowly torn away from her, even as a fist smashed into her torso. Swearing and screaming, Maria Escarra lost herself in her rage at the unfairness of it all, slamming her *Rifleman*'s foot down on the *Trebuchet*'s to pin it in place for another body slam, this one sending it staggering backward enough for a quick kick to send it crashing to the ground.

Something tore loose as damage began to work its way into her internals. Captain Escarra screamed along with her systems as she stomped on her fallen foe. It was not meant to be like this! She was better than this! Than them! She would *not* die here! She couldn't! Not a legend like her!

The *Dervish* tackled her off the mangled *Trebuchet*, even as she continued to swear and lash out. The barrel of a Gauss rifle drove into the smaller machine like a spear before twisting out of shape. The other three guns unloaded on the retreating *Catapult*. She didn't notice if she hit or not.

She didn't even notice the *Dervish*'s fist slam into her cockpit.

In the end, Captain Maria Escarra of the Fourth Amaris Dragoons, survivor of Gorst Flats, died screaming.

ON1-K_B ORION

Mass: 75 tons
Chassis: General Mechanics-2A
Power Plant: Vlar 300
Cruising Speed: 43 kph
Maximum Speed: 64 kph
Jump Jets: none
    Jump Capacity: none
Armor: Leopard V Ferro-Fibrous with CASE
Armament:
    1 Lubalin Ballistics LB 10-X Autocannon
    1 Holly LRM 15 Launcher
    2 Magna Mk. II Medium Lasers
    1 Hovertec Quad SRM 4 Launcher
Manufacturer: General Mechanics
    Primary Factory: Mars
Communications System: OmniComm 3
Targeting and Tracking System: Starbeam 3000 with Artemis IV FCS

For more than six centuries, the *Orion* has been a mainstay of Inner Sphere heavy military forces and a deeply respected machine across the known breadth of humanity's domain. Its Hegemony-era ON1-K model was so effective that no other variant was produced for centuries. Even the Terran Hegemony's Royal Divisions found so little need for a custom variant that only a few of the enhanced ON1-Kb units were ever produced, all in the 2760s. Lost to history for centuries, this so-called Royal *Orion* was briefly attested in the New Dallas Memory Core, proving the elusive 'Mech's existence—if only via quartermaster footnotes, administrative overviews, and a few truncated maintenance briefs.

Capabilities

The ON1-Kb's most significant upgrade—though mundane by modern standards—was an improved cooling system that made overheating nearly impossible. Other improvements used advanced and expensive components to incrementally increase survivability and effective firepower.

The *Royal Orion* inherited the ON1-K's finicky ammunition feed, despite the autocannon itself being from an entirely different manufacturer. In the ON1-Kb's case, both ammo bins had to be short-loaded one round to avoid the risk of malfunction when switching between bins—a far more common occurrence with LB-X weapons than the ON1-K's standard autocannon. The problem was noted and reportedly described to General Mechanics, but if the history of the ON1-K is any indicator, the issue remained unresolved.

Battle History

In light of the information recovered from the New Dallas Core, a number of recorded engagements involving the legendary General Aleksandr Kerensky have been re-reviewed. In several instances, Kerensky likely used an ON1-Kb instead of what was previously thought to be a single, repeatedly customized ON1-K.

Despite the fall of its capital of Apollo in 2768, the Rim Worlds Republic remained in a state of political flux for some time as various factions sought to gain control and curry favor with the Star League Defense Force. In 2769, while visiting Erin to inspect SLDF repairs to the vital shipyards, General Kerensky went groundside to get some cockpit hours along with his command lance.

Advance scouts had failed to detect a contingent of Rim Worlds Army commandos who had sensibly evaded pitched battle during the SLDF invasion. Being fed intel by sympathizers in the new Rim Republican government and waiting for a chance to strike, these insurgents remained hidden in the wilderness. Their opportunity arrived when Kerensky's custom ride was hangar-bound due to a software glitch, forcing the general to switch to what appeared to be a standard ON1-K.

While traveling between outlying staging depots, Kerensky was waylaid by a full lance of EXT-4C *Exterminators*. The *Exterminators* used their stealth systems to remain concealed until they had clear shots at their only target: Kerensky himself. Focused fire from the ambush sent Kerensky's *Orion* crashing to the ground before his lancemates could react. A lucky missile hit penetrated the *Orion*'s torso, triggering an explosion that should have blown the entire machine, and its pilot, to bits. With the element of surprise now gone and their objective obvious, the Rim Worlds lance was dealt with in short order by Kerensky's escort of heavy and assault BattleMechs that shielded his shattered 'Mech while carving up the lighter *Exterminators*. The Rim Worlds' pilots died, with some satisfaction at having completed their mission and avenged their fallen nation. However, as records show, Kerensky's cockpit was miraculously undamaged; and the general mostly unharmed. Historians of the late Succession Wars have assumed Kerensky had luckily chosen to travel with nearly empty ammo bins, but it is now apparent he had, by 2768, switched his backup to an ON1-Kb; the Royal variant's visual similarity to the standard model resulted in the assassins' single, critical mistake. However, it remains morbidly intriguing to consider, as many historians have, how the course of history was so nearly derailed by a case of mistaken identity—and how many other such minor errors have led us to where we are today.

Although the ON1-Kb itself is functionally extinct, parts of a few SLDF-era examples have been identified, using lot ID codes from the New Dallas documents. Several well-preserved components come from a machine encountered in 2995 on Here. Hauptmann Rhivallo Morton's detached garrison of Third Lyran Regulars was tasked with intercepting a pirate raiding force and engaged a heavy lance including what appeared to be a standard ON1-K. As battle commenced on the outskirts of a remote industrial depot, Morton noticed the *Orion* was sustaining a staggering volume of fire. Initially crediting an unusually skilled pirate MechWarrior, Morton was surprised to see the *Orion* using an advanced autocannon. He focused his lance's fire on the 'Mech until it collapsed, legless. Other pirate 'Mechs and vehicles took advantage of the Lyrans' preoccupation, grabbing as many supply crates as they could carry and running for their DropShip rendezvous. Fixated on the lure of *lostech*, Morton ordered his forces to let them go.

Wary of additional surprises, the Lyrans put several more shots into the downed machine before sending in a capture team. The pilot, apparently named Hobart Spicer the Eyeball Slicer according to his forehead tattoo, did not survive his attempt to fight his way out of his 'Mech, and much of the cockpit was damaged by the grenades the Lyrans dropped inside to effect the aforementioned failure to exit. What remained was shipped to Tharkad University for study. Lyran researchers had some idea that the newly promoted Morton had actually recovered a *lostech*-equipped *Orion*, but for many years they lacked the software and documents to properly classify or repair the 'Mech's systems. Even then, they assumed the components were custom upgrades. It was not until the relative calm of the Republic era that historians had time to comb through far-flung scrap warehouses to catalog remaindered bits of ancient salvage (rendered irrelevant as research subjects after the 3030s, when the Inner Sphere could simply manufacture these items anew).

Notable 'Mechs and MechWarriors

Commanding General of the SLDF Aleksandr Kerensky: Though Kerensky is known to have piloted several BattleMechs during his long career, he is inextricably linked with the *Orion* chassis. His famous customized *Orion* has been retained in history largely because of the interest in its extensive modifications and the copious recordings of its most notable deployment, the final assault on Unity City that ended the Amaris Civil War.

Based on the standard ON1-K, the custom unit (simply referred to as "the Kerensky") was extensively and repeatedly modified, most notably to accommodate an experimental snub-nose PPC and enhanced heat sinks. Centuries later, when House Kurita discovered the 'Mech's stripped hulk, technicians were able to use the base chassis' fittings and ports to restore the machine to its baseline configuration.

The experimental machine's numerous customizations made maintenance unpredictable at best. After being forced to switch BattleMechs during a scramble due to lockups in both the PPC gimbal mount and the Gauss rifle's feed system, Kerensky kept a standard ON1-K as a backup ride, reserving his distinctive custom for deployments with sufficient preparation time and logistic support. It is now apparent he *also* used a -Kb variant at times, adding to the long-standing uncertainty regarding his exact ride in many battles for which only spotty or degraded footage remains.

Type: **Orion ON1-Kb**
Technology Base: Inner Sphere
Tonnage: 75
Role: Brawler
Battle Value: 1,617

Equipment		Mass
Internal Structure:		7.5
Engine:	300	19
Walking MP:	4	
Running MP:	6	
Jumping MP:	0	
Heat Sinks:	10 [20]	0
Gyro:		3
Cockpit:		3
Armor Factor (Ferro):	231	13

	Internal Structure	Armor Value
Head	3	9
Center Torso	23	36
Center Torso (rear)		10
R/L Torso	16	22
R/L Torso (rear)		10
R/L Arm	12	24
R/L Leg	16	32

Weapons and Ammo	Location	Critical	Tonnage
Medium Laser	RA	1	1
LB 10-X AC	RT	6	11
Ammo (LB-X) 20	RT	2	2
Ammo (LRM) 16	RT	2	2
Ammo (SRM) 25	RT	1	1
CASE	RT	1	.5
LRM 15	LT	3	7
Artemis IV FCS	LT	1	1
SRM 4	LT	1	2
Artemis IV FCS	LT	1	1
Medium Laser	LA	1	1

Notes: Features the following Design Quirks: Easy to Maintain, Rugged (1).

Type: **Orion Kerensky**
Technology Base: Inner Sphere
Tonnage: 75
Role: Brawler
Battle Value: 1,821

Equipment		Mass
Internal Structure:		7.5
Engine:	300	19
Walking MP:	4	
Running MP:	6	
Jumping MP:	0	
Heat Sinks:	10 [20]	0
Gyro:		3
Cockpit:		3
Armor Factor (Ferro):	231	13

	Internal Structure	Armor Value
Head	3	9
Center Torso	23	36
Center Torso (rear)		10
R/L Torso	16	22
R/L Torso (rear)		10
R/L Arm	12	24
R/L Leg	16	32

Weapons and Ammo	Location	Critical	Tonnage
Medium Laser	RA	1	1
Gauss Rifle	RT	7	15
Ammo (Gauss) 16	RT	2	2
Ammo (SRM) 25	RT	1	1
CASE	RT	1	.5
Snub-Nose PPC	LT	2	6
SRM 4	LT	1	2
Artemis IV FCS	LT	1	1
Medium Laser	LA	1	1

Notes: Features the following Design Quirks: Easy to Maintain, Rugged (1), Prototype.

SECOND EXODUS

ALAYNA M. WEATHERS

For after the Usurper's fall,
A first Exodus
to new worlds, and new stars,
clinging to the chance
for a new beginning.

The soil is rich,
much like the planet is new,
though foundations are laid
with blueprints from before.

Prosperity, though,
cannot grow
from the same seeds
that once reaped war.

A new generation of leadership sees it.

A Second Exodus begins.

May Unity be found in
the shedding of tradition.

Give up the plans of your forebears
for something truly new.

ACE DARWIN IN PARADISE

JAMES BIXBY

"Never attribute to malice that which is adequately explained by stupidity."

—HANLON'S RAZOR

**GEMINI STABLES TRAINING FACILITY
BLACK HILLS
SOLARIS VII
LYRAN COMMONWEALTH
18 DECEMBER 3092**

Annabelle Darwin-O'Bannon leaned against a support column, watching a gaggle of technicians raise a BattleMech from the massive flatbed recovery vehicle. Uncle Andrew said this was a special 'Mech, and had insisted Annabelle be here to see it returned to its rightful owner. Annabelle assumed that meant either her mom or Auntie Tanya, but neither was present right now.

"Make sure those knees are locked!" Andrew Sevrin shouted at the top of his lungs as he waved his hands back and forth.

A loud *thud* rang through the hangar space as gravity took over and the BattleMech slid from its bed and landed on the ferrocrete pad below. The arresting hoist pulled taut, keeping the machine from tipping forward. Techs in scissor lifts attached myomer-strengthened

chains to anchor points on the war machine's shoulders, suspending the 'Mech upright.

She could see why such a move was necessary. Normally a 'Mech in standby mode would still generate enough electricity to feed power to its myomer musculature to keep the machine upright and locked. This 'Mech, however, had no engine to speak of. The entire torso cavity was empty, with no gyroscope or heat sinks, to say nothing of the lack of armor over the torso. As massive clamps locked the bipedal machine in place, technicians used hydraulic tools to force in place the locks in the key joints to allow the machine to stay upright. The clamps and cables would still need to be used, at least until an engine and gyro were installed.

Across the arms, legs, and hips, sandblasted and partially corroded metal was broken up by a heavily matted, but still garish, pink. Across the left arm in a heavily reinforced vambrace was mounted a particle projection cannon of some type. It was more compact than a Ceres Smasher or Lord's Light, and the muzzle device resembled the standardized form on most Clan OmniMechs, but beyond that, she could not identify it. On the shoulder pauldron was a two-toned pink cat's pawprint, still pristine and somewhat glossy, despite the wear and tear over the rest of the dilapidated 'Mech. It was the same pawprint that was on her T-shirt.

"Okay, so...who are we giving this piece of junk to?" Annabelle asked her adoptive uncle.

"Annabelle," Sevrin said with a smile on his face, "this piece of junk is *yours*! This is—well, *was*—your father's PNT-9R *Panther*."

Annabelle laughed at the notion. "I already own a 'Mech, Uncle Andrew."

"No, you mooch off your mom's *Marauder II*," Sevrin retorted. "And as much as you drool over Seanoa's *Onslaught*, that 'Mech belongs to the stables. This *Panther* is legally yours. Your father wanted you to have it when you were old enough. And we are going to fix it up just for you, exactly to your taste."

Annabelle looked at the BattleMech with even more concern on her face. The head module was entirely missing, and the skeleton had several connection points shredded or missing. "I have to ask, why a *Panther*? Surely, he had a chance to upgrade more than once in his career."

Annabelle saw her Uncle Andrew smile wide. "You know it's funny you should mention that," he said as he popped a stick of chewing gum in his bearded mouth. "So, no kidding, there I was..."

CURTISS HYDROPONICS MANUFACTURING ANNEX 03
PARADISE
FREE WORLDS LEAGUE
13 MARCH 3052

I have traveled across the Inner Sphere, serving contracts in all five Successor States, and even one Periphery state. Through it all my loveable *Panther* has been as much of a loved, well-worn companion as my indelible partner and tech Andrew Sevrin. Later on in my career, some mercenary journalist even went so far as to call my *Panther* iconic. Personally, I never saw it: seeing things as icons only tends to paint big targets on your back. But it is true that the old battle cat has been an important fixed point in my career. So it may surprise you that for a minute I was looking to replace it. The fact of the matter was the Clan Invasion scared the ever-living hell out of me. And after helping Wolf's Dragoons prevent the theft of some of their rare Clan OmniMechs, I felt my *Panther* was too slow and too lightly armed to face the new threat—if I was going to face them at all. That brought me to the aptly named world of Paradise, thankfully far from the Clan front.

Curtiss Hydroponics needed additional security for one of their secret projects. That alone was odd. Their headquarters on Paradise was hilt-deep in Free Worlds space, a jump or two away from Atreus itself. On the other hand, water is a much-needed commodity even on so-called Goldilocks worlds, where alien microbes and flora can sometimes cause unfortunate digestive issues even in apparently clean water. Pirates and colonial militias have historically staged raids on Paradise to secure parts for purifier systems, or even whole systems themselves, to keep their meager outposts survivable. The release of the Helm Memory Core and the dissemination of less specialized means of purification eased the pressure on water supply chains by an order of magnitude. Despite this relief, it was still popular for independent contractors and small-scale mercenaries like myself to occasionally "take a vacation to Paradise" for an easy payday.

I was accompanied on this sojourn by three distinct groups. The first was some pure independents, ostensibly led by an old acquaintance of mine from nearly a decade ago. Allejandro Cortez did indeed replace his BattleMech, and was now operating a *Wolfhound*. Apparently, he was taking to my method of hiring out independents and filling out smaller-time contracts like cadre and security detail. The problem was that with the Clan Invasion in full swing, mercenary commands needed to be company-strength to even get noticed. Even with the onslaught being well coreward from the Free Worlds League, spooked employers felt the need to hire larger and larger forces. This meant my old playbook of conglomerating indies and lance commands into a larger force was becoming more and more common, and the *Wolfhound*, *Blackjack*, and *Shadow Hawk* Cortez brought to the group were welcome.

The second group was led by a native Terran named Nicky Dansereau, something of a portly and jovial man. At some point in his career a bad ejection led to scarring on his face, which he covered with a luchador leather mask adorned with all sorts of purple and silver flair. His command, called the Deep Ones, brought a couple heavies to the party, and even an *Atlas*. Apparently, this group was double company strength at one point, but combat losses and a contract default left them depleted to two lances and needing to rehab their image. I hired them during a year-long training stint on Outreach, where they saw their first combat half an hour later. Individually, their skills were about average, but their teamwork was incredible. In simulations and battleROMs, I was shown proper fire convergence, as well as physical combat maneuvers that could make Zeta Battalion's infamous charge tactic look like child's play. With cohesion like that, I was more than willing to offer a cushy job and the second chance they needed.

Finally, there were the folks I brought on directly from recruiting from Outreach barrooms and folks coming in from the rain. The only MechWarrior in that group was Nyla Zaveski, a brown-skinned, hyper-muscled woman from the Federated Suns. She got injured in the same action Dansereau's group participated in on Outreach, and was unable to exercise heavily or drive the *Crusader* we brought with us. Instead, she had poured herself into "untangling the administrative mess" that was the paperwork I tended to ignore. I kept threatening to make the Amazonian my executive officer, which she disturbingly smiled at. There was also a pair of Striker tanks crewed by a multigenerational family unit. They swore up and down on Outreach that I hired them the same day Sevrin bought the IndustrialMech dealership that became my headquarters, though I personally had no memory of it. Had Nyla not shown me the contract paperwork, I would've told them to pound sand.

On the first day of official duty, I saw Captain Dansereau's *Archer*, adorned in his unit's black, silver, and purple paint, move from its parked positions to begin a wide patrol of Curtiss' property. Accompanying it was the *Atlas*, *Warhammer*, and *Phoenix Hawk* that made up the Deep Ones' heavy lance.

"Clear from your docks, boys," I said over the radio. "Your patrol is scheduled for four hours. Have fun!"

The amount of real estate Curtiss owned for two factories of industrial equipment was massive. Thirty square kilometers of open space across the drier parts of wetland, parked just outside the limits of a town I suspected was built exclusively to support the industrial plant. For as much security as Curtiss demanded, it just made me curious as to what the hell was going on there.

Confident Nyla would have the rest of the operation going smoothly enough, I could go back to purchasing a new BattleMech.

"So when last we talked," I said to Sevrin, "we were talking about a medium BattleMech. What are our opportunities?"

A cloud of nicotine smoke and steam from three coffee cups surrounded my irritable aide. Before him were tech printouts, splash sheets, brochures, and magazines covering the glut of new BattleMechs available to the wandering mercenary.

"What about a *Phoenix Hawk*?" Sevrin said as he ashed his habitual cigarette. He was holding a paper magazine with Achernar's newest upgraded '*Hawk* on the cover. Even the magazine's editor couldn't help sarcasm, with the legend NOW WITH TWO LARGE LASERS! on a yellow splash next to the posed BattleMech. Personally, I was less than impressed.

"Come on, Andy," I replied, bored already with the conversation. "*Everyone* pilots a *Phoenix Hawk*. Silver out there pilots a *Phoenix Hawk*."

Cortez spoke up while pouring himself a cup of coffee. "My two-year-old daughter has a bright-pink *Phoenix Hawk* stuffie," he said through a thick Spanish accent. "So, your paint job would work!"

"See what I mean? Even a child has a *Phoenix Hawk*! Thank you, Cortez." I turned to Sevrin. "Point is, the *Phoenix Hawk* is so bland everyone pilots them. I want to stand out! You know, in the AFFC it is a joke among Dispossessed warriors..."

"Yeah, yeah, 'I'm not Dispossessed, I am just on my way to my *Phoenix Hawk*,'" Sevrin finished the old saw before he lit a new smoke. "You already rejected a newer *Shadow Hawk* as being a logistical nightmare."

"Three different types of ammunition, all the wrong amounts. I never understood how *Shadow Hawk* pilots could manage all those guns!" I said to Sevrin, collapsing in a chair across the table.

"There is a new firm, Bander BattleMechs just released this new heavy, based on the *Marauder*, called a *Bandersnatch*."

I glanced at the advert and winced immediately. If this was built on the GM *Marauder* Chassis, I could not see it. The gait was so wide and the hips spread out I wondered how the 'Mech could even walk. The early publicity photos were taken at a weird angle. Maybe the marketing department was trying to convey a sense of motion, but it made the lines and proportions look all wrong.

"Now we're running into the opposite problem. Sure, I wanna stand out, but this would draw so much attention I might as well have a neon pink sign saying, 'Shoot me, I'm here!'" I said, causing Sevrin to spit up his coffee.

"No sense of irony, eh, boss?" Sevrin said. "What about one of those Outworlds heavies, the *Merlin*? Tough as hell, has a PPC we can use our Dragoon toys on. Similar handling profile?"

"Too far away, it's not in standard supply chains," I said. "Do *you* want to fly out to Alpheratz to take delivery? Besides, I'm looking for a speed upgrade and a durability boost. That incident on Outreach spooked me, even if the Dragoons patched my girl up as a thank you."

"There's a bunch of *Scorpion*s lying around. We can upgrade them right at the dealership, I got this neat idea—"

"NOPE!" I blurted out, barely suppressing a laugh at such an asinine idea as to operate a four-legged BattleMech. *Scorpion*s were fast and had a certain amount of agility with their four legs. To my mind, the fixed forward weapons mounts cramped my style. On top of that, the quadruped 'Mech was notorious for being a rough ride on the move.

"Look, Ace, we gotta think of *something* here. Unless we want to spring for one of those extra-light engines, our upgrade options for your *Panther* are limited. It's not like the chance to test a new, top-of-the-line BattleMech is going to just fall into our lap out here..." Sevrin's communications app on his noteputer chimed. "Sevrin... Yeah... Uh huh... Are you *kidding*? Yeah, Ace and I will be there in thirty minutes."

"What was that about?"

"I will tell you before we get there if you *promise* not to say a single word," Sevrin replied, a jet stream of tobacco smoke firing from his nose.

After I nodded, he said, "How would you like to test-drive a brand-new, top-of-the-line BattleMech?"

I said all of the words, of course. The timing was just impeccable. Apparently, Curtiss Hydroponics had created a subsidiary to get into BattleMech production, and a batch of test machines was ready. Curtiss' owner thought that since their security force included a semi-famous mercenary MechWarrior, they thought it kind to give me a chance to test-drive one. I am sure the cadre of test pilots they had on staff just *loved* that.

I certainly was not going to complain. The assembly facility looked small for BattleMech production. I learned that the chassis were actually assembled in orbit, and then shipped down for final assembly. Combined with the buildings clearly under construction in the surrounding area, it made sense that this whole operation was popping up all at once. Once I was inside, the building revealed its purpose not as assembly, but research and development.

I must say the pair of BattleMechs in maintenance cradles certainly *looked* impressive. Tall for a medium 'Mech, the claws on its feet reminding me of a desert arachnid. Its armored hide was heavily curved, only enhancing the insect-like appearance, as did the twin antennas on the back of the head. The T-shaped cockpit canopy sat recessed underneath a large, armored hood. On its back was an oversized jump pack; seven actuated thruster nozzles spoke to the 'Mech's maneuverability.

"When you said they had fifty-five-tonners, Andy, I was thinking *Griffin*s or *Shadow Hawk*s. What on earth is this?"

"This, Commander Darwin, is the TRX prototype," a burly, bronze-skinned man in last year's fashionable businesswear said. "Designed to use all the newly rediscovered technology to maximum effect, the TRX provides maximum maneuverability, battlefield accuracy, and strike capability in a fast, light, and unpredictable package. Techs call it a *Wraith*." The man walked up and extended his hand. "I'm Mathieu Kassel, executive vice president of Curtiss' brand-new military division. The *Wraith* here is my baby."

"Ace Darwin." I took the man's hand and received a surprisingly firm shake. For an executive, he was neither dainty nor trying to engage in a petty test of strength. "Just Ace, by the way. The WhipIts do not have a rank structure."

The correction got a smile and a nod from Kassel.

Sevrin walked up close to one of the prototypes, watching techs armor the machine. "So what are these things packing? Something bigger than the usual CoreTek 275?"

"We sourced a new 385 grade Extra-Light, so this puppy can run just shy of 120 kph. We want to try and squeeze in some of that new myomer-booster technology, but our computer models predicted we would run out of space.

"Space?" I asked. "Couldn't you just design around it?"

"To a certain extent, but with the advanced materials we'll be using, we have to be mindful of our physical volume as much as anything." Kassel pointed to an armor panel that was being removed from one test 'Mech. While the space between 'Mech and armor is always tight, the thigh of the TRX looked particularly thick, much thicker than on the *Chameleon* trainers at the Nagelring.

"Our first and second test platforms were built using conventional materials. They were there to make sure the new engine, gyroscope, and electronics all worked. Putting that many jump jets on a 'Mech so large had never been done before, so we had to write the control programs from scratch. You should have seen the flame-outs when they first jumped."

Kassel turned to the third 'Mech. "Our third platform uses our new zero-G-forged endo-steel chassis. Half the weight, but it takes up significant volume, so you've got to design the chassis with extreme precision. We have an orbital foundry up and running, designed from

Helm Memory Core blueprints. All of it was built in-house, spared no expense."

Were this a children's cartoon, I am sure my jaw would have dropped right to the floor. To engage in such a massive investment to start BattleMech manufacturing from scratch was more than impressive. To have the organization's first offering be a ground-up design instead of licensing an existing machine would have been considered insane a mere decade before. I quietly wondered how the board meetings of Curtiss Hydro went, with Kassel seeking another billion here or there for what amounted to a hot-rod garage.

Walking up, I glanced at the weapons pods. Thanks to the outer armor being removed from the left arm, I could see the mounting bracket for multiple weapons in an over-and-under configuration. The right arm was dominated by a large rectangular box that reminded me of a *Vindicator* with a three-meter-long laser barrel jutting out most of the space, and there seemed to be no hand actuator on this example. "Energy-based armament?"

"That's right. We got a large laser and two medium lasers for now. Our engineers are experimenting with tertiary weapons, though some insist a PPC should be considered. or a large pulse laser is the way to go." Kassel was clearly proud of the warhorse he was breeding, I'll give him that.

"Why is there only one hand actuator?" I asked. "If this thing moves as fast as you say, it will make an excellent raider, and you'd need two hands to maximize external stowage. Plus, in my experience, if you're moving a 'Mech flat out and need to turn, a hand can help balance against terrain."

Kassel pulled out a small notepad and scratched a few words. A stack of well-used pages smudged in blue ink said he took recommendations seriously. "Honestly this has not come up. Our test operators were gladiators pulled from Solaris, so perhaps it did not cross their mind."

That made sense, of course. The gladiators of game worlds fought first and asked questions later. Unless you were doing 'Mech sports on Noisiel, you rarely thought about what you had to make your machine hold, if anything.

"Well, Mr. Kassel. You got a very impressive machine here. I just have one last question," I said while pulling off my jacket. "Where's the keys?"

The 'Mech was not keyed to a specific MechWarrior, so only a simple alphanumeric code and five minutes synchronizing to the neurohelmet were needed to get the *Wraith*'s myomers flexing beneath me. The Star League-period neurohelmet I was using for several years spoiled me, since the old Marik Militia reservist model rested directly on my shoulders and weighed four times as much. The dried leather pads spoke of future chafing. As heavy as the helm felt though, the 'Mech's controls felt light and soft to the touch. Lifting each arm felt effortless and smooth, and its single hand flexed as I gripped the actuator control yoke.

"Okay, Andy," I said, "set the Augmented Reality course. Let's see how this bug handles."

Pushing the throttle to its maintenance-bay thrust, I felt the *Wraith* seemingly float on the ferrocrete pad. Even shifting my body weight side to side, I could feel the 'Mech's gyroscope hum to maintain center of balance. Having piloted half a dozen different BattleMechs in my career, I'd only felt such responsiveness when piloting a Clan *Black Hawk* on Outreach. The smooth ride from that experience I chalked that up to the Clans' techno-sorcery. Now I wondered just how much of the soft factors that make BattleMechs loved or loathed were lost from the Star League's collapse.

After a brief stroll, I pulled the TRX to the starting position for Curtiss' test range. Multiple green dots overlaid in the *Wraith*'s head-up display, each with a letter next to it to indicate order to travel.

Over the comm, Sevrin spoke into my ear. "Okay, Ace, I got the course set up. Basic maneuvers test first. You will see on your navigation screen a high-speed octagon course. Make one circuit, then cross between as many straight lines as possible in less than five minutes. You get a bonus of ten seconds if you jump through the hoop in the middle of the octagon."

"Copy that. Darwin ready," I said, tightening my piloting gloves and taking a deep, centering breath.

After three beeps over the radio, I rammed the throttle forward to its physical limit. The sensation of hitting 120 kilometers per hour in less than two seconds is hard to describe. My mind wandered to images of old cartoons where a character is sitting on a shed-built spaceship, and when the engine lights, they stay still while their ride shoots off screen, and their arms stretch ridiculous length to accommodate.

A BattleMech was still a BattleMech though, and in no time, I managed to get a feel for the speed. As the *Wraith* galloped to Waypoint Alpha, I counted down seconds until the waypoint was just thirty meters ahead of me, and I could start the turn. After crossing Waypoint Delta, I slammed my feet down on the jump-jet pedals. I let out a yelp of excitement as the air-breathing rockets brute-forced the BattleMech into near flight through the projected ring marking the halfway point. As I ended the circuit, I pulled on the throttle and pressed the left foot pedal, twisting my body hard to match the mechanical inputs through the neurohelmet. Almost as though it were controlled by thought, the *Wraith* underneath me shifted its posture and maneuvered into a pivot stop.

"Very impressive," I said over the radio. "It's not just the speed and maneuverability. The controls are more responsive than anything I have encountered. Doing that stop on my *Panther* would have taken another fifteen meters."

"Glad you approve, Ace," Kassel called. "Maneuverability and responsiveness were our principal benchmarks. The goal was to make a BattleMech that could flow like water across the battlefield."

"Well, it's not like in the kiddie cartoons, but close enough," I said. "Andy, give me Dansereau's location. I wanna poke the bear a little."

"Ace," Sevrin said with the disapproving tone of a parent watching a child about to cause chaos. "What are you thinking?"

"Just watch and see," I said as I followed the navigational marker to a point near where Dansereau's patrolling lance was expected to cross in half an hour. By the time they crossed where my 'Mech lay in wait behind a hilly outcrop, I was giggling like a madman.

"Captain Dansereau, report in," I called, using a line-of-sight laser comm.

Apparently, he didn't pick up what the source was and replied as though I was calling from our billet. "All quiet on the western front," Dansereau said. "Just the marsh, its wildlife, and valuable boredom between us and a paycheck."

I lined up the TRX to maneuver right between the four 'Mechs of the lance. Vance's *Atlas* was pulling up the rear, while Reynolds' *Phoenix Hawk* was up front. Dansereau's *Archer* and Angel's *Warhammer* were on the sides of the classic diamond formation, giving me a nice, wide fifty-meter gap in the middle. I set the laser weapons to training power levels and pressed the throttle.

"Well, if you need a little excitement..." I said. *"Trainingbeginsnow!"* I belted out as loud and fast as possible and depressed the triggers to the large and medium lasers in the 'Mech's arms.

The emerald and sapphire beams splashed heat and color across Vance's *Atlas* enough for him to know he got kissed, but by the time he turned the 100-ton behemoth around, I was already past him on the opposite side of his turn. I spread the *Wraith*'s arms wide like a kid pretending to be a superhero and continued firing laser pulses at the lance's two heavies before reaching out to the *Phoenix Hawk* with the left hand. A loud clang of metal on metal sounded as the *Wraith*'s hand slapped the *Phoenix Hawk*'s backside and I shouted "Tag! You're it!" and bolted the *Wraith* back to Curtiss' R&D bay.

The cursing and howls of rage over open comms was quickly overcome by laughter. Even Reynolds' *Phoenix Hawk* delayed chasing after me long enough that I was out of reprisal range. Not that Kassel would have appreciated one of his prototypes being shot up.

The following days went by without incident. I honestly spent more time in staff meetings than on training maneuvers with the Whiplts. When not doing that, I was making sure the neon pink paint on my beloved *Panther* was buffed, waxed, and shiny before the sand ablated it again.

At first, I was genuinely interested in getting on the *Wraith*'s waiting list when it reached full production. Then I found out I could purchase a *Zeus* and enough spare parts to half build a second one from Defiance Industries for what Curtiss Militech was looking to charge for one of their *Wraith*s. At that price, I decided maybe the *Panther* wasn't so bad after all.

After ten solid days of nothing in particular actually happening, I decided to go out on patrol personally. Really, it was a weak excuse to go outdoors. The marshlands stood in stark contrast to the cold mountains of Tharkad. It may have been humid as hell, but it was sunny and warm enough that I was feeling nostalgic for my childhood years.

Reading the map, I saw a plateau overlooked almost the entirety of the plains Curtiss owned and were using as proving grounds for their hot rod of a BattleMech. And most importantly, Sevrin and I had made some additions to the *Panther*'s head module that needed testing.

So that was how I wound up lying on a lawn chair, slotted into some brackets on the top of my *Panther*. A tester can of ice-cold margarita-flavored Coolant Flush in a cup holder, my trusty flight jacket and coolant vest hanging off a hook on the chair back. A pair of binoculars dangling from a neck strap aided me in my job keeping tabs on Curtiss' property. Dansereau's heavy lance was looping around to the south, testing some small-unit maneuvers during their sweep. To the east and well out of range, the two lighter BattleMechs of Dansereau's unit were holding the entryway to Curtiss' property from proper civilization, the nearest large city some fifty kilometers southeast. Out to the northwest, Cortez's block camo painted light 'Mechs jogging were supposed to be jogging their assigned route.

"Andy, from my vantage point it is all quiet," I called out through a handset radio keyed into the *Panther*'s communications system. "I'm gonna go radio silent for half an hour."

"Roger that, Ace. Enjoy the nap." The bastard didn't even try to hide it.

"You may want to check the source of the lime syrup on that soda flavor. It was more bitter than sweet, like an officer who was called out for impropriety on an open channel."

"Putting it into the tasting notes. Will reach out in three-zero minutes."

As it stood, I only got to enjoy ten minutes of clear skies and warm sun before Cortez called me. "Ace, I got an unknown contact to my east. Looks like some blowers are shooting up a lot of water. Can you see from your position?"

I stood up and lifted the binoculars to my eyes. Sure enough, there was a large plume of water being kicked up. Through my binoculars I could see a convoy of hovercraft, some being large cargo trucks. Dotted around them were nearly a dozen fanboats or personal skimmers.

"Darwin to base. Prepare for company. I see a column of conventional vehicles making for the water-treatment grounds. No BattleMechs yet, but that doesn't mean they're not there. Dansereau?"

"Go ahead, Ace."

"Take your group to six klicks out from the factory. Establish a perimeter. I expect these pirates to scatter when the BattleMechs show up. Cortez, meet you there. Let 'em dismount and then secure their vehicles. Should be easy pickings."

"Copy, Commander. Cortez inbound."

There was one last thing I needed to secure. "Andy, inform Mr. Kassel that pirates are inbound. Have his security teams hold at the factory. We'll ambush them in the middle of the pillaging."

I pressed a button on the lawn chair, and a small electric motor reeled in the umbrella and folded the chair into its storage compartment. The soda can got knocked over and leaked all over the paint, but there was nothing to do about that now. I yanked the canvas cover over the contraption and hooked it in place.

"Not sure he'll like you letting bandits walk into his factory, boss."

"Well, unless he has other BattleMechs onsite, I do not see an alternative. We won't be able to intercept until they're already there. Best to keep 'em pinned."

One of these days I will learn to keep my big mouth shut.

Even jumping from the plateau and moving my *Panther* at a full sprint, it took me ten minutes to get to the pirates' target. Both tankers were backed up against a large commercial-storage tank and were pumping water into each vehicle's spacious trailer.

Meanwhile, the flatbed trucks were backed into the loading dock, the rolling doors were clearly ripped off their tracks. That they were ready for a quick exfiltration showed these people were at least smart. That nobody was outside to stand watch showed they were not *too* smart.

Cortez's *Wolfhound* moved up 100 meters to my left, the lasers on its chest adjusted position to target both trucks simultaneously. "Water and industrial parts, the story of this planet, eh, *amigo*?" he said over the radio.

"So it seems," I replied. "Where are the rest of your guys?"

"Ed and John are half a klick back, their 'Mechs ready to plink from range. Rico's *Shadow Hawk* is by the east side, making sure the side door is secure."

"Good, let's go introduce ourselves."

I nudged the throttle forward, the *Panther* beneath me moving at a casual parade walk. Two pirates carrying boxes from inside the warehouse to the flatbeds froze halfway through delivering their pilfered cargo.

"Good afternoon," I said via my external speakers as I pointed the *Panther*'s PPC right at the first tanker. "I take it you folks are thirsty?"

Poor bastards didn't even fight back, just jumped from the top of the trailers and scurried into the nearest building.

"Cortez, knock over their trucks, and make sure they can't leave with anything," I said before putting paid to my orders, kicking over the tankers in turn.

By the time the second truck was rolled over, a forklift had reached the gate before immediately turning around, its yellow caution light illuminating the warehouse interior in brief pulses.

"Sevrin," I radioed, "the pirates aren't going anywhere. Tell security to move in and make the arrests."

Before Sevrin could reply, a panicked woman called the general frequency. "WhipIts, this is Anna. I got three BattleMechs on my tail. Christ, these things are fast! Never seen them before!"

"This is Ace. Stay cool, we're on our way. Cortez, hit it!"

The problem with large industrial facilities is that, if you are paid to defend them, you can't just roll through or onto buildings. You could easily find yourself liable for damages, and battlefield insurance just does not exist in most circumstances. So, while I *could* have jumped my *Panther* onto the roof of the building, alongside the two mediums accompanying me, the damage to the facility would have cost us more than it was worth. All the while Dansereau's medium lance leader was a mere 200 meters from us and panicking like the Clans had crossed half of the Inner Sphere in the last month. It took three excruciating minutes spent maneuvering around warehouses, offices, and other drek before I witnessed the battle at hand.

There was Anna, her *Phoenix Hawk* dancing as best it could against the three *Wraith* prototypes, her medium lasers and machine guns blazing away, occasionally interrupted by a sapphire beam from her large laser. Across the entryway, I could see the Striker tanks trying to pin the machines with long-range missile fire, but only succeeding in cratering the area around them.

"You gotta be kidding me!" I said, before switching to the general frequency. "Curtiss pilots, Curtiss pilots, stand down! *Phoenix Hawk* is friendly, say again, we are all friends here!"

Whoever was at the helm of those 'Mechs made no indication they heard me, and two of the prototypes instead flashed their paired large lasers my way. Cursing in a manner that would make my grandmother wince, I rammed the *Panther*'s throttle forward and shifted laterally, putting distance between myself and Cortez.

"Those things are Curtiss' new babies. Try not to shake the lightbulbs too hard. Anna, book it to the loading bay. Dansereau!"

"Kinda busy, bossman. Six Bravo-Mikes, including a *Hunchback*. Need to humble them."

I slammed a fist hard against a hand-painted EMERGENCY IDIOT button on the bulkhead of my cockpit. The pirates had BattleMechs in reserve, and here I was dealing with overeager idiots who were supposed to be on *my* side.

"Curtiss test pilots, this is Ace Darwin of the WhipIts! You are engaging your own mercenaries! Respond!"

Static met my pleas to stand down, and more inaccurate laser fire crisscrossed either side of my *Panther*.

"Sevrin," I said, "I am invoking our contract's escape clause. We are under friendly fire, and are no longer liable for damages to Curtiss property."

"So noted, boss. Nyla is securing our documents."

"Ace," Dansereau said, "we're not outgunned, but we *are* outnumbered here."

"Do your best, Nicky," I replied. "We are also engaged. Cortez, forget being gentle. Leg those things!"

I lined the *Panther*'s PPC on the rearmost *Wraith*. This particular prototype was experimenting with short-range missiles, and I was well out of its range. As a bolt of man-made lightning briefly connected our BattleMechs, the knee joint of the prototype fused from melted armor plate dribbling between gaps. The 55-ton machine turned right toward me, hobbled, and fell, its chest armor crumbling like paper under the impact.

Off to my left, autocannon tracer rounds from the *Blackjack* streamed while trying to connect a more mobile *Wraith* prototype while Cortez and his *Vindicator* lancemate were grappling with number three.

"*Wraith* pilots," I said, "stand down *now*! We already downed one of you, and we are friendly! Respond!" I swapped channels quickly "Andy, what the hell is going on?"

"Aside from Kassel saying he had three 'Mechs and they started shooting at you? I have no idea. Their radios must be jammed on transmit or something."

At that point, Cortez's lance managed to knock over a second *Wraith*. The *Vindicator* held its PPC to the new machine's faceplate to keep it incentivized. I turned my own BattleMech to the third, who saw it was all alone, and immediately turned tail to the 'Mech Factory wing.

"Tell Kassel two of his prototypes are severely damaged, and the third bugged out. And next time not to put amateur MechWarriors into a combat zone." I growled. "Dansereau, you need assistance?"

"Thanks, but it's all over but the crying here. Their bruisers are down and the zoomers ran off."

By time the smoke had cleared, two-thirds of the pirates were arrested or killed in a firefight, and I was in possession of two slightly used and dented BattleMechs on top of everyone else's equipment. And, not for the first time in my life, I was ready to punch my employer.

Mathieu Kassel saved me the trouble of having to hunt me down, though the presence of my equally irritable partner standing next to him told me he may have been dragged down to the employee lounge that served as the Whiplts' makeshift offices. God bless Sevrin, he knew how to effectively take power away from people.

I slammed my neurohelmet and coolant vest onto one of the cafe tables, and gently took off my sunglasses. Taking a deep breath and counting to fifteen, I took a seat in one of the many wire-frame chairs. "So, Mr. Kassel, you mind telling me what the hell happened out there and what you were thinking, sending your 13 million C-bill prototypes into a combat zone?"

"You let those brigands into my factory! Someone had to do something–!"

"You were being a fool," I interrupted. "None of those 'Mechs had been combat tested yet. And while I didn't know this at the time, your pilots were clearly amateurs." I took a long, slow sip of water before letting myself get too riled up. "I do not know *what* caused the communications screwup, nor do I really give a damn. The fact of the matter is that those three 'Mechs of yours, and the lives of their pilots, were *your* responsibility, not mine, and you are damn lucky you only have two partially destroyed 'Mechs and a broken clavicle to answer for."

"Ace," Kassel said, "you are being paid to protect Curtiss Military factories, a mission I could argue—" But I cut him off again. I was not in the mood.

"If you want to get into contract language, I can have Nyla pull up our paperwork. To my memory, we were contracted to guard 'Curtiss Hydroponics' factory and warehouse facilities.' 'Curtiss Militech' was never mentioned. Hell, I was not aware your division even *existed* until two weeks ago!" I turned to Nyla. "Is that correct?"

"Contract parties are listed as 'Ace Darwin's WhipIts,' and 'Curtiss Hydroponics,'" Nyla said, after donning a pair of reading glasses. "Nowhere in the contract does it mention 'Military division,' 'Manufacturing Annex 3,' 'BattleMech production facilities,' or the like. Assets to be protected are specifically stated as 'water-purification manufacturing facilities and product storage.' There is no mention of protecting offices, onsite water-storage tanks, construction equipment, or the row of Porta-Johns used by construction workers."

"Thank you, darling," I said, turning back to Kassel. "You want to argue that the WhipIts defaulted on our contract by letting the raiders into the facility. Fine, you can take the damaged garage door out of our contract insurance. Now I don't know if you ever served a single day as a MechWarrior, or in any military capacity. Back at the Nagelring, I learned multiple raid and counter-raid tactics. BattleMechs are *phenomenally* bad at chasing down and dealing with dismounted people. The best thing to do in a raid like that is to damage transportation, so the raiders cannot escape with any pilfered goods. As you will see in our after-action report, we accomplished just that. Your raiders were trapped, they were not going anywhere. And when they called for reinforcements, my people intercepted them, and those BattleMechs didn't get within a kilometer of your facility. Your actions distracted my people that *were* onsite and made it likely that the raiders could escape."

"This was a perfect time to combat test our machines! Simulations are all well and good, but..." Kassel continued babbling, moving from one lame excuse to the next. "This is all a simple communications failure, you cannot expect—"

"Mr. Kassel, if you wanted to combat test the *Wraith*, you should have consulted me on a training and cadre assignment. I would've been more than willing to negotiate a subcontract for that. Instead, you wanted to wander off and be a damned cowboy. I am open about my team being a cooperative of independent contractors. That arrangement can lead to a mishmash of markings and colors. We are not the Kell Hounds or the Eridani Light Horse, after all. So I am willing to state that, despite a clear-cut friendly fire incident, covered from multiple angles by multiple units of my team, this was a *completely unintentional* mishap."

I took another long, slow gulp of water to lower my heart rate, and make sure every word I said was precision crafted. "I mean, if I had Nyla interview the test pilots and find out they were not briefed on the Whiplts' markings, colors, or composition, and were told to maintain radio silence with any other entity but your test bunker, that would make life a *lot* more complicated for everyone." I spoke levelly, as neat as you please, the placement of my canteen punctuating the threat.

The tick of the analog clock on the wall was the only thing that made a sound in the next minute, and I could see Kassel glance toward my waist, looking for a nonexistent gun holster. By the Gods, I think he believed I was going to hurt more than his pride today.

"Mr. Darwin, I will see to it personally that your BattleMechs are refit. If you excuse me, I have an injured MechWarrior of my own to attend to." And with a nod, Kassel walked off.

Sevrin stared at me slack jawed, his habitual cigarette burning close to the filter, a centimeter of ash dangling from the burning leaves.

"Ace, do you want to try a hostile takeover of the company while we are at it? Own your own BattleMech factory? I am pretty sure you could've convinced him to sign over the deed at this point."

I let out a stuttering belly laugh at that, sitting back down. "Heavens, no! You're the entrepreneur in this outfit. I just shoot things."

"All tallied up, we were rather fortunate. No injuries, and only Rico's *Shadow Hawk* was seriously damaged. With two weeks left on our contract, I figured we would have no more serious duty ahead of us," Sevrin said, tossing the noteputer onto the coffee table

"That may be, Andy. Either way I get a feeling we should not show our face around this planet for a good long while though."

"Oh, I agree," Sevrin said as he lit up another cigarette. "I'll ship Cortez and his crew back to Outreach, since they only signed up for this contract. Nicky wants to re-up, however, and I didn't think you'd object to that. In the meantime, Nyla found us a gig that is a nice, low-risk job that pays ridiculously well."

"I am all for low risk. Where are you thinking?"

"Have you ever been to Solaris VII?" Sevrin said with a smile.

I never had, not finding the appeal of 'Mech combat for sport. Fate would have other plans for me though. That contract would become one of the most important of my career, if not for the professional chops, then for meeting the most important women in my life.

But that is another story.

GEMINI STABLES TRAINING FACILITY
BLACK HILLS
SOLARIS VII
LYRAN COMMONWEALTH
18 DECEMBER 3092

"Hold it, hold it," Annabelle objected. "Maybe I got my dates wrong here, but I was born in 3068. You're saying Dad came here and met Mom over a decade earlier?"

Sevrin popped a stick of gum in his mouth and smiled at the young woman. "You really think your mother and father fell in love right away and had a fairy-tale romance? Oh sweetheart, I thought Elizabeth told you that story already."

"Not...really. Just that she saw Dad, said to herself, '*Mine*', and got him." Annabelle shrugged. "I'm sure a lot of the details weren't suitable to tell your child."

Sevrin let out a big belly laugh. "On again, off again, aborted, restarted, occasionally diverted by your aunt... There was the time with the Steel Viper Clanswoman..." He cleared his throat at Annabelle's baffled look. "That contract in 3053 was what got your dad the first taste of fame, becoming a footnote in Solaris history. And for once, it wasn't even his fault."

"Wait...you mean Mom dragged him kicking and screaming into fortune and glory?" Annabelle asked.

"No, believe it or not..." Sevrin pulled out an old cigarette lighter and glanced down at its battered brass casing. The action confused Annabelle, who never recalled her godfather lighting a cigarette in her conscious lifetime. His hands were shaking, as though bad memories were trying to compel indulgence in an old habit.

"That time," he said wistfully, "it was all *my* fault..."

HYPERPULSE GENERATORS

MICHAEL MILLER

LECTURE AT ARC-ROYAL INSTITUTE OF TECHNOLOGY
PROFESSOR EMERITUS DIETRICH MATHERS
13 MARCH 3152

Hello, class. I'm Professor Arthritis...I mean, Emeritus Dietrich Mathers, visiting from Tharkad with that mob of academics Grand Duchess Kell invited. Your Adjunct Professor Maklin was kind enough to bribe me with a meal at an authentic Grateful Burger franchise, and I'm happy to repay her by giving a quick introduction to hyperpulse generators from my *Empire Technologies* series.

Hyperpulse Generator Origins

To start with the basics, hyperpulse generators are, in so many words, "faster-than-light radios." For about 500 years, they were absolutely vital for knitting together humanity's far-flung worlds, even though humanity spent most of those 500 years trying to kill each other.

HPGs, like JumpShips, are based on the hyperspace theories from Thomas Kearny and Takayoshi Fuchida. Kearny and Fuchida had originally observed hyperspace translations of particles in prototype fusion reactors—deep in gravity wells, where JumpShips could never operate. As a footnote in a paper published in 2022, they speculated about the creation of artificial jump points and provided the governing equations.

Artificial jump points attracted interest as far back as the Deimos Project in the early 2100s, because hyperspace travel would be much faster if ships could arrive and depart deep in gravity wells rather than beyond a star's gravitational proximity limit. However, multiple impracticalities stymied dreams of planet-based "stargates" or orbital "jump stations." First, fusion-like conditions were required, which were not compatible with most ships and passengers. Second, a ship-scale artificial jump point would require fantastic amounts of energy and money even by the Terran Hegemony's standards.

The Star League's quest for faster-than-light communications found a use for microscopic (and thus affordable...or at least tolerably expensive) artificial jump points, specifically faster-than-light communications without lag from natural jump points. History books usually record the Star League's HPG research program as lasting fifteen years through 2630, but the last decade was spent standardizing the design, mass-producing HPGs on Terra, and finally distributing them across known space.

Formally on New Year's Day in 2630, Nicholas Cameron sent the first HPG message, a prolix epistle about the peace, prosperity, and glory of the Star League that you may have had to memorize in secondary school if you were as unfortunate as me. In truth, Dr. Cassie DeBurke was transmitting incoherent noise from her kludge of an off-the-shelf hyperspace research chamber and assorted experimental transceivers by 2616. Her memoirs claim the first coherent message (29 January 2619) was "KF wer rite agin." Well, as coherent as byte limits of the crude device allowed. This was sent from the University of Terra to the Deimos Hyperspace Research Center. The arriving pulse, which did not target another HPG's core, also drove the passing Phobos Skyhook into safe mode with its electromagnetic pulse, which was quite a scandal. Accordingly, the 2630 New Year's Day massive...I mean, missive... usually gets lead billing in history books.

Hyperpulse Generator Operations

After the HPG establishes an artificial jump point (which looks like any other fusion plasma, if you were wondering), the field initiator creates a hyperspace field and begins rotating electromagnetic signals through hyperspace to a light-years distant destination, typically another HPG facility with a shielded receiver chamber where the signal arrives without distortion.

Like a jumping K-F drive ship, the hyperspace pulse does not travel in a "hyperbeam" or pass through a wormhole or rip holes through the space-time continuum. The pulses are "jumped" from the transmitting HPG to the reception point without passing through intervening space.

An interesting aspect of HPGs is what they transmit: radio signals, just like the personal communicators that everyone's reading rather than listening to what's going to be on today's pop quiz. Oh, got your attention now? Yes, HPGs translate millisecond bursts of mundane radio waves through hyperspace, not exotic particles or "hyperwaves" or something similar. While modest data is delivered per millisecond, equivalent to a few pages of text, HPGs can pulse rapidly, allowing delivery of large holovids or even—in command circuits of two chains of HPGs—providing almost real-time holovid communications.

The receiver chamber of an HPG not only allows undistorted reception, but it shields the hyperspace ripple of the arriving pulse, which is as powerful as a small JumpShip's arrival pulse. Since the side effects are similar to a small nuclear weapon's EMP and planetary HPGs are usually near or in cities, the damping is critical. (Again, refer to the Phobos Skyhook incident, or see what happens to ships along naval HPG command circuits.) Bonus: Targeting an HPG core also assures the HPG's owner controls the information.

While planetary HPGs normally deliver their pulses to well-known targets with centimeters of accuracy—far better than even the finest K-F drive navigation—mobile HPGs are less discriminatory. In fact, they typically target pulses out in the open. Command circuits of ships equipped with mobile HPGs were rendered nearly blind by repeated EMPs.

Take a moment to consider what that means: An HPG does not need to target an HPG, and you only need a radio to capture the signal. We'll get back to that later in this lecture.

Beyond individual HPG operations, there's the matter of organizing HPGs. I mean, back when humanity had enough working HPGs to organize into networks. The Star League, ComStar, and Clans built their planetary HPGs in two classes: A and B. A-class HPGs are...*were*...are hub installations found on key planets, able to send transmissions up to fifty light-years and capably handling distribution of signals to all other HPGs within their range, sequentially transmitting to all B-class stations in range multiple times per day. B-class HPGs transmitted only to specific A-class stations, but had ranges of twenty to thirty light-years. The Star League class B HPGs transmitted twice daily to up to three A-rated stations, while ComStar slowed that to once every few days to a single A-class.

The Star League and ComStar generally kept costs modest: one C-bill (when those were a thing) for a single holograph or two pages of text. (Big customers could get huge discounts for data-intensive transmissions like holovids.) One could even arrange priority transmissions, interrupting transmission queues to rush a message across the Inner Sphere. However, such priority transmissions were expensive: they required the HPG network to realign the A-class stations during transmission, meaning the message might bounce across dozens of relays, and ComStar charged 1,000 C-bills per relay involved. At the other extreme, the Clans mostly ran HPGs as a public service, so many Chatterweb users were never directly billed.

Anatomy of an HPG Station

Planetary-based HPGs are massive installations that became veritable fortresses during the Succession Wars. The actual HPG core is a relatively small portion of the installation, a meters-wide containment vessel looking like an over-instrumented fusion engine. Conventional communications gear, administration offices, and customer service areas composed most of the facility. ComStar often deliberately encouraged businesses near its HPGs, with hotels, conference centers, banks (especially ComStar) and other enterprises that utilized interstellar communications.

A common feature is a large dish antenna on the roof, which interfaces with planetary satellite networks or even punches radio signals to standard jump points with enough megawatts to frazzle nearby 'Mechs. This dish antenna is often mistaken for part of the HPG. In fact, ComStar would emphasize that falsehood during Interdictions by dramatically turning aside the dish, but truthfully, the dish has almost nothing to do with the generator's hyperspace activity. (You wouldn't want a hyperspace pulse arriving in the open and EMPing the nearby city, and like JumpShips, signals from the core can be sent in any direction.)

A fusion power plant is almost universally present on site to give a compact, independent power supply, but a robust utility grid connection is satisfactory.

On the note of fusion power, while fusion-like particle energies are maintained in an HPG's core, it is not a power plant. Any means of power extraction ruin the required multi-dimensional smoothness of particle energies in the core. An outside power plant is necessary to maintain the "fusion" conditions.

An artificial jump point is highly dependent on local conditions: gravity, planetary mass, and planetary mass distribution and masscons (e.g., a nearby mountain range or dense ore bed). Because the Star League and ComStar were not interested in having the Houses steal HPGs (as the pirate Helmar Valasek was known to do), the cores of planetary HPGs were tuned for specific locations on a planet, making them hard to relocate after being constructed.

More to Come

All right, let's take a quick break. When we come back, I'll talk about some HPG applications you're probably not familiar with.

DEEPER INTO THE MACHINE

LORCAN NAGLE

OVERLORD-CLASS DROPSHIP RSS *RIGHTEOUS FURY*
EPSILON ERIDANI ORBIT
REPUBLIC OF THE SPHERE
11 FEBRUARY 3141

This isn't like the sims at all…

Sergeant Alison Reeves clutched the sides of her chair in a white-knuckle death grip as the sounds of a combat drop played out around her. The dull thrum of the *Overlord*-class DropShip's weapons batteries firing, the crash of weapon hits to the outer layers of the ship's hull, the rattling as the ship began to descend into the atmosphere, each time causing a cascade of panicked thoughts like *oh shit, this time it's gonna breach*.

She was glad the consoles in the control room were configured in a cross shape, so none of the other operators in the room—her subordinates—could see how badly the battle was affecting her. They'd done simulated drops back on Terra, of course, but even though she and her fellow recruits felt they'd come through those exercises with flying colors, she now couldn't comprehend how anyone in the training corps could think they'd prepared anyone for an aerospace fighter making a close pass by their ship.

Like so many other young people, she'd been enticed to sign up with the promise of protecting what remained of the Republic from predation by the nefarious forces beyond the Fortress Wall—the Capellans, Kuritans, and even worse, the Clans—but now she found herself facing death in the skies over a Republic world. She was part of a task force sent to defeat the Blessed Order, a covert militant secret society within ComStar—a domestic enemy. A battle she wasn't adequately prepared for against a foe she wasn't aware of... Not the best start to a career in the military. She was so caught up in her reverie that she barely noticed the message coming over the 1MC applied to her.

"All hands, this is the Bridge. We have entered the atmosphere. We will be grounding near New Copley within three minutes. Begin preparations for deployment as soon as possible."

"Okay, that's us," she said to the room, loud enough to be heard over the commotion as the ship's passengers began to act. "Let's get the consoles up and running and connected. By the book, guys."

She and her crew got to work, bringing the advanced electronics in the control room online. Each of the four consoles resembled a BattleMech cockpit, with a full array of controls and a series of extra screens in the controller's peripheral vision. When Alison's central monitor came to life, she could see the inside of a cradle down in one of the BattleMech bays deep in the DropShip. Techs were moving, wary of the ship's motion in the atmosphere, but they were prioritizing working on other bays before removing to the one she could see out of.

Another call came over the 1MC: "Grounding in thirty seconds... twenty...ten..."

The bay doors opened almost immediately, and Alison could see a lance of BattleMechs stride out of their bays and down onto the planet's surface as soon as it was safe.

As she watched, the voice of one of the bay personnel came over the team's comms. "Sergeant, bay master's regards, and she says your primary lance will be free of the cradle in about two minutes. You'll get the green light on the cradle mount as per the book, and someone will be in place to guide you out."

"Right, you heard the man, same as in the drills." *Hopefully.* "We'll be on rapid response when we get out there, and as soon as the perimeter is secure, we bring the second lance out."

Her team—Corporals Anthony, Yoshino, and Dubois—all gave an affirmative and got ready to move. When the time came, the quartet of UBM-2R *Revenant* drone BattleMechs emerged from their cradles and awkwardly stepped out of the 'Mech bay into the light of Epsilon Eridani's sun. While most four-legged 'Mechs aped a mammalian shape, the *Revenant* stood on segmented, insectoid legs—long and spindly. This motif continued across the rest of the 'Mech, the "head" resembling more of a chitinous protuberance with sensors poking out, constantly moving and flexing. The weapons jutted out of either side of the main body, creating a truly alien appearance.

The *Revenant* was originally developed by Word of Blake, the fanatics who had bathed the Inner Sphere in nuclear fire in the 31st century. A desperate bid to increase their numbers as Blakist territory shrank, their version of the 'Mech had an onboard AI, allowing them

to be fully autonomous units on the battlefield, but they were only deployed during the Word's last stand on Terra in 3078. Even then, the system was deeply flawed, making poor choices on the battlefield and becoming highly erratic when exposed to enemy ECM.

Facing a similar crisis to the Word of Blake—though the Fortress Wall that prevented K-F jumps afforded them more time to rebuild—the Republic resurrected the drone project, but ditched the AI-control system in favor of remote control. Republic engineers had not been able to fully mitigate the ECM vulnerability, however, so the jamming would disconnect a drone from its operator and leave the machine inert on the battlefield. Fortunately, the drone system didn't require the same rigorous standards of its operators compared to the MechWarrior elite—no neurohelmet tests, relaxed physical standards, an easier time in training—so the Republic Armed Forces could cast a wider net both inside their ranks and in recruitment. Alison had shown high-tech aptitudes in her tests and was expecting to become a BattleMech technician until she was recommended to the drone program, and it came with a promotion, so she was happy to take it. *Until now, at least*.

As the drones moved to their designated staging ground, Alison noticed a few of the first units out—a lance each of light 'Mechs and hovertanks took off at high speed to set up the picket line until the rest of the unit was ready to move out. The XIV Hastati Sentinels had been hunting these new Com Guards for months now, and there was an anxiety among the entire force to get the job finished. Alison hadn't been part of the drop on Luyten 68-28 that began this hunt, but she felt a lot of the same nervous energy, and found herself gripping the control sticks on her console and releasing them subconsciously. However, it wasn't long until the call came up for the drone teams to move in— leading elements of the force had run into heavy resistance, and needed immediate assistance. So Alison and her lance, plus a regular 'Mech lance and two lances of tanks, dashed out from the drop zone to assist.

The relief force didn't need their nav computers to zero in on the fighting—tall plumes of smoke stretched into the sky, coalescing into explosions, tracers, spiraling missiles, and flashes of lasers and PPCs as they closed on the forest where the fighting was taking place. Fires blazed as they transitioned from the idyllic scenes near the drop zone into what felt to Alison like a Boschian depiction of hell, minus the torture victims.

"Okay, team," Lieutenant Okube's voice came over the comm, "we've got to move fast and decisively. Striker Lance and Drone Lance, you're on harasser duty, hit and fade, keep them off balance. 'Mechs and Heavy Armor Lance, we're the line. Advance and engage in force.

All the lance commanders, Alison included, replied *"Roger"* almost in unison. Her training was kicking in, so maybe the sims were good for something after all.

"Okay, guys," she said to her team. "You heard the LT. Let's concentrate fire on a single target at a time where we can and coordinate our movement. We're gonna prove this experiment right today!"

As she finished her sentence, the tree line ahead of them broke apart, a Republic *Lament* walking backward through it, steadily firing its heavy PPCs in a one-two rhythm. A *Pack Hunter* came flying over the forest, firing its own Clantech PPC down toward the *Lament* before landing in the open.

"That's our first target, engage, engage!"

The *Revenant*s surged forward. Alison squeezed the trigger that fired the 'Mech's four Martell extended-range medium lasers, and smiled as three out of the four beams splashed coherent light over the enemy 'Mech. The combined fire of the four drones dug deep into the Com Guard's internal structure, and the *Pack Hunter* sagged to the ground, waste heat from its crippled fusion engine blooming red on a thermal scan. She set a waypoint in the forest for the lance to head toward, as they couldn't rely on the enemy to come to them, and the hovercraft couldn't follow the other lances into the forest to provide support. The *Lament* pilot raised their 'Mech's right arm in an approximation of a salute as the drones passed, but as her 'Mech had no arms, all Alison could do in response was flash her running lights to return the gesture.

"Contact, Sarge," Yoshino called out in the control room. "Seismics say it's a medium, so we should be able to take it. It's about 120 meters ahead. I'm tagging it on everyone's screens now."

"Good work," she replied. "Let's move to envelop. Hit them from three sides and hopefully the confusion will work in our favor. Doubly so if the pilot knows their military history and recognizes the 'Mechs, right?"

That got some laughing acknowledgement from the team.

"Let's go!"

The *Revenant*s moved through the forest, catching sight of their target as they approached a clearing. It bore a distinct appearance—digitigrade legs, angular lines, the cockpit a narrow, triangular shape with a truncated front... The most hated and feared of BattleMechs of the Jihad: the Celestial series.

"What the hell is that?" Dubois cried out. The confusion, fear, and anger of all three of Alison's lancemates was palpable.

"It's not a Manei Domini 'Mech!" she shouted at them. "Look at your warbook! Computer's IDing it as one of the 'Mechs they had on Wyatt. Keep moving and engage!"

The moment of shock was enough, however. The Com Guard 'Mech—a *Kheper*—lined up on Yvonne Anthony's 'Mech, and in a split second a Gauss rifle shot streaked across the open space between them, smashing clear into the four-legged drone's front-left leg. Laser fire crisscrossed the 'Mech's torso before a cloud of short-range missiles exploded across the entire body.

"Shit! I've got an actuator hit!" Anthony called out, panic rising in her voice.

"It's okay, Yvonne!" Alison called back. "Concentrate fire and fall back when you can. And don't worry about losing the 'Mech. We have spares in the 'Mech bay."

Oddly, having to calm down one of her team helped Alison calm down herself. She lined up on the ComStar 'Mech and fired a full barrage. Even with her full team's fire, it wasn't enough to destroy the enemy in a single volley like they had the *Pack Hunter*, but it did seem to unnerve the pilot and they clearly had to put an effort into staying upright after a significant chunk of the 'Mech's armor evaporated under enemy fire. A snap shot from their Gauss rifle flashed past Alison's *Revenant*, and then the enemy melted back into the forest.

Lieutenant Okube's voice came back over the radio: "All units, fall back. I say again, fall back. The advance team has extracted and the enemy is pulling back. Let's get back to base ASAP."

Alison breathed a sigh of relief. Not the best first outing for her team, but it could've been far worse. They got back into formation and headed for the designated rally point, slowing to keep pace with Yvonne Anthony's damaged unit.

EIGHTEEN HOURS LATER

Alison skittered her *Revenant* to the left, narrowly avoiding a stream of autocannon fire from a Com Guard Demolisher tank. She speared it with her lasers as Yoshino, now controlling a -2R2 version of the *Revenant*, fired his LRMs into the same target. She smiled as the DI computer on her 'Mech estimated the tank's left treads had been shattered, and continued to dash out of range of the enemy's big guns before the turret could traverse to track her.

She angled her *Revenant* toward a lighter enemy 'Mech—a Jihad-vintage *Thorn* she figured was an easier match for her light drone's capabilities. The enemy MechWarrior spotted her on the way in and launched a quick spread of SRMs, but most of the missiles exploded around the *Revenant*'s stalk-like legs.

For this sortie, Corporal Anthony had also switched out the drone she was piloting for a testbed drone armed with a PPC, and she sent an azure bolt of energy right into the *Thorn* from across the battlefield.

Alison dashed toward the 'Mech, smoke pouring out of the side where the PPC had hit it. Her lasers splashed damage across the smaller 'Mech's body, but a stream of tracers from her light machine guns found their way into the damaged section of the 'Mech. The *Thorn* stumbled to a halt and shuddered as a series of explosions consumed its side, clearly the result of an ammunition hit. CASE panels blew out the back of the *Thorn*'s torso, venting most of the blast away, preventing the 'Mech's total destruction. The *Thorn*'s remains spun with the force and fell to the ground, the explosion having gutted the extralight engine to the point it could no longer function.

Alison smiled in satisfaction as she orbited the battlefield, looking for her next target. Personal victories aside, the fighting had not been going well for the Republic forces over the span of a very long day. Every advance out of the landing zone had been met with ambushes and heavy resistance, and Alison was on her fourth sortie now, with very little rest in between. Yoshino and Anthony had to switch to the other drones because their original ones had been destroyed in previous missions, leaving only two spares to replace any further losses. They were bogged down now; any operational tempo General Rehagen had hoped for was clearly gone, and they needed some sort of unqualified victory before morale started to slip.

"I've been tagged!" came a cry over the general comm circuit. "TAG on the field!"

Within seconds, the ground rumbled as a Republic Demon tank was hit by a pair of Arrow IV missiles drawn to their prey by a targeting laser somewhere on the battlefield. When the smoke cleared, the vehicle was a twisted wreck, the devastation so complete that any fires started in the explosions had been put out by the sheer force of the blasts.

"All scout and harasser units, this is Vulture Lead," said Captain Orcini, the commander of the most recent push. "Intel has confirmed none of the armored units on the field are equipped with TAG, so there have to be infantry spotter teams out there. Go hunting where you can, expect them to have sneak suits to remain concealed. We're counting on you to keep this artillery off our heads."

As one of the faster units armed with anti-infantry weapons among her 'Mech's arsenal, Alison was one of the soldiers to acknowledge the command directly. She quickly flipped through visual and infrared sensors to see if there was any obvious sign of the Com Guard troopers—but nothing showed up, of course. Even if they didn't have advanced systems like optical camouflage or sneaksuits that prevented heat emission, they'd be covered in thermal blankets or other simple methods of hiding themselves.

She crested one of the small hills that characterized the landscape for kilometers around the landing zone—making herself a target for a

Com Guard *Crab* that turned away from the grander battle, hitting her with one of its ER PPCs. Alarms blared in her headset, as the shot had almost penetrated her front-right leg.

Alison turned and fired on the 'Mech, causing minor damage in return, but that gave her enough time to get into motion. First of all, she had to get off the hill so she could get some hard cover between her and her assailant, and then up onto the next one and into the woods that obscured much of the ground there. A chill spread down her spine as a secondary monitor displayed the enemy 'Mech's specifications: It was a CRB-30, and more than the weapons or armor, the ECM suite was what worried her. Stray too close to that 'Mech, and her *Revenant* would be cut off from her control console—it would be little different than if a regular BattleMech were to overheat and shut down, an easy target to quickly destroy. Intel confirmed ComStar had been using remote drone technology as well, so they knew how vulnerable the control system was to interference. She took a pair of deep breaths to try calming her nerves, hunched over her controls, and tried to urge a little more speed out of the drone, to keep the distance open.

A pair of PPC blasts narrowly missed her as she completed her planned maneuver; she was unable to fire back though—while the ability to fit a turret to BattleMechs was long-available at this point, the *Revenant* had not been designed with this flexibility. She drove farther into the woods, so intent on avoiding the next volley of enemy fire that she almost didn't notice when her computer picked up movement and placed an inset display on her main screen.

Enemy soldiers.

Not just soldiers, but ones fleeing a prepared position she'd just stepped right into. *The spotters!*

She opened a general comm line. "This is Ghost Lead. I've found a spotter team, but I'm under heavy fire. Someone get this *Crab* off my back!"

Her computer was still tracking them, but in this tree cover they'd be able to escape her quickly. She twisted the 'Mech around as quickly as possible, right as an actinic PPC blast passed through where she would have been if she hadn't changed course. The *Crab* was suddenly wreathed in explosions. A *Jackalope* in Republic colors landed beside it, speared it with a pair of medium lasers, and turned to run around to the Com Guard 'Mech's rear, forcing the pilot to turn and face the more dangerous, immediate foe.

"Move, Ghost Lead. I've got this," a voice said over the comm. The line was so full of static thanks to the *Crab*'s ECM, Alison couldn't tell if she even knew the person.

She didn't reply to her savior as she focused on the infantry trying to melt into the forest. The computer still had them though, and she stalked after them. When they passed into a clearing, she selected her machine guns, lined up her shot, breathed out, and squeezed the trigger.

And they were *gone*. Replaced with streams of gore, the Bosch scene now completed in a split second of supreme agony for the people she'd just killed. Her 'Mech halted, she sat at the console, breathing heavily. She barely even noticed the call over the comm that the Com Guards were falling back and they were to return to base.

She didn't speak on the way back, either.

She had to get out.

For those first sixteen hours on-planet, Alison had been aboard the DropShip. Sitting at the console, napping in her rack, grabbing food, bullshitting with whoever was around. But now that their 'Mechs were back from this mission, she couldn't do it. And so she sat on a crate outside the ship, taking in Epsilon Eridani's air for the first time.

She couldn't escape the fighting, of course: the artillery battery was set up not far away, and they were firing constantly, a reminder she was in a war zone, even if there wasn't the bustle of a military outpost happening all around her.

A hand appeared slap-bang in her field of vision, an open pack of cigarettes in it. "You look like you could use one of these, Sarge," a brusque voice said.

She looked up to see a rugged man in full infantry battle dress, forest camo, an Intek laser slung across his chest. Lieutenant Denisov, she remembered. His platoon had come in on the *Righteous Fury* as well, all boisterous and boastful about how they were going to take the Robes down quick and painful. He looked like he'd been dragged through the mud a few times, white teeth gleaming through a face that needed at least three showers.

"I don't smoke," she replied, brushing her hair out of her eyes.

"Maybe not, but you look like you need it. And maybe someone to talk to?"

"Sure, why not." She took one of the slim paper cylinders out of the pack.

Denisov produced a lighter, pocketed the smokes, and pulled another crate over with some impressive dexterity, a smooth movement that suggested he'd done this sort of thing many times before.

Predictably, her first inhalation of the cigarette led to a minor coughing fit. "I don't know how anyone does this for pleasure!"

"It's an acquired taste." He smiled, then took a long drag on his cigarette. "And it helps with my nerves, especially after a fight."

She took another drag, kept from coughing this time, and exhaled.
"This your first deployment?" Denisov asked.

"Yeah, first time on another world, too. Literally, I didn't step foot on the planet until a half-hour ago. First time breathing another planet's air, first time I..." She shook her head, unable to finish the thought.

"You killed someone, and it felt too real, didn't it? Even through those fancy screens?"

She kept silent.

"You don't need to talk if you don't want to. And if you want me to shut up, I'll just sit here. And if you don't want that, I'll go."

Still nothing.

"A lot of the troopers in my platoon, they're in the same boat. And they're trained, indoctrinated really, to fight and kill in a personal way. MechWarriors tend to not get that because their fighting is more abstract. And you guys, with the drones? That's more abstract again. It's like a video game, you ask me."

That was how the first few missions had felt to Alison, a video game. She wasn't at risk the same way Lieutenant Okube or Captain Orcini were. Definitely not the same way Denisov and his men were. A single 'Mech with a machine gun or a flamer could sweep across his platoon and...*and...do what I did to those poor bastards on that hill.*

She started to cry.

He put his hand on her shoulder. "It's okay, you're safe here, you can let it out."

"Does it get easier?"

"For some people, yeah. I've been doing this for a few years. I've been outside the Wall. It's easy for me...now."

"I don't know if I want it to get easier for me..." she said, getting the sobs under control.

"That's fine too. I know one 'Mech jock who can't make it through a fight without getting sick after they get home. But they clean up, get back in that cockpit, and do it again and again."

"That's nuts."

"Maybe, but it's also dedication. The mission means a lot to them, so does the regiment, and the Republic means a lot to them too."

"Me too. The Republic, I mean."

"That's why we all signed up, right? The last line against the barbarians at the Wall."

"And here we are. We're not keeping the barbarians at bay, are we?"

"Not right now, but we can't leave ComStar at large inside the Wall anymore. We've got to get our house in order so when the Exarch says it's time to go, we're ready to liberate all our lost prefectures."

"Yeah, I know what you mean. It's still a dirty fight, though."

"Sometimes that's what we gotta do. And speaking of dirty, I'm off rotation for the next few hours, and I really need to clean up."

"Yeah, you really do." She smiled. He was pretty stinky as well as dirty.

"You're gonna be okay?"

"I don't know... Probably."

"I'm not going to tell you your business or anything, but you should talk to a combat-stress instructor, sooner rather than later. You've got three people depending on you for leadership back in there—" He jabbed a thumb at the massive *Overlord* DropShip looming behind them. "—and we need all the firepower we've got in the field. This fight is nastier than we planned for."

"Okay, I'll think about it."

"That's what I like to hear. I'll take off then, Sarge."

"Hey, call me Alison, or Ali. You outrank me, for heaven's sake."

"Rank comes with respect in my book, especially noncoms. I'd be nowhere without my sergeants...Ali."

"Thanks for the talk, LT."

"Hey, no problem. And maybe don't make a habit of smoking those things? I hear they're bad for you, even in a war zone!"

He ambled off into the DropShip laughing, leaving her sitting there. But she was smiling a little, at least.

SHAMUS MOUNTAINS
EPSILON ERIDANI
REPUBLIC OF THE SPHERE
16 FEBRUARY 3141

The last two *Revenant*s advanced slowly across uneven terrain, ranging ahead of the combat engineers they were assigned to protect. The Com Guards had fought the Hastati Sentinels to a standstill, but elements of Stone's Brigade had landed the day before and pushed hard. The ComStar forces fell back into the mountains, sacrificing their aerospace fighters to bomb the passes and seal them off before the now-overwhelming RAF troopers could swarm through. And so the engineers were slowly moving forward to plant explosives to make new paths through to the enemy base.

As the area was treacherous to begin with, on top of being full of debris from the extensive bombing runs, it fell to the Hastati's light 'Mechs and infantry to stand guard in case of a push by the Com Guards. By virtue of being more stable four-legged designs and disposable technology, the drones had pulled advance picket duty, in this case having carefully navigated to the far side of the ridge the engineers planned to remove. The heavy fighting over the five days on-world had left the unit with only a baseline -2R and the last of the PPC-carrying test beds left in operation. Yoshino was the best marksman in the unit, so he took the latter 'Mech for this shift, while Alison controlled the -2R.

Somewhere in those days, the drone control room and the console had become "the Machine" in Alison's mind. Less a remote-control system and more a portal to another, horrible world outside the DropShip's metal shell. She hadn't needed to fire on any more infantry since that fight in the foothills, but she'd even hesitated to use the machine guns when she was running a standard *Revenant*. It was too real, the thought of rounds ricocheting off a target and hitting someone who strayed too close. In the abstract, she recognized that anyone on the battlefield was making a choice to be there and accepted the risks, but the visceral feelings outweighed any detached logic.

She hadn't spoken to anyone about it since her conversation with Denisov. Even now, running half watches, there always seemed to be something more important to do—paperwork, rack time, food, or exercise—running down the clock until they were done on this damned planet seemed appealing for some reason. If something, anything, would happen on this mission, it might help.

Alison was just staring at her screens, eyes darting between the view from the drone's cameras and the radar screen, half listening to the comm chatter, her concentration fading and returning. She was half relying on Yoshino to raise the alarm, or a sudden change to jolt her back to full awareness.

Not a good place to be as a team leader, she thought ruefully, piling on the internal pressure. Here she was, back in the Machine, ready to kill again.

"Oh, hell," Yoshino said. "I think I see something near that tree line, about three hundred meters out on my nine."

Alison set her primary screen to focus on the same spot. "Yeah, I think you're right. Looks like a scout car to me."

"Do you think they've spotted us?"

"I can't imagine they haven't," she replied. "No emissions detected, so I guess they're maintaining comm silence, but we're screwed if they get away. Let's call this in before they realize we've seen them." She flipped over to the general frequency. "Turnkey, Turnkey, this is Ghost Lead. We have spotted what appears to be an observation team that has eyes on us."

"Acknowledged, Ghost," came the reply from the team leader. "We're about a half hour away from being ready to blow the ridge. Keep them under observation and—"

There was a sudden glint of metal in the trees and then obvious movement on Alison's screen. "Wait—shit, they're onto us!"

"Roger, move to engage. Do *not* let them get away."

Both drones were already moving. Yoshino fired his PPC, a spectacular blue flash illuminating the camouflaged Fox armored car hidden behind the trees for a second and starting a small fire. If that thing got moving, they'd only have a few seconds to take it out, and it could withstand even a couple of PPC hits unless they managed to concentrate on a damaged section of the hull.

Alison snap-fired her lasers, one cutting a glowing scar along the hovercraft's air skirt. And then she saw the people in the woods running toward the car. It was five seconds until they'd be in range of her machine guns, only a few seconds after that they'd be in the Fox, and then how long until they escaped?

Maybe this decision would save or doom the entire Republic. She had signed up because she truly believed in the cause, in protecting her family and friends back on Terra. Could she live with herself if letting these scouts escape meant this battle was prolonged even further? If that led to the Republic's defensive posture being weakened to the point they couldn't defeat the various wolves at their door?

In the end, it wasn't a choice at all.

She lined up the targeting reticle on the retreating figures and squeezed the trigger.

It was easier this time.

QUIETING THE ROAR:
A TIME OF WAR MISSION SEED

TOM STANLEY

This adventure is for use with *A Time of War: The BattleTech Role-Playing Game* (*AToW*). While possible to play with *MechWarrior: Destiny*, most of the opposition and equipment listed here are built with *A Time of War* in mind.

MISSION OVERVIEW

Voting on the Dominion's fate over joining the ilClan-created Star League caused great civil upset on many worlds. Disturbances ranged from fistfights to open warfare with military-grade hardware. When Prince Hjalmer Miraborg enforced the Unity Council's vote, supporters such as Star Colonel Reidun Støle upheld that decision on every world they landed. Dominion Watch assets on Karbala were contacted to put down both Joiner and Denier groups; the message clear: Support the Prince and lay down your weapons. Technician Anton rose to popularity with a Denier mob calling itself the Karbala League of Freedom (KLF), which desired to throw off any potential shackles of Clan Wolf control.

Using his connections and charisma, Anton slowed down work in cities that voted in a Joiner majority, while quickly servicing Denier-sympathetic areas. The KLF escalated trouble with the death of a Watch member and numerous civil servants when an explosion near a Joiner celebration was claimed by them. Watch agents working with local *polis* forces were constructing a case on terrorists like Anton when the Star Colonel's message came to the system. Now armed with better hardware to face both sides of this civil war, Inquisitor Lorenzo and Detective Tameca cooperated fully with the Star Colonel's demands. The assistance could not have come at a better time considering the rumors of the KLF obtaining contacts that could supply them sneaksuits and powered armor. Joiner factions were fixated on obtaining more military hardware, such as combat vehicles, due to a lack of sufficiently trained MechWarriors joining their ranks.

ASSETS

The players are citizens of the Dominion. Their professions can vary from military to civilian due to their official position as Watch agent assets or even agents themselves; those with family ties to Mimir are also a viable idea to incorporate into the character. Player characters must have a minimum of +1 toward combat-oriented Skills such as Martial Arts, Small Arms, Melee Weapons, or Thrown Weapons. This adventure will not use 'Mechs but, at most, will allow combat support vehicles or medium-sized combat vehicles.

OPPOSITION

Technician Anton is a Grade 20 worker with contacts in higher circles of the lower castes. He hates the idea of Clan Wolf ruling over all other Clans, and sees the Dominion as beyond the "petty dreams of long-dead Russians." He's vocally against the idea of ruling Terra and creating an ilClan state, because the Dominion, to him, is a good example of the Clans ruling by might without the unnecessary need for wasteful rituals of old.

When creating Anton's stats, use the Boss stat block (p. 339, *AToW*), giving him at minimum +3 toward Intimidation, Protocol, and at least two tech Skills. His forces consist of two Knox Armored Cars (p. 18, *Technical Readout: Vehicles Annex Revised*) and one Burro II (p.

22, *TRO: VA Revised*) as his "traveling command center" with a Military Comm Hub installed in it for his transmissions (p. 301, *AToW*). Though he has numerous supporters, he can only count on three platoons of Foot Rifle troopers as his most fanatical bodyguards, Skill range from Green to Regular; at best they have flak armor on them when on duty. They all cannot follow him around, since some patrol territory or keep watch at Anton's primary base, an old vehicle shop just outside of Bestla.

SUGGESTIONS FOR THE GAMEMASTER

Anton will fall in due time to Star Colonel Reidun Støle. A couple civilian vehicles and a handful of foot trooper washouts cannot stand against the might of properly trained Clan warriors.

When running this adventure, advise that merely running at Anton will not solve the problem of his image among the Deniers, and how he's a famous villain to the Joiners. Information gathering, sabotaging his efforts to strengthen his image, and finding out any rumors of obtaining power armor are the keys to taking him down. The Watch agents are here to be the eyes and ears of Star Colonel Reidun Støle, and she will be the hammer at the end of it all.

If the players are a bit bloodthirsty, perhaps the Star Colonel has them assisting in battle against Joiners and Deniers later in another adventure, as a reward for their hard work.

OBJECTIVES

Find him, find him! Talk with locals, scan news reports, do whatever they can to get information on Anton's whereabouts. If he's traveling in his Burro II, find out where his base of operations is outside of the capital. Use Thug NPC stat block (p. 337, *AToW*) for anyone not within his inner circle and Soldier stat block (p. 338, *AToW*) for his more fanatical supporters.

"Can we come in and talk about Kerensky's plan for you?" While walking up and knocking on the door is direct, it is also brash. Have the team sneak in somehow to see what Anton has planned in his offices. Information on his computers, conversations overheard by supporters, or even people locked up as "prisoners" can be useful in finding out where the rumors lead to any power armor or sneak suits. Anton might even have dirt on his Joiner enemies for the Watch Commander to use!

"That loose sprocket, that's why your Knox ain't working!" The team is in the building, or at least knows where it is. Time to sabotage some of the equipment Anton has for when the big moment occurs. The main goal of the adventure isn't to kill Anton or capture him outright, but get information on him and get out so the Star Colonel can do her job. Breaking a few of Anton's toys is just a wonderful side benefit of the mission. The team could also plant Joiner evidence, causing more chaos. If the GM thinks now is a good time to introduce some power armor, have those sabotaged too.

The adventure is considered a success if either there's information to present the Star Colonel or the team did enough damage at Anton's base to cripple his ability to mobilize his forces when the time comes.

AFTER MISSION NOTES

Award the players 5 XP for their success. This adventure may lead to another one featuring Joiner forces or even a military scenario featuring the Star Colonel taking these factions down, thanks to the efforts of the player characters today. This adventure could also be a stepping stone into an exciting career of being a Watch agent and navigating the balance of honor versus service in the life of a Clansperson.

NOT WITHOUT SACRIFICE

GILES GAMMAGE

SAMARKAND-CLASS CARRIER DCS TOGURA
HIGH ORBIT, NEW SAMARKAND
DRACONIS COMBINE
8 OCTOBER 3072

"Talk to me, Kanegawa."

A black dot inched along the hull of the carrier. Below, far, far below, swept the vast arc of New Samarkand—with Luthien under siege, now functioning as the capital of the Draconis Combine—wispy dragon tails curling across a canvas of ochre, rust, and mahogany.

All was motion, storm fronts rolling across the plains, the plains themselves marching steadily toward the terminator, the planet orbiting about the distant star, and high above, the dilapidated museum ship that had once been the *Samarkand*-class carrier DCS *Togura* hurtling through orbit. It was enough to make you dizzy if you ever looked down. Or up. Or anywhere, really.

Kashira Ion Kanegawa very carefully, and repeatedly, did not look up. He glanced back at his magnetic boots, burning the comforting green of a secure contact, before looking ahead to find his next handhold.

"I just want to talk, Kanegawa. Stop this foolishness and respond."

—Bit chatty for a traitor, isn't he?

And you're pretty talkative for a dead guy, Dad.

—Not like you have a lot of options for conversation partners: Your commanding officer has already killed your only friend on the squad and is now trying to kill you, you have no idea if the three others are on his side or not, or if they're even still alive, and the short-range radio in this suit isn't going to let you ring up the Coordinator's office and let them know there's a treasonous murderer on the only WarShip in the

system. It's either talk to me or enjoy the scenery. So, unless you're a fan of vertigo, let's talk.

Calling the *Togura* a "WarShip" was being generous. The carrier was almost four centuries old—and looked it. The hull was pitted with micro-craters, tiny divots where centuries of space dust and debris had abraded the armor plating. The weapons had been removed, the gun ports sealed; a hollow warrior, empty save for fading memories of glories long past. It was a tourist attraction now, a place where schools brought bored children as part of their patriotic education, and occasionally where the Internal Security Force's Draconis Elite Strike Team commandos ran field exercises.

Talk about what?

—For example, we could speculate about why your instructor decided to shoot one of his trainees in the middle of an exercise. Why now, why here? What does he hope to gain? This thing is about as well-armed as a halibut.

"Give me a chance to explain, and I think you will understand," his instructor, *Chu-sa* Hudson Maine, radioed again. "Look, you're going to run out of air in about thirty minutes. What do you think you can accomplish?"

Kanegawa had already been keeping an eye on the air gauge in his helmet HUD and didn't need the reminder. Space suits normally had enough air to last up to two days, but as part of the training they had initially—with what in hindsight was clearly a deliberate move to prevent Choi or himself from trying to escape—each been limited to two hours instead.

—Keep moving, his father's voice advised. *Just keep moving.*

The flattened blister of an escape pod hatch filled his forward view.

—Just a little farther.

"I did what I did for the benefit of the entire Combine. You must believe that."

—Benefit? His father snorted. *I'm sure factory laborers on Pesht will be ecstatic to know DEST instructors have taken to shooting their own trainees. "At last! This makes my fifteen-hour shifts worthwhile! Dragon be praised!" they will say, no doubt.*

Kanegawa pictured the body of Anwar Choi, endlessly tumbling head over heels over head over heels, maskless, lifeless, comet-tailed with a haze of shattered glass and frozen blood. Kanegawa had been out of position during the exercise: He wasn't supposed to have seen Maine take the shot, but he *had* been out of position, he *had* seen Maine kill his fellow trainee, and had been seen in turn. Now here he was.

There was a ragged edge of damaged hull ahead. He curled his fingers about it.

"We are at *war*, Kanegawa. Not with the Word of Blake, or the Clans, over mere territory, but with traitors in our midst for the spirit of the Combine itself. And wars demand sacrifice."

—*The spirit of the Combine. Ah, now where have we heard that rhetoric before, son?*

The Kokuryu-kai. *The Black Dragons.*

The Black Dragon Society was a cancer eating away at the soul of the Combine, spreading dark tendrils throughout the Draconis Combine Mustered Soldiery, growing back each time they thought it had been cut out forever; extremists, traditionalists who violently rejected change, positioning themselves as the defenders of some imaginary golden age of *bushido*. The Combine's elite DEST commandos, whose whole *esprit de corps* rested on being the ultimate expression of *bushido*, had proven especially susceptible to the Black Dragons' flavor of toxic nostalgia.

—*That gives us a motive, but not an objective. What does the BDS want with a geriatric space hulk?*

Kanegawa lifted a foot. The metal handhold beneath his fingers warped, bent. The sudden lurch detached his other boot. His legs swung wildly away. The brittle metal bowed, almost apologetically, starting to tear along the new fold.

Kanegawa flailed, scrabbling for another handhold. Fingers slid across the smooth hull. With a snap, his other hand came free, clutching at a knife-edged shard of plating. The force of it threw him off balance, starting to tumble, only centimeters off the hull but floating free, torso pitching backward, legs flying out before him, now upside down, helmet almost scraping the ship, now right side up again.

Kanegawa tensed, waited for the tumble to bring him feet-down to the hull. Thruster microburst. Tiny jets built into his backpack fired, whistling plumes of propellant, kicking him back "down" toward the ship. His feet moved closer, got a lock, and glued to the hull, slamming him to a stop. He bent over backward and managed to fold his knees instead of breaking both legs. He sat down heavily, breathing hard.

The suit chimed to inform him he was down to fifteen minutes of air, and precisely two seconds of propellant.

Kanegawa glared at the dagger of metal.

—*Ought to be more careful,* his father chided. *You could hurt someone with that.*

Kanegawa cocked back an arm to hurl it away, then rethought. Gave it a nod of grudging respect and tucked it into a side pouch, carefully, slowly, so as not to cut himself.

"*Chu-sa*, permission to exit and hunt him down," said another voice.

"Patience, Odita."

—*Well, at least one of your teammates is a co-conspirator.*

Never liked Odita much, Kanegawa groused, which was true enough: Odita had been the star pupil—bossy, arrogant, the one clearly destined for command, and that had rankled.

"I'll take an EVA unit. Nowhere to hide out there."

Kanegawa grimaced. That was true enough. A *Samarkand*-class carrier was a 350-kiloton cylinder of metal with stumpy, bulging wings running along either side, which themselves sported further blisters, swellings, and protrusions, but all rounded and smooth and with a distinct lack of nooks and crannies to hide in. With only two seconds of hydrogen peroxide propellant in his maneuvering pack, he could only fling himself away from the carrier, with no way of ever coming back.

Pointless self-sacrifice would be very on-brand for the DEST, wouldn't it, Dad?

—Unfair, Son. Now, focus. This is not a good time to panic.

Panic? Like by hearing voices in my head?

—As if that is a bad thing.

Well, you died when I was eight.

—Third Man Syndrome. You're alone, about 500 kilometers up in orbit and talking yourself through a problem. And who better to talk you through this than Daddy DEST? Take a moment. Breathe. Now, move.

He breathed. Moved. The escape pod hatch was before him. There was a maintenance handhold, an elongated U of metal, beside the hatch. Kanegawa yanked on it, testing it cautiously a few times to see if it would bear the strain, then slipped an elbow under it to anchor himself.

"He can hear you, Odita."

"He has a door breacher and a de-powered training laser. What's he going to do, tickle me with it? Let him hear. I don't care who his father was."

—Oh, bless my scales, not Irece again. Sorry, son.

Irece, invaded by Clan Nova Cat in 3051. Site of a daring raid by DEST commandos that had killed the Nova Cat leader, Galaxy Commander John Rosse. And died themselves, in turn.

Not like you could've predicted the Clans would invade the place. Not your fault, however much I might wish for someone to blame.

Kanegawa detached the door breacher from its magnetic seal on his back. It was a fist-sized square of black polymer, a training device equipped to transmit a code to a receiver on the other side, trigger open the carrier's airlocks, and simulate a boarding action without having to blow up several billion ryu of hardware and cultural heritage in the process. He set it next to the escape pod hatch, just above where he estimated the control circuit would be inside, and clamped it to the hull. Thumbed the switch and watched the digital display begin its countdown.

Five minutes.

"*Chu-sa*, door breach in progress, escape pod H-7." A third voice, Alis Keene.

—*That's cheating. No surprises there.*

Kanegawa nodded. The OpFor wasn't supposed to be able to detect a door breach during this exercise. The screen on the breacher read *"4:50."*

"Oh, yeah? Persistent, isn't he?" That was Niko Vong, the final member of the five-person team that had begun this exercise.

—*So they're all in on it, everyone but you and Choi. Not great at making friends, are you, Son?*

I thought you were helping me.

—*I'm helping you see how screwed you are.*

Great. Mission accomplished.

"Proceeding to deck C airlock."

"I said *wait*, Odita."

"*Chu-sa*, I serve the *Kokuryu-kai* because we serve the true spirit of the Combine. We do not run. We do not hide. I will face him."

Four minutes.

"Not on comms, Odita."

"Why not? He only has a short-range radio. Nobody can hear him now, and nobody ever will if he's dead." There was a series of metallic *thuds* over the channel, the sound of Odita grunting, an electronic chime. "Entering airlock."

"Happy travels," said Vong.

"You hear that, Kanegawa?" *Chu-sa* Maine sighed. "You hear what your stubbornness has forced us to do? Choi's death was regrettable, but necessary. You, I had hope for. Your father was the hero of Irece. I thought if anyone could understand, it would have been you. If only you'd let me explain. He would have been so disappointed in you."

—*Oh, stick a yellow bird in it, Maine. What would he know?*

You were not an easy man to please, from what I recall.

—*It's a tough universe. And look how well you turned out.*

Oh yeah, right: Alone, stuck to the side of a spaceship, about to have my head blown off by a maniac with a laser rifle. Kanegawa sighed. *Look, Dad, I made it.*

"The fault is yours, Kanegawa. I never wanted this. Sometimes sacrifices must be made. Your father would have understood."

—*I understand all too well.*

Is he right, though? Kanegawa wondered. *You were the DESTest of the DEST. Led a suicide mission to take out the Clan leadership, never mind leaving behind a wife and son. That kind of self-destructive heroism is right up the Black Dragons' alley.*

—*The willingness of a Combine warrior to sacrifice themselves isn't some kind of aberrant personality disorder, whatever the Federated*

Suns might claim or however much the Black Dragons try to turn it into one. It's a belief that the state, the community, the lives and safety of strangers can be as—if not more—important than your own, or even your family's. Is that really so terrible? Or is it the basis for all military service, taken to its logical end?

So it all comes down to being willing to die for the cause, is that it?

—If you think of an alternative, be sure to let the rest of the Inner Sphere know.

Kanegawa couldn't answer, aware he'd just lost an argument with himself–though perhaps that counted as winning. He reached to his ankles and clicked off the magnetic seals, letting the boots float free, keeping himself anchored with the arm under the stanchion. He planted his feet against the hull and squatted, bringing his knees up to his chest.

The display on the breacher ticked past the two-minute mark.

"Cycling airlock. ETA two minutes."

—Damn. This'll be close.

"A clean kill, Odita. We owe his father that. Keene, Vong, get down to deck C for retrieval."

"Yes, *Chu-sa*."

Kanegawa drew the sidearm he'd been issued for this training exercise, a de-powered Sunbeam laser pistol, little more than a bulky laser pointer now. It was a good bet Odita's and the others' wouldn't be. Kanegawa shrugged inside his suit. You didn't get to be a DEST trooper by whining whenever things weren't perfect.

One minute.

There was movement down the hull, near the bow, about 300 meters away.

Odita's space suit was identical to Kanegawa's, black on black, black-booted, black-helmeted, black-visored, glittering like obsidian in the starlight, and Kanegawa could see the chilled puffs of propellant from the man's EVA backpack unit.

Thirty seconds.

As Kanegawa watched, Odita glided out from the hull, brought himself to a gentle stop, then rolled and turned, orienting so he was feet-down to the hull. He hung there for a moment, no doubt scanning for Kanegawa.

The breaching unit flashed to announce it was done. A bright white strobe, like a beacon. *Shit.*

The silhouette of Odita whipped around. Perhaps a little blinded by the sudden light.

—Good to know. Useful.

The escape pod doors snapped open.

Odita blinked hard against the flash of light, shouldered his Starfire laser rifle, and blindly squeezed off three rapid shots in the direction of the flare. When his eyes could focus again, he saw the escape pod doors, two semicircles of metal now standing perpendicular, straight out from the hull. Three orange-red dots glowed where his shots had impacted. No sign of Kanegawa, but it didn't take any imagination to know where he was hiding.

"Peekaboo, Kanegawa, I see you."

Odita jetted forward at a leisurely speed. There was no rush. If the escape pod was intact, there would be no room for Kanegawa to squeeze inside its launch cradle. If it had been removed, which was more likely, there would be nowhere for him to hide. A fish in a barrel.

"Ten minutes of air, Kanegawa. I'm doing you a favor, really."

He was facing "down" now, toward the hull of the carrier, drifting laterally as it seemed to slide beneath him. He kept the Starfire aimed at the growing oval of the aperture, smile of anticipation on his face. Only a few more seconds.

The hole gaped wide. No escape pod. Odita fired and fired, not waiting for visual confirmation, filling the narrow space with a grid of deadly green hail. Metal glittered and glowed, slagging where his shots landed. He blinked, released the trigger, frowned in puzzlement. No escape pod, but no Kanegawa either. Just a round hole filled with nothing but billowing shards of hot-white metal fragments from his laser fire.

A light stabbed into his eyes again. Something rocketed up at him from behind the far side of the escape pod door. He had time for a yelp, a wild shot, and then Kanegawa cannoned into him, hurled forward by the last reserves of his maneuver pack. He slammed into Odita's waist, sending them both cometing back, away from the ship.

They were tangled, spinning, the world revolving and revolving beneath them. In his visor Odita saw the ship, the planet, open space, the ship, the planet, open space, wheeling and wheeling. Kanegawa hooked a leg behind Odita's knee, desperate to keep them locked together. Odita wriggled, tried to kick, but there was no leverage, and he only made the tumble worse.

"Did you find him?" Maine's voice crackled. "Odita? Report."

Kanegawa got a hand on the barrel of the rifle, wrenched it to the side, tried to get his other hand under the rim of Odita's helmet and force his head back. Odita got a forearm up, batting Kanegawa's hand away, then crashed his own fist into the side of Kanegawa's helmet. The blow was muffled and padded and only jerked his head sideways, but he lost his grip on the rifle.

"I have him, just one—"

Odita yanked the gun free but too fast, too hard. It slipped from his fingers and flew up, tethered in place by the cord attached to its power pack on Odita's belt, adding a third element to the chaotic whirl of motion. The cord stretched taut and then rebounded, the rifle careened down, smacked butt-first against Odita's helmet, and bounced away again.

"One what? Stop playing games, Odita."

Kanegawa let go of Odita's leg, pushed off against the man's chest, flung himself not toward where the gun was, but where it would be just, right, about—*now*.

Almost.

The gun slipped past his flailing arms, impacting against his shoulder, spinning him half around. He got a hand on the stock just as it yanked and jerked away from him.

"He's dead," Odita seethed. "He's dead, he's *dead*."

He was reeling in the power cord like a fishing line, hand over hand. He got a hand on the trigger and Kanegawa lunged, stabbing a finger into the guard, behind the trigger, the padded gloves stopping it from firing.

In rage and fury Odita swung his head back and then launched forward, head-butting Kanegawa in the chest. He was losing his hold, his finger was slipping. There would be nothing to stop Odita from shooting.

"Is he?" Maine said. "Well, good. Now enough screwing around and bring the body back here."

With his free hand, Kanegawa grabbed for a side pocket. Ripped it open. His finger on the trigger guard came free.

Odita howled in triumph.

And never saw the shard of metal hull plating that stabbed down, tearing through the neck of his suit in a sudden spray of blood and escaping air.

Vong watched the black-suited figure of Odita approach the outer airlock doors, body in tow, while Keene waited at his side. Keene was big, muscular, with her head shaved; Vong, half a head taller still, his face half-hidden behind a black, tangled beard. Magnetic boots kept the two clamped firmly to the deck.

"*Tch,*" Vong clicked his tongue. He couldn't resist the temptation to bait Odita a little, even at a time like this. The man was simply insufferable. "What took you so long?"

Odita only shook his head and mimed rapping on the outer airlock door. *Knock, knock.*

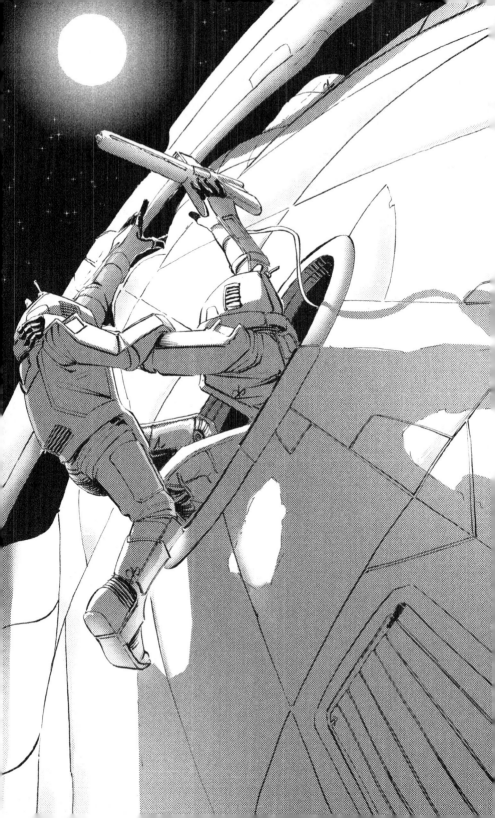

"What a mess," Keene exclaimed, leaning forward to peer at the grainy image on the monitor. "Looks like you took his head half-off. The *chu-sa* said do it *clean*, Odita."

Odita just shrugged.

"Opposite Day," suggested Vong. He was grinning, as usual. He was congenitally incapable of taking anything seriously—the universe was a joke, was his philosophy, and humanity equally absurd. He'd joined the Black Dragons more out of the desire for iconoclasm than anything else.

"Do we have an Opposite Day?" asked Keene.

"No, which means today we do."

"Huh."

Outside, Odita cocked his head to one side, looking pointedly at the airlock.

"All right, all right," Keene grumbled as she worked the airlock controls.

On the monitor, Vong watched Odita float inside the airlock chamber, then haul the stiff corpse after him, and lean it at an angle against one of the bulkheads like a piece of discarded statuary. Odita staggered a little, put one hand out to steady himself, and helicoptered one finger at eye level. *Hurry up.*

"*Hai, haaai*, keep your hair on." Keene continued to grumble as she swung the outer lock closed and flooded the inner chamber with air.

"Too late for you," Vong joked to Keene.

"Yeah." Keene ran a hand over her scalp. Paused. "Shut up."

"Who would you talk to if I did?" Vong nodded towards the airlock. "Chirpy in there?"

Odita had loosened his helmet seal and was now bent double, shoulders heaving, evidently sucking air as fast and deep as he could.

"He *has* been kind of quiet. Odita, you okay?"

On the viewscreen, Odita gave a thumbs-up.

"See?" Vong laughed. "Our very own Sparkling Conversation-*san*."

Keene didn't smile. She was frowning at the image on the display. Muttering, she stepped away from the controls and approached the airlock door itself, gun in hand. Keene and Vong both carried Sunbeam laser pistols in hip holsters. While the Starfire rifle was the weapon of a marksman, a Sunbeam was the opposite; almost more of a high-powered blowtorch than a laser, capable of burning extraordinarily large holes in people in extraordinarily short spans of time.

"Odita?" Keene called.

The airlock door pinged. Began to slowly hinge open.

"Odita?"

Keene's head flicked back, then nodded slackly forward as a brilliant lance of green light erupted from the back of her skull, splattering

Vong with brain and bone, burning a neat round hole in the ceiling just above his head.

Vong dropped as a laser rifle barrel poked from the crack between the airlock door and its frame, and fired a fusillade of wild shots, sparking and slagging the metal where he'd just stood. His Sunbeam was in his hand, firing just as Keene's body went limp and she floated, almost lazily graceful, into his line of fire, incidentally taking Vong's shots to the back of her suit, burning straight through to bone.

Vong cursed, ducked under another spray of fire, and then launched himself at the control panel. He hammered the outer door release, then swore as a curt message informed him: FORBIDDEN OPERATION, INNER AIRLOCK OPEN.

Vong backed away slowly, crouching, keeping the Sunbeam trained on the door. The corridor was beginning to fill with smoke. An ancient fire alarm gave a trill, then crackled silent as its wiring failed. Disused fans chugged, laboring to draw off the smoke.

"Come on..." Vong growled through clenched teeth. "Come on."

There was a hollow *clang*, something smacking into the airlock door on the other side. The door sprang wide. A black figure filled the opening. Vong fired twice, taking it once in the head, once in the heart. The head lolled strangely and slackly sideways. Then Odita's body pitched forward, like a felled tree, stiff as a board.

Behind it stood Kanegawa.

Vong opened his mouth to shout, and a laser beam took him through the back of the throat.

"This has quite ruined my day, I don't mind telling you," *Chu-sa* Maine's voice rasped from the carrier's intercom system.

—*Good. It's about to get worse.*

Kanegawa squinted at the power cell reading on the Starfire, then sighed and tossed the rifle away. He crouched first by Keene, then Vong, retrieving their Sunbeam pistols, holstering Vong's depleted one, keeping Keene's at the ready.

"No questions, Kanegawa? No comment? No curiosity?"

Kanegawa craned his neck and scanned the ceiling, quickly spotting the tiny black blister of a monitoring camera almost directly above his head. He pursed his lips for a moment. "Are you telling me there is some explanation for this, *Chu-sa*?" He waved his pistol at the general destruction surrounding him.

"Of course there is."

Kanegawa toed Vong's body with his boot. "I'll bet."

With a last look around, he panthered down the corridor, keeping the Sunbeam in his hands and hugging one of the walls.

"The shuttle we came in is still in Bay Two. Take it, go, report me if you want."

—*And let Maine do whatever he wants with the biggest hunk of metal currently in orbit? I don't think so. That does mean he's confident he can do whatever he's planning to do before you can warn anyone, though. I'd hurry.*

"Sorry, *Chu-sa*, but I have my duty."

"Your duty to whom, Kanegawa?"

"The Coordinator—the Dragon," he replied automatically, not looking up. "The Draconis Combine."

"Ah, but what is the nature of the duty we owe to the Combine?"

The corridor had been part of the museum tour. It was lined with the portraits of the Combine's Coordinators over the centuries in a mishmash of artistic styles from each era. There was the founder of the Combine, Shiro Kurita, in a black and white 2D photograph, beside a 3D solidograph of his heir, Tenno. The only one missing was the last, Theodore Kurita. A shattered frame hung on the wall over a plaque bearing his name.

"To serve House Kurita?" Maine said. "The ambitions of one family, however noble? No. No, I say. There is a reason our leader is called the 'Coordinator of Worlds,' not a 'Prince' or 'Archon.' They coordinate, they build harmony, they safeguard the spirit of our people. Those who threaten that spirit must be removed, no matter the cost to ourselves."

—*These people are emotional masochists, aren't they? Typical abusers: "Look what you made me do." Always the victim, their every crime an act of glorious self-sacrifice.*

"You shot Choi for being insufficiently harmonious?" Kanegawa reached the end of the corridor, where a ladder ran through the deck. He edged forward, peering up at the circle of light where the ladder pierced the deck. The bridge would be two decks up. Satisfied, he grabbed a rung with one hand, the pistol trained straight upward in the other as he climbed. "Listen to yourself, *Chu-sa*, how crazy that sounds. Do you have even a shred of self-awareness?"

"We are at war for the soul of the Combine, Kanegawa."

"I'll take that as a 'no.'"

"What Theodore Kurita called 'modernization' was nothing less than spiritual annihilation. The erasure of everything that makes us *us*."

—*Suicide and samurai swords? Is that all we are? The man's appreciation of the Combine's culture is as deep as a puddle.*

The theme of the next deck was the First Succession War, when the *Togura* had seen action. Animated, 3D holographic star charts highlighted the sweeping advance of the Combine deep into the heart of the Federated Suns. Video clips played and replayed Minoru Kurita's proclamation of himself as the new First Lord of the Star League. Weapons, uniforms, mess kits, and other bits of soldiers' gear stood entombed in glass cases.

"Some of the ancient samurai didn't want to modernize either," Kanegawa told a MechWarrior's uniform with a laser burn in its back. "Look what happened to them. Is that what you want? To be left on the garbage heap of history?"

"Listen to me, Kanegawa: *They gave the planet your father fought and died to defend back to the Clans*!" Maine suddenly shouted. "Your father's team was sent to kill Galaxy Commander John Rosse. They succeeded, at the cost of your father's life. Now go to Irece. Go there. Touch down at the spaceport in New Barcella. Yes, go to *Rosse* Spaceport. Go there and listen to them spit on your father's sacrifice. Go there, and see what the Combine has left on the garbage heap of history."

Kanegawa's inner voice was still and made no response. There was silence in his head. An emptiness where the sound and memory of his father should have been. There always had been, of course; he'd been talking to himself the whole time. His father had died a hero when he was eight. Eight. That was a hole that would never, *could* never be filled.

Kanegawa bowed his head in memory. "I admit, that hurts," he said at last. "That hurts a lot. But then, maybe it's also the answer to his sacrifice. We won by *not* taking revenge on the Nova Cats. Sometimes the only way to win a real and lasting victory is not by being willing to die ourselves, but by being willing to let others live."

There was no answer from either Maine or his father. He would have to wrestle with this one alone. Kanegawa shrugged and sighed, looked around the chamber one last time. On the hovering holo-map there was a world, at the edge of red-tinted space, called Kentares. Accursed Kentares. Where a Coordinator had been killed, and the Combine had murdered a world in retaliation.

They say it represents everything wrong with the Combine, that we're nothing more than an interplanetary death cult...and they're right, he thought. *It shows my father's beliefs taken too far. But then that's the problem with extremes. Too much Davion-style individualism is bad; look at their civil war. Too much Word of Blake faith is bad; look at the Jihad. Too much anything is bad, that's precisely what "too much" means. Water is essential to life; drinking too much water will kill you.*

The ship stretched and groaned about him. Kanegawa felt a vibration in the rungs under his hands and feet. The *Togura* had needed only a gentle nudge from station-keeping thrusters from time to time to keep it in orbit, but now there was a noticeable and steady thrust.

Although the *Togura* had once possessed respectable acceleration for a carrier when it was in pristine condition, it wasn't even within jump distance of "pristine" any more. The main drives had long since been reduced to little more than ballast by the Inner Sphere's technological decline, leaving only the reaction control thrusters that kept it in orbit. Yet even so, Kanegawa could feel an insistent pull, faint but growing steadily stronger, like a hand at his back and under his arms, pulling him "up" toward the nose of the vessel.

Deceleration? But slowing down will knock us out of orbit.

"It's good that you and I think so highly of sacrifice, Kanegawa."

Kanegawa holstered the pistol and began to climb faster, darting up the ladder with both hands. He was almost at the bridge deck now.

What is Maine trying to do? Ice ran along his spine. *What would a man who idealizes self-sacrifice want with a glorified flying tomb?*

Kanegawa got his shoulders over the rim of the ladder hole and hauled himself up onto the bridge deck. The massive slab of the door to the bridge barred his way, but to his surprise the lock status showed green, unlocked.

Kanegawa flattened himself against the adjacent bulkhead, took a deep breath, then shouldered open the door, lunged into the bridge, weapon sweeping the room.

Chu-sa Hudson Maine had been a big, beefy man, with a wide round face, hands the size of dinner plates, arms the size of cast-iron cannons. He lay in the captain's chair, stripped to the waist. Both hands were wrapped around the hilt of a short, curved sword. The blade had been plunged halfway into his stomach.

"Ah, you're—aah, just in time—" Maine twisted his neck to look at Kanegawa, teeth clenched, grinning with manic intensity, sweat beading on his brow. "—to be my second."

Of course, the sentimental idiot tried to kill himself. Kanegawa snarled and leveled the Sunbeam, started to squeeze the trigger—

—Suicide and samurai swords? Is that all we are?

—then checked himself, jerked the barrel aside at the last instant, and blazed a hole in the couch mere centimeters from Maine's temple.

Kanegawa took a breath, another. He had his answer.

"The Combine is not a death cult," he said, more to himself than Maine.

"Do it," the man rasped. "Do it, kill me and I die in glory. Do it."

Kanegawa stalked past the *chu-sa* to the navigation controls and saw Maine had programmed the carrier to slow down enough that it would fall out of orbit, at which point gravity would take hold, yanking the WarShip violently down through the atmosphere and sending it plunging straight down onto Yamashiro, the capital city. While the carrier carried no munitions, Kanegawa didn't doubt that hundreds of thousands of tons of metal and machinery impacting the ground at ten thousand kilometers per hour would make a mess.

He punched in the command to deactivate the engines, on the slim chance Maine had forgotten to lock out the controls, and was rewarded with a flashing red text message telling him where to stick that idea. Overriding the lockouts might have been a fun exercise under other circumstances—such as not being approximately thirty minutes from a violently abrupt and unscheduled visit to the roof immediately above the Coordinator's office.

"Can't stop it, you—*hrrn*—have to kill me."

"Should have done it properly yourself," Kanegawa said, not looking back at him. "In *seppuku,* you're supposed to cut crosswise."

"Kill me, go on, kill me, *kill me.*"

Kanegawa tried the comms, but they were disabled as well. No doubt alarms all over the planet had started ringing the moment the *Togura* started braking. Aerospace fighters would be scrambling. By the time they were off the ground though, the *Togura* would be screaming down toward it.

Maine's breath was coming in hoarse, panting rasps now, his commands now reduced to pleas: "Kill me, please kill me, *oh, please* kill me."

"Stings a little, does it? I'll give you an honorable death if you unlock the controls."

A shudder ran through the ship, metal aged beyond ancient grumbling and groaning as it was subjected to new stresses for the first time in centuries.

Maine cried out as a tremor rattled the captain's chair. "Kill me, shoot me, kill me, do it, do it, *do it*—"

"Oh, I'll do much worse than that," Kanegawa threatened, turning, and advancing on the *chu-sa.* "I'll make sure you live. Get us both off on the shuttle. No public trial, no fame, no martyrdom for you; the ISF will make sure you die in darkness. They'll hang you like a traitor. Like a peasant."

"No, no, nonono, you have to, have to, have—"

Alarms began to hoot as automatic systems warned their absent operators of the growing danger. *How much time before this is beyond recovery?* Kanegawa pushed the thought from his mind. With an evil grin, he yanked off his gloves and pressed the recline button, laying Maine flat. Maine's hands, once so strong, now beat at Kanegawa with butterfly futility. Kanegawa bent down and tore out the first aid kit located under the chair, ripped it open. With deliberate malevolence he snapped on one surgical glove, then the other.

"You coward, you gutless coward, you foreigner, you stinking foreigner!" Maine shouted as Kanegawa worked, applying pressure, stemming the bleeding, cleaning the wound.

"You're welcome," he told Maine, working quickly, trying not to think how little time was left. "Lucky for both of us, you didn't have the guts to, you know...slice your guts."

The man wailed in denial. The deck plates were vibrating more intensely now, dust shifting across the bridge like snow warning of an oncoming avalanche.

Kanegawa forced another smile. "Think I've done all I can here. Have to leave the metal in you for now." He drew a Sunbeam, carefully sighted to avoid accidentally hitting Maine despite the constant bouncing, and burned through the blade of the sword, leaving only a small stub jutting from Maine's belly. "There. Now let's get you down to the shuttle."

"No, *no!*" Maine's eyes bulged. He'd screamed himself hoarse.

Kanegawa reached down and hauled Maine from the captain's chair and, despite the man's bulk, hoisted him over one shoulder, trying to avoid the stubby sword-end. The carrier shuddered and Kanegawa swayed, but stayed standing. "Not to worry, *Chu-sa*. Today, the Combine warriors win by *not* killing ourselves, just for a change."

"Stop, *stop, STOP*—"

INTERNAL SECURITY FORCE HEADQUARTERS
NEW SAMARKAND
DRACONIS COMBINE
10 OCTOBER 3072

Ion Kanegawa sat in the interrogation room. It was windowless and bare; the door was steel and heavy and locked. He sat on a molded plastic chair, the kind of thing you might find in cheap roadside eateries, in front of a plain steel desk.

On the other side sat the ISF agent. Her face was severe, her hair pulled back from her scalp so hard and straight it made Kanegawa uncomfortable just to look at. Her eyes were obsidian, and watched him the way a scientist might an underperforming lab rat.

Kanegawa tried a smile. She raised an eyebrow.

"Aren't you going to ask me any questions, Agent?"

"What should I ask you questions about, *Kashira* Kanegawa?"

"About my instructor and fellow soldiers trying to murder the Coordinator along with the entire government of the Draconis Combine, perhaps?"

"An interesting thought." She nodded, then leaned forward and Kanegawa instinctively drew back, spine hard against the back of his chair. "As it happens, there are more important matters to consider."

"More important than an attempted coup d'état?"

She continued as if he had not spoken: "*Kashira* Ion Kanegawa, as of this moment you are the only one in the Combine, indeed, perhaps the only person in the history of humanity, to board and capture a WarShip single-handedly."

He had to chuckle at that, and rubbed the back of his neck, a Combine *aw-gee-shucks* gesture. "Hadn't thought about it like that."

The agent said nothing and did not return the smile. The silence stretched thin enough to become uncomfortable.

Kanegawa coughed once, looked around the room and said, "So, it was an unusual situation, I agree. Is that all?"

"It may not be all," she said, and finally did give him a smile of alabaster and ice. Kanegawa wished she hadn't.

"The *Togura* was not the first time the Black Dragons have stolen a WarShip." The agent turned her noteputer around to face him. On the display was the bullet outline of a Draconis Combine Admiralty corvette. On the nose was her name: *Amakaze*, the *Winds of Heaven*.

"It will be a risky mission. But our war against the Black Dragons is far from over, and it will not be won without sacrifice."

Kanegawa couldn't help it. When she said the last word, he laughed in her face.

UNTIL DELIVERANCE COMES: AFFS EFFORTS TO STEM THE TIDE, 3144–3146

EDWARD MCENEELY

"For now, all we can do is hold on as best we can until, by some miracle, deliverance comes."

—FIELD MARSHAL CLAIRE WINTER, 23 SEPTEMBER 3144

"I am not a military man. A teenager during the Victoria War, I never seriously considered the possibility of a major conflict in my lifetime. The last twenty years have shattered many illusions. My life's work was lost with the destruction of the Gogh-Bukowski campus. My beloved daughter Megara, so clever and so funny, who idolized her mother and dreamed of being a soldier just like her, is now a name on a memorial on Robinson with no known grave.

"This short summary of the earliest phase of the war that brought this nation so close to the abyss could never be definitive, but I hope it will spur the penning of more comprehensive works. I am indebted to my wife, Leftenant General Heather Zibler (ret.), and my daughter, Major Alecto Zibler, for their assistance with terminology and concepts.

"Last, I must humbly thank the unknown Robinson Ranger in Atlas III 023/'AJAX,' who gave their life to buy time for my evacuation from New Avalon."

—JEREMIAH RANKIN, NEW VALENCIA, 28 JUNE 3152

On 19 June 3144, the Federated Suns suffered the worst defeat in its history. The Palmyra Disaster claimed thirteen of the best and most prestigious commands in the Armed Forces of the Federated Suns, the irreplaceable FSS *Lucien Davion*, the vast majority of the AFFS High Command, and First Prince Caleb Hasek-Sandoval-Davion himself. With them died any hope of coordinated or effectual resistance to the invading Draconis Combine. This is the story of the AFFS's efforts to preserve itself and the nation in the face of an overwhelming and triumphant foe during the hard years before Julian Davion's return.

3144–3145: PALMYRA'S CONSEQUENCES

The first intimation the wider AFFS received of the disaster at Palmyra was the sudden appearance of a dozen JumpShips at Tsamma's zenith jump point. Stripped of transports in service to First Prince Caleb Davion's counteroffensive, the militia lacked the ability to investigate the situation. Tsamma Crucis March Militia (CrMM) commander Leftenant General Yamini Garg-Davion was forced to ask for aid from Tsamma's largest exporter, Crystal Sky Water Interstellar. The conglomerate subcontracted a mercenary aerolance in their employ and loaned a *Merlin*-class DropShip to transport it. Before the JumpShip could depart, however, the militia's K-6 "Black Box" picked up an in-the-clear Kuritan transmission providing proof not only of the death of Caleb Davion, but also of most of the AFFS High Command. It is believed the unencrypted transmission of an image of the severed heads of the First Prince and seven AFFS marshals was intended to be received by Federated Suns forces as part of the Draconis Combine's psychological warfare efforts. Leftenant General Garg-Davion correctly assumed her command would be next. In less than a month, she and many of the Tsamma CrMM were dead.

From Tsamma, the news spread rapidly throughout the AFFS. In 3144, K-series transmitters were still widely utilized in the absence of a functioning HPG network, despite strictures on their employment due to Caleb Davion's distrust of them. On Palmyra, the First Prince ordered all units to turn their transmitters over to his headquarters for secure storage in the name of operational security, ensuring no messages were sent during the disaster. Usage and transmission errors increased dramatically in the wake of Palmyra, enabling the Draconis Combine to use captured AFFS codebooks to decipher many messages before their intended recipients had even received them.

This brought the first major AFFS counterstroke, the hastily planned Operation Ardent Spirit, to grief in late July of 3144. Upon receiving word of the disaster, Milligan PDZ Commander Marshal Colleen Estrada bought out the contracts of over a dozen company-sized mercenary commands in service to minor nobles or corporate employers in the region. Staging from Milligan, this heterogeneous force was intended to strike the worlds of Greeley, Adrian, and Chanute simultaneously, cutting the developing Kuritan penetration into the Federated Suns off at the base. Alerted by the flurry of Black Box messages required to coordinate an operation of this scale, the Combine was ready for them, and battalions from the fearsome Wolf's Dragoons lay in wait on all three worlds. At Chanute, the aging commercial JumpShip leased by the AFFS misjumped and was lost with all hands, by grim happenstance furnishing the Federated Suns with their only success of the operation: The Dragoons' Tarantulas Battalion remained fixed in position for a further six weeks to ambush foes who never arrived.

Though both less ambitious and less disastrous, other AFFS attempts at offensive activity followed similar patterns, relying heavily on mercenaries. As the usage of Black Boxes increased, the reliability of their transmissions dramatically decreased, and increasingly, Regent Erik Sandoval-Groell required JumpShips to transport orders if there was any hope of them remaining intelligible. This ended the Combine's string of signals-intelligence successes, but it left the regent tied to a single location to ensure communiqués from the fronts reached him.

As the situation deteriorated through 3145, control of mercenary hiring was successfully centralized by Erik, as the regional commanders' "panic-buying" was threatening to price the Federated Suns' faltering economy out of the market. One near success during this time, not known until 3152, came in September of 3145, when the Sky Kings, a mercenary unit, jumped into Tsamma on an intelligence-gathering raid, catching *Gunji-no-Kanrei* Matsuhari Toranaga's DropShip in the process of transferring between JumpShips in his command circuit. Disoriented from the jump, the mercenaries mistook the *Avenger* for a similarly shaped and obsolescent *Sholagar* aerospace fighter and scrambled their aerolance to engage, only to hastily order a retreat when the error was realized.

3146: NEW AVALON'S FALL

As the Kuritans drew closer to New Avalon, the regent's concern grew. Since Palmyra, the AFFS had been afflicted with a critical shortage of JumpShips, exacerbated by Chancellor Daoshen Liao's offensive into the Capellan March. By early 3146, the fall of New Avalon was considered inevitable. Sandoval-Groell, wary of a repeat of Palmyra, moved his headquarters to Remagen. It was not until 3152 that POW interrogations revealed that the Combine suffered from a serious ammunition shortage for its capital and subcapital weapons, due to the inadvertent destruction of the principal naval ammunition depot at Avon in 3142, during the Nova Cat Rebellion. Production of new munitions had been restarted, but the prioritization of troop transportation and the maintenance of the command circuit to transport the *kanrei* to and from Luthien meant little reached the front lines before the end of the decade. Keenly conscious of the continued existence of the *Fox*-class corvette FSS *Admiral Michael Saille*, the Combine conserved its remaining munitions for antiship work.

The *Saille*, as the last operational WarShip of the Federated Suns Navy, was arguably more important as a symbol of the nation's status as a great power than it was as a fighting vessel. Nearly ninety years old, it was maintained in operation by spares drawn from its hulked sister ship, the FSS *Brest*. While the *Saille* was kept to defend New Avalon for morale purposes, in practical terms, it was incapable of defeating the Combine's two WarShips, both known to be in the Dragon's Tongue thanks to a daring joint raid on Mauckport by MI6 and the Sixth Crucis Lancers at the start of 3146. While the regent wavered on whether New Avalon's importance merited the sacrifice of the Federated Suns' last WarShip, the matter was taken out of his hands when the *Saille*'s maneuver drive broke down in April 3146. The crippled WarShip limped to Kathil in the hope repairs could be effected.

When the invasion of New Avalon came on 8 July 3146, Sandoval-Groell's response was hamstrung by uncertainty as to the location of the Combine's WarShips. Postwar, it was learned they remained in reserve at Coloma, one jump away, before being recalled to Luthien by the Coordinator in late August. The ongoing JumpShip shortage played a major part in the regent's selection of the Second Robinson Rangers for New Avalon's attempted relief, as the regiment could be transported in a single lift.

With New Avalon under blockade, the remnants of her defenders would unlikely be able to escape. But Erik Sandoval had one ace up his sleeve. The *Admiral Michael Saille* had completed temporary repairs over Kathil under conditions of the utmost secrecy throughout August and September. While only barely able to maneuver under its own power, the WarShip was still potent. On 3 October, the daily courier JumpShip in the system received the signal Erik had been dreading and preparing for since Wolf's Dragoons were unleashed.

On 4 October 3146, the two-pronged Operation Azure Temple commenced, when at New Avalon's nadir jump point, the *Saille* materialized, accompanied by the assault DropShips of the mercenary New Medusans and the Third Crucis Lancers' aerospace wing. Though almost helpless against others of her own kind, the crippled WarShip could still damage lesser ships, and a picket *Okinawa* was destroyed before it could react. Across New Avalon and throughout the system, every Draconis Combine Admiralty aerofighter and combat DropShip scrambled to engage the WarShip, only to be left empty-handed when the severely damaged *Saille* jumped out of the system once the bulk of the Combine's forces were committed to high-velocity passes. Upon the WarShip's departure, carefully husbanded JumpShips appeared at a pirate point to evacuate the fleeing Davion Assault Guards. Their departure from the conquered capital marked the close of the bitter defensive phase of the war.

With the evacuation concluded, the *Saille* returned to Kathil for more substantive repairs, where she remains still. The Assault Guards traveled to Remagen, where they were greeted by electrifying news: First Prince Julian Davion, feared dead, had at last finished his long odyssey home from the Lyran Commonwealth, halting the invasion of the Capellan March as he passed. The First Prince's return marked the end of the long, hard years of defeat. The AFFS, despite agonizing defeats and humiliations, was not destroyed. Its survival contained the seeds of a future victory.

HARD TARGETS

O. J. S. GOODMAN

BRUNNAMORE
THE EDGE
CLAN HELL'S HORSES OCCUPATION ZONE
16 JANUARY 3146

The speed was incredible. The VTOL's pilot was pushing the aging Anhur transport to its maximum velocity, producing a mighty roar from the jets and making the transport bay shake and rumble as though it were a building during an earthquake.

Buried deep within her Elemental battle armor, however, Star Commander Ariadne felt only a dull tremor, just enough to upset her sense of balance. For a moment, she watched the Anhur's gray-bearded loadmaster deftly riding the pitching deck as though he were a wet-navy sailor aboard an ancient wooden boat, before turning to address the rest of Alpha Point. Out of habit, Ariadne twisted her face into a frown of command, even though none of her warriors could see her face—nor she theirs—behind their imposing helmets.

"Remember the plan!" she barked over the comm, the deep contralto of her Elemental voice penetrating the overpowering din of the jets. "We drop in at Location One! Destroy the pirate filth holding position there! If the other Points also do their jobs, the tanks will have a clear advance into the town! Alpha Point understands our task, *quiaff*?"

A grumble from the rest of the warriors of Alpha Point was the response. Each was already two and half meters tall, and the battle armor added yet more height, such that the shoulder-mounted SRM launchers on each suit scraped the ceiling of the transport bay. Each suit's right arm mounted a 'Mech-scale flamer unit, while each left arm terminated in an anti-personnel submachine gun slung beneath a wicked-looking battle claw.

The Elementals were a motley lot, typical of Iota Galaxy. Each warrior's black armor was personalized: Harriet's helmet was painted like a grinning skull, painted fire blazed across Ellis' and Meilong's armor in idiosyncratic patterns, while for some reason Piotr had written "*HAVE A NICE DAY*" across his breastplate in blood-red paint. Only Ariadne's armor was without ornamentation, unchanged from its standard Iota Galaxy black.

Despite their fearsome appearance, however, Ariadne's Pointmates did not seem to share her enthusiasm for the battle to come. This, too, was typical of Iota Galaxy, widely scorned as the dumping ground for failed or over-aged warriors. Ariadne herself was twenty-seven, which was hardly the prime of youth for a Clan warrior, even as the youngest of her Pointmates was pushing forty. Iota was the graveyard of warrior careers.

That will not be my fate, she told herself.

"I said, we understand our task, *quiaff*?"

"We heard you, Slayer," said Piotr.

Ariadne bristled at the nickname. Piotr's face could not be seen behind his visor, but no doubt he wore his characteristic sneer.

The Branding ritual four years past should have been the platform that propelled her from promising *ristar* to proud officer on a path toward earning a Bloodname. All she had needed to do was work with the others to capture and brand a hell's horse. Instead, believing herself the most capable, she had dominated the group in contravention of the Clan's ways, and when her plan to snare the horse failed, she had sought to capture it single-handedly. The ensuing struggle had left the beast dead and Ariadne in a two-week coma. On waking, she had found that she, like the others, had been branded with the Mark of Hell for their shameful failure. She alone, however, had been transferred to the Sixty-First BattleMech Cluster, Iota Galaxy, as punishment for her undue seizure of command and the resulting catastrophe. An example of the deserved fate of those who could not cooperate.

Such an individual had no place among the premier Galaxies of Clan Hell's Horses. Now, every time the Iota Galaxy trash called her "Slayer," she could swear she felt the Mark of Hell on her shoulder twitch.

She opened her mouth to retort to Piotr when the pilot called out "One minute, warriors!" over the comm. His voice was momentarily swept away by a wash of grating static. "—ground fire, Star Commander!" yelled the pilot, his panicked voice underlaid with residual static. "Need to set her down!"

"*Aff,*" growled Ariadne, although they were barely within the town limits. "Drop us now, and we will get to Location One on foot."

"Coming in for drop!" responded the pilot.

Ariadne's stomach turned a somersault as the VTOL dropped altitude sharply. *Those must have been PPC bolts*, she thought grimly.

The pilot guided the VTOL down to a ruined town square and dropped the bay hatch. Hardly needing the loadmaster's direction, Ariadne raced down the ramp and into cover, turning to see her Pointmates disembark with somewhat less enthusiasm.

It is too late for them, she thought, watching the others jog half-heartedly into their own cover. They were old, and age had made them apathetic. They would be in the Sixty-First for life, which would not be long.

But there was a way out for Ariadne. One that only she among them had a chance at. A Bloodname.

She was a Trueborn of Bloodhouse Seidman, and while she was still young, she stood a chance of winning a Bloodname. She just had to perform some great heroic feat for a Bloodnamed Seidman to notice her down here in Iota and sponsor her for the Trial of Bloodright. Then she could win, and become Ariadne Seidman.

"*Ariadne Seidman*," she whispered. It could happen. *Ariadne Seidman*. Once she was Bloodnamed, she would get out of Iota Galaxy. Even if she did not, promotion to Star Captain would swiftly follow. From there, why not challenge Star Colonel Samantha Johnston for command of the Sixty-First? And there were heights to aim for beyond that. As a young Bloodnamed warrior, it was quite possible she could one day become Galaxy Commander. *If* she won the Bloodname.

Ariadne Seidman.

The whine of the VTOL's jets increased in volume, shaking Ariadne from her reverie. She watched the Anhur ascend and turn away, only for a sudden PPC bolt to strike it viciously in the starboard side. It wobbled in the air, and another PPC bolt struck the same location a moment later, blasting open its armor and exposing its transport bay to the clouded sky. The craft's ascent faltered and it quickly fell, its steel belly grinding hard against the roof of a civilian dwelling. A great cloud of dust arose as the Anhur made its deathbed in the ruined house. The roar of the jets died, and it was still.

"Pilot, report!" Ariadne ventured.

After a moment, a faint reply came over the comm. "Ugh... Still alive, Star Commander," he said, the pain in his voice evident.

"Status?"

"Power's dead, and I think my arm is broken... Jamie is unconscious." There was a moment's silence. "Not much left of Reuben."

Frowning, Ariadne tagged the wreck for later salvage. "Stay close to the VTOL. Once we clear the approach to the town, I will direct a relief truck to this position. The rest of you, follow me. We still have a job to do!"

Her locational sensor told her Location One was around half a kilometer up the road, through winding civilian streets flanked on both sides by houses, bars, and small shops.

"All right, Alpha Point." she said, scanning her surroundings. "Whatever downed our transport is still out there, and more besides. We move fast and quiet to Location One and clear it out. None of you will get me killed before my Trial of Bloodright."

There was a chorus of undisguised chuckling from her Pointmates.

"Whatever you say, Slayer," said Piotr.

Ariadne marched over to him. "What is the matter with you, Piotr? Ashamed to be ordered around by someone who still has a chance of promotion from this *dezgra* unit?"

Piotr's reflective visor was as impassive as her own. "Nobody gets out of Iota, Slayer. Especially not with *that*." He nudged her shoulder with his battle claw, right where the Mark of Hell was. "You're here till you die, like the rest of us."

"No, *you* are here until *you* die, Piotr." Ariadne stepped closer to him until their breastplates were touching. "Do you want to make today your last day?"

After a moment, he looked away. "*Neg*, Star Commander."

"Good," said Ariadne. "They will be sending soldiers to inspect the wreck. We will ambush them before they reach it."

Alpha Point dispersed, Harriet and Meilong darting to the other side of the street while Ellis, Piotr, and Ariadne spread themselves out along their side.

A voice came over the comm—Point Commander Aaron, of Epsilon Point. His five warriors had been deployed elsewhere in the town, tasked with locating the remains of Brunnamore's garrison, which had apparently folded under the pirate attack.

"Sinner Two-One, this is Sinner Two-Five. Acknowledge."

"Accept transmission," Ariadne said, a *bleep* from her suit informing her the channel was now open. "Two-Five, this is Two-One. Send traffic."

"Be advised, Two-Five has encountered pockets of heavy resistance inside the town. Heavy combat vehicles and light BattleMechs are confirmed. We have taken casualties."

"Acknowledged, Two-Five. What is the status of your mission?"

"We located what was left of the garrison. No survivors."

Ariadne grimaced. "Proceed south, out of the town. Clear another entry corridor for the tanks."

"Confirmed. Sinner Two-Five out."

Alpha Point, spread among the alleys and abandoned buildings of the street, moved cautiously toward the source of the anti-aircraft fire.

Before long, Ariadne's prediction was vindicated, and she signaled the Point to halt. Ten pirate soldiers wandered down the middle of the road toward the wreck of the VTOL—and, unknown to them, the concealed Elementals. The pirates were unarmored and carried automatic rifles, and bantered to each other instead of maintaining silence.

"Prepare to fire," said Ariadne. "On my mark. Wait until they are in the kill zone."

"Aff," said Meilong, while the rest readied their submachine guns in silence. The pirate infantry continued their inattentive advance until they reached the area surrounded by the waiting Elementals, who had taken positions among the abandoned buildings.

"Fire," said Ariadne.

The pirates had no chance. A fusillade of submachine-gun bullets from both sides of the road caught the unarmored infantry in a lethal crossfire. In seconds, all were dead.

"Ten kills confirmed," said Harriet, a hint of savage joy in her voice.

"They don't count," responded Piotr. "Killing animals is easy."

Ariadne shot him a glare, while Ellis coolly swept the barrel of his submachine gun up and down the killing field, watching for any sign of a target playing possum.

Alpha Point continued up the road, checking their sensors. Eventually, the repeated thundering of PPC fire became clearly distinguishable from the background din of battle.

"New sensor contact, Star Commander," ventured Harriet, who was the farthest ahead. "BattleMech approaching."

"Tonnage?" asked Ariadne, instantly tense. Elementals were famed for their ability to swarm BattleMechs and destroy them in close quarters, but even so, *not* facing one was simpler than facing one.

"Getting a reading... Thirty tons. Approaching from the northwest."

"We push forward to the source of that PPC fire," replied Ariadne. "If this 'Mech wants to add itself to the scrap heap, we will oblige it."

Before long, the rest of Alpha Point picked up the 'Mech on their sensors as well. It was a ponderous thing, the signal moving slowly down the street toward the Point's target. Even so, its speed indicated it would reach Location One, and whatever was firing those PPCs, before Alpha Point did—the Elementals would have to contend with both of them.

A bend in the road displayed a row of houses in various states of damage on the left side of the street. The sound of the PPC discharges was massive, each one a roar of energy that sounded like an entire thunderstorm concentrated into half a second. The machine that mounted them was now also showing up on Alpha Point's sensors—a large vehicle positioned at a three-way junction just around the bend in the road that faced the Elementals.

From its position at Location One, the vehicle was situated to provide a sustained bombardment beyond the town, across the open field that surrounded Brunnamore, making any ground approach by the Sixty-First's limited ground forces a dangerous proposition. The vehicle was also capable of frightening anti-aircraft fire, as Alpha Point had already seen, and there were several such positions covering the southern approaches to the town. The 'Mech was also nearby, about to link up with the vehicle.

"Forward!" commanded Ariadne.

Alpha Point moved faster, picking their way through the buildings and up the street. They rounded the bend and finally caught sight of the vehicle—a long-bodied thing with armored treads and a rectangular turret that mounted three imposing barrels. It was a Schrek PPC carrier, painted a dark military green. The 'Mech was also coming into view, a stubby, cylindrical body atop bulky humanoid legs. The *UrbanMech* had no real head to speak of, merely a domed cap on the fat barrel of its torso. Nor did it have true arms—instead, one shoulder mounted a stocky laser housing, while attached to the other shoulder was an even larger housing that contained a twin-barreled autocannon. Ariadne's suit informed her that this particular *UrbanMech* was a UM-R69 model. It was a scarred, ugly beast, spray-painted dark gray and covered in battered patchwork armor from an evident variety of sources. A series of kill markers were daubed on its autocannon in white paint, and the flag of Clan Hell's Horses, defaced and inverted, drooped mockingly from beneath its laser housing.

"That is a lot of metal," muttered Piotr dourly.

Ariadne was forced to agree. Even one of those machines would be a match for her Point, but both at once could pose a distinct threat, especially if they lost the element of surprise.

"Keep to cover," she said. "Move through the buildings wherever possible. I want total radio silence until we engage. That includes you, Piotr."

"*Aff*," he replied, before the unit began to creep the final thirty meters to Location One. As they got closer, the communications suite in Ariadne's suit informed her it was picking up enemy comm chatter.

"Intercept," she whispered, although there was no possible way either the Schrek or the *UrbanMech* could hear her. The pirates' radio chatter came through, distorted by a harsh layer of static, but Ariadne could still strain to hear their voices.

"...got some weird sensor readings coming from down the road behind you. Don't see where they went."

"Copy. Keep an eye on it while I keep hitting these shitheads."

Ariadne frowned. The ECM equipment in the Elementals' suits was clearly doing its best to mask their presence, but apparently it could not fully hide them from the *UrbanMech*'s sensors.

Alpha Point kept creeping forward until they were a scant twenty meters from the two machines. Ariadne moved through the smashed ruin of a café, stepping over the low remains of a broken wall—Ellis was moving through the floor above her, with Piotr behind him, while on the other side of the road Ariadne caught glimpses of Meilong moving between houses.

Meanwhile, Harriet was sneaking across the upper floor of a burned-out house, clearly searching for an access to the building's ceiling to find a place from which to jump onto the pirate machines. She took a step across the damaged floor, then another…then her third step splintered the weakened floorboards, sending her foot through it. Harriet grunted as she fell, her armored body smashing through the floorboards to land in a heap on the ground floor of the building.

"Harriet!" called out Piotr over the comms. "Are you good?"

"*Aff*. Just a little fall."

"Quiet!" cut in Ariadne. "I said radio silence!" She glanced fearfully at the end of the street, and saw the *UrbanMech* and Schrek both rotate their guns down the road toward Alpha Point.

"Found 'em!" said the pirate comm chatter. "Battle armor on our asses!"

The Schrek turned its massive turret toward the Elementals. In the heat of the moment, it was impossible to tell which warrior it was aiming at.

"*Stravag*! It sees us!" shouted Ariadne. "Use your jets!"

No sooner was the order given than the Elementals all fired their jump jets. Ellis and Piotr leaped up from the upper floor of their building, punching through the thin ceilings, while Meilong emerged from behind the house she was sneaking past. Ariadne charged out of the café and fired her jets, rocketing up into the air and landing on the roof of the structure in front. Harriet was still righting herself as the Schrek fired, three massive PPC bolts flashing down the street and blasting apart huge sections of building she was in. Harriet emerged from the explosive chaos in a jet-powered leap to land in a fighting crouch on the roof of the next house.

Then the *UrbanMech* fired, the heavy *thump-thump-thump!* of a rapid-firing Ultra-class autocannon. Harriet, having just recovered from her hasty jump away from the Schrek's fire, was too slow to avoid the shells slashing toward her. They hit her directly. To Ariadne, it was over in less than a fraction of a second: One moment, Harriet was crouching on the roof, and the next, she simply disappeared amid the explosions.

"Missiles, now!" roared Ariadne over the radio, drowning out Piotr's cry of horror. "Hit that 'Mech!"

The remaining Elementals fired their mounted SRM packs, eight missiles streaking out from their firing positions toward the *UrbanMech*. The missiles struck the 'Mech head on, blowing craters across its torso armor. It retreated slowly from the onslaught, crushing a discarded civilian motorbike underfoot. The remaining warriors of Alpha Point charged forward over the rooftops, blasting sheets of flame at the pirate machines in desperate covering fire as their missile packs reloaded.

The Schrek fired again. The bolts lashed out at the buildings she, Piotr, and Ellis were running across, blowing apart massive pieces of brick and metal. None of the powerful energy blasts struck the Elementals, but the rooftops began to crumble beneath them.

"Jump and hit that 'Mech again!" ordered Ariadne, her jump jets already propelling her into the air. "Quickly, before it fires!" She fired her own missiles while she was still in the air, and landed a second later behind the smoking ruin of a civilian cargo hauler. Her missiles struck from on high, slamming into the *UrbanMech*'s right-side torso and blowing chunks of armor plating away. Depleted, her missile launcher fell from her suit with a pneumatic *hiss*.

She watched the *UrbanMech* turn to react, shielding its damaged right side and sweeping its left arm around, seeking Ariadne with its laser. Two more pairs of missiles struck from above as Ellis and Piotr fired, hitting the 'Mech's stubby left arm in a mirror of Ariadne's attack on its right. From her position behind the ruined truck, Ariadne saw Meilong crouched atop the last remaining building on her side of the street, lining up a shot with her remaining missiles. Meilong fired, her shots flying past the Schrek and striking the *UrbanMech*'s left arm near where Piotr had hit it. The remaining armor gave out under the twin explosions of Meilong's missiles. When the smoke cleared, Ariadne saw the weapon housing was crumpled and twisted, exposing the fragile components beneath. The Schrek brought its great turret about, attempting to get a bead on Meilong.

"You three, destroy that vehicle! The 'Mech is mine!" shouted Ariadne, and she closed the channel without waiting to hear her warriors' acknowledgments.

Above her, Ellis and Piotr leaped from the roof of their building, flying across the street to engage the Schrek. Meilong was already on it, her spent launcher forgotten as she scrambled atop the tank.

Not wanting to give the *UrbanMech* time to come to the Schrek's aid, Ariadne fired her jets and leaped out from behind the truck. The 'Mech took a ponderous step toward its comrade before it caught sight of her, but Ariadne was already overhead. The 'Mech stepped backward and turned as Ariadne flew over its head and landed atop a house behind it.

For a split second, it aimed its autocannon straight at her, and Ariadne let out an involuntary cry of terror as she jumped again—a moment before it fired. Up close, the noise was incredible, and even the audio dampeners in her suit could not prevent the deafening *boom* of the cannon from shaking her teeth in their sockets.

Ariadne landed atop the *UrbanMech*'s head and dug her battle claw into a depression in its patchwork armor for purchase. Flattening herself against the front of the thing's head, just above its cockpit visor, Ariadne did her best to try and grip some of its domed armor between her ankles and thighs, spying the crude, improvised replacement hatch that capped the UrbanMech's head, a primitive handle jutting up from the beaten metal surface. She freed her battle claw from the depression in the 'Mech's armor and closed it around the handle, but the flimsy thing snapped off under the strength of her battle claw. Surprised, Ariadne lost her balance as the 'Mech twisted beneath her, and she fell from the top of the *UrbanMech to the ground*.

She landed on her back, the impact driving the wind out of her and sending spikes of pain up her spine. She quickly pushed herself to her feet as the 'Mech stepped toward her, its foot landing barely a meter from her leg. The 'Mech aimed its cannon at Ariadne and she ducked to the right, growling in frustration as it fired again, punishing her with another deafening thundercrack and sending stone shrapnel bouncing from her armor as the round detonated behind her.

The *UrbanMech* stepped backward to put some distance between itself and Ariadne, but she sprinted around it, leaping over its outstretched back leg and ducking underneath its torso, spying a hole in the armor on its right side where Alpha Point's missiles had struck. Across the street, Piotr, Ellis, and Meilong engaged the Schrek, crawling over its turret and tearing into its thin dorsal armor.

Ariadne jumped and grasped the *UrbanMech*'s upper thigh with her battle claw. She tried to climb higher up its body, but it surprised her by twisting its torso faster than she thought it was capable of. A protruding section of its hull came about and collided with her helmet, stunning her and throwing her off the 'Mech to land on her back at its feet.

Blood filled Ariadne's vision as she struggled to right herself. Before she could, the *UrbanMech* stepped forward and fired its left-arm laser. Ariadne cried out in pain as the laser scored a wicked line across her torso, burning away layers of armor. Although her breastplate held, the heat transferred from the 'Mech-scale laser was excruciating.

Tears and blood clouding her vision, Ariadne desperately rolled to her feet as the 'Mech again tried to crush her under its foot. She turned to it as she ran, firing half-blind at its torso with her flamer and submachine gun, desperately seeking the damaged right torso. The anti-infantry submachine gun washed inconsequentially over the *UrbanMech*'s hull, but each blast from her flamer stripped more armor away. The 'Mech kept its distance, but Ariadne, mad from pain and anger, harried its every step with more bursts, burning away armor with each shot while she desperately danced away from her opponent's laser fire.

The *UrbanMech* kept backing up until it plowed into the house behind it, stumbling against an uneven wall and falling back into the building, coming to rest half sitting against the ruined brickwork. Sensing her chance, Ariadne used her jump jets to leap forward and onto the supine 'Mech. Taking care to avoid the laser, she braced her feet against its torso before going to work on the damaged right side, weakening the remaining armor with flame before tearing away glowing chunks of metal with her battle claw. Its laser fired, missing Ariadne, and she scrambled over and promptly smashed its lenses with repeated blows from her claw. She took a moment to rip the tattered, burning remains of the defaced flag from beneath its left arm, snarling in satisfaction as she did so.

The *UrbanMech* sat up jerkily as its pilot wrestled with the controls, and Ariadne peeled back the final layer of armor on its right side with her claw before plunging her flamer into the 'Mech's innards beneath. Gripping onto its torso with her claw, Ariadne fired point-blank into the *UrbanMech*'s internal structure as it stood, bringing a quake of protest from the 'Mech as she damaged critical internal components. Blinking blood from her eyes, she pushed her flamer farther inside and kept firing, not caring what she hit, as long as it damaged the 'Mech.

She discharged one last burst of flame and tried to withdraw her arm, but it would not come free. Bracing herself against the hull, she pulled with all her strength, but to no avail. Her arm had become stuck inside up to the elbow.

Suddenly, a wave of cold panic ran through her as she realized the magnitude of her mistake. This *UrbanMech* model carried the ammunition for its main weapon in the right torso, which she had been liberally filling with burning gel. That ammo bin was now an oven, and the contents would surely explode in a matter of moments, annihilating the 'Mech—and Ariadne with it, if she was still mounted.

The pirate Mechjock had clearly come to the same conclusion, because the *UrbanMech* began to twist violently, rotating its torso madly in a desperate attempt to shake Ariadne loose before she could do any further damage. Ariadne was thrown around like a ragdoll, her right arm lodged inside the *UrbanMech*. She howled with agony as she felt her elbow snap under the force. At once, her suit began to pump powerful anesthetics to the wound.

Abruptly, the 'Mech shuddered and stopped moving. Somehow, Ariadne thought she could hear the pirate banging against the ruined hatch, desperately trying to escape before the 'Mech could explode.

Ariadne knew what had to be done. Gritting her teeth, she brought her battle claw over, seeking the vulnerable elbow joint in her own armor.

She took a deep breath, and severed her arm above the elbow.

Instantly she fell, the impact with the ground drawing another cry from her before she madly scrambled away from the *UrbanMech* and stumbled to her feet. She fired her jets on pure instinct to get away from the danger, her armor already secreting HarJel to cover her wound.

"Clear the *stravag* 'Mech!" she yelled over the comm as she shot upward. "It is going to blow!"

The rest of her Point had dealt with the Schrek, having ripped the hatch open and saturated the crew compartment with napalm. They jumped, and the four warriors of Alpha Point fled Location One just as the *UrbanMech*'s ammunition finally cooked off. It detonated with enough force to annihilate the 'Mech.

Ariadne jumped over to where the rest of Alpha Point crouched in cover. Blinking blood and tears from her eyes, she keyed the comm. "Sinner Two, this is Sinner Two-One. Report."

Aaron and the other Point Commanders spoke over the comm, confirming the successful capture of the locations they had been assigned to.

Ariadne switched channels to contact the Star Captain in charge of the Binary. "Sinner actual, Sinner Two-One. Entrance to the town is secure."

The Star Captain's gravelly voice came back after a moment's delay. "*Aff.* Not bad, Slayer. Armor is moving in. We will have these wretches in the ground by sunset."

"*Aff,* Star Captain. Be advised, Sinner Two has taken significant casualties. Request medics to this position." Ariadne indicated Alpha Point's downed VTOL.

"Understood, Two-One. Support vehicles en route."

"*Aff.* Sinner Two out."

Ariadne indicated the rally point to the other Point Commanders, and turned back to Alpha Point. "We must return to the VTOL. Medics are on the way."

"Ariadne, your arm..." ventured Meilong.

Ariadne looked down at her right arm. Severed messily by her battle claw, the wound had been sealed with HarJel and was now a stump. Despite the best efforts of the anesthetic, Ariadne stumbled, suddenly feeling the effects of the blood loss. Her Elemental physique meant she was unlikely to die from such an injury, but even so, the adrenaline withdrawal nearly put her on the ground.

"I will be fine," she grunted, shaking her head. "Let us go."

"Have to hand it to you, Slayer," said Piotr, as they withdrew back to the rally point. "You slew that 'Mech but good. Maybe that Bloodname is not so unlikely after all."

He gestured to the stump of her arm, and Ariadne looked down at it again. It terminated just below her biceps, not far from the Mark of Hell. It would require a myomer prosthetic, or a budded, tank-grown replacement, which might make combat more difficult—including the Trial of Bloodright, when it came.

"When," not *"if,"* she thought. If she had lost a limb to earn the distinction she needed, it was a price she was willing to pay. She would give all her remaining natural limbs for the Bloodname, if required to. Had not Khan Malavai Fletcher been extensively reconstructed with prosthetics? Mad as he had been, had he not still been the most fearsome Elemental of his generation?

It was still possible. The Bloodname, and all that it promised. Once she was Ariadne Seidman, there would be no limits to what she could win. The mere loss of an arm was immaterial next to that.

It will be mine, she told herself, touching her battle claw to her shoulder. *I swear it on this Mark of Hell. This is only the beginning. Soon, Bloodhouse Seidman will be bidding among themselves to nominate me.*

It will all be mine...

MARKET READY

BRYAN CARTER

DISTRICT CITY
KATHIL
FEDERATED SUNS
23 MAY 3105

Director,

As instructed on the 17th of May last, we have completed our investigation into why we lost an entire team of research and development techs last year, and separately the investigation into what caused the *Blackjack* BJ-5 research and development project for the Armed Forces of the Federated Suns to run over budget last quarter. It turns out the answer to both of these questions is the same. Please find below the extracted internal mails we have managed to piece together from backups. This goes a large part of the way toward explaining what happened. The report concludes with our recommendation for further possible courses of action. For your convenience, we have also attached the live-fire testing reports from the test pilots involved at the end, and the itemized list of project costs it was possible to verify.

* * *

To: Bill Knipe
From: Amit Schäfer
Subject: How come we don't do this?
Sent: 23 December 3104, 04:23

Hey Bill,

   I was at the Christmas party tonight talking to some of the military liaison guys, and one of them, Colonel something-or-other, can't remember, gave him my card anyways, asked why we don't have a *Blackjack* with a rotary autocannon in our catalog? After all, the AFFS loves autocannons and the RAC is the most autocannon there is. Every decent 'Mech that can be refitted to have one has at some point, *JagerMechs*, *Enforcers*, *Centurions*, etc. The *Legionnaire* is even built around one of our Mydron Model RCs! We make both kinds of RAC! So why haven't we put them on a *Blackjack* yet? I said we're working on it and the prototype was basically ready to go. He's out of the city until the new year, but he wants to see it by the end of Week 1, 3105. You can get this done, right? Probably a drop-in upgrade for the new BJ-5 model you guys're working on. I'll make sure to get the project budget cleared with Geoff when he gets back.

Best regards,
Amit Schäfer, Marketing Manager, House Contracts

* * *

To: Amit Schäfer
From: Bill Knipe
Subject: RE: How come we don't do this?
Sent: 3 January 3105, 09:37

Hi Amit,

I've been out of office until today, and am just getting to this email now. You promised someone we'd have a working prototype of a RAC-armed *Blackjack* by Friday? I don't think that's possible. Can we push the deadline back?

Regards,
Bill Knipe, R&D Engineering

* * *

To: Bill Knipe
From: Amit Schäfer
Subject: Automatic reply: RE: How come we don't do this?
Sent: January 3rd, 3105 09:38

I am out of office until 9 January 3105, with
limited access to email. I will respond to your
message upon my reply, but if it is urgent, please
contact Andrew Harlon who will be able to assist.

Best regards,
Amit Schäfer, Marketing Manager, House Contracts

* * *

To: Amit Schäfer
From: Bill Knipe
Subject: RE: RE: RE: How come we don't do this?
Sent: 3 January 3105, 09:42

What the hell, Amit? You're not even back until
the Monday after the deadline you committed to?
How are we supposed to meet this?

Regards,
Bill Knipe, R&D Engineering

* * *

To: Amit Schäfer
From: Bill Knipe
Subject: RE: RE:
RE: RE: How come we
don't do this?
Sent: 4 January
3105, 09:42

Hi Amit,

I know you're not
going to read this
until the 9th, but I've
shelved everything on
the BJ-5 project for
this week and spent
yesterday evening
talking to the guys in
supply. They've got a
pair of antique BJ-1s
and one of the old BJ-
3s St. Ives handed over
to us back in the day
which we can use for

this project, but they won't be dragged out of mothballs and in the bays until tomorrow at the earliest. We've got plenty of access to our Mydron model RACs, so at least that's not an issue. I've got someone digging in stores for some Supernova-2s too, but they're license-built, so we may not have the spare stock. Looks like my tech teams are gonna be pulling double shifts to try to get something in the field in time. It's gonna be close if we manage it at all. Either way, you owe the guys a case of beer for this.

Regards,
Bill Knipe, R&D Engineering

* * *

To: Bill Knipe
From: Amit Schäfer
Subject: FW: Blackjack RAC product demo.
Sent: 10 January 3105, 09:42

Bill,

What the absolute [REDACTED BY CORPORATE CONTENT FILTER] is this?

Best regards,
Amit Schäfer, Marketing Manager, House Contracts

> To: Amit Schäfer
> From: Leftenant Colonel Alex Calhoun
> Subject: Blackjack RAC product demo.
> Sent: 9 January 3105, 17:18

> Dear Amit,

> Regarding the live-fire demonstration of the new RAC carrying *Blackjack* variant you mentioned at the GM Christmas party, I have to express my disappointment with the state of the project as it currently stands. The 'Mech we saw today definitely had RACs mounted in the arms, but very little else. This doesn't meet the standards we've come to expect from GM here at AFFS procurement. For a project you described to me as "market ready" I find myself having doubts. Can you explain what

happened and assure me that any issues have been corrected?

> Leftenant Colonel Alex Calhoun, AFFS Procurement

* * *

To: Amit Schäfer
From: Bill Knipe
Subject: RE: FW: Blackjack RAC product demo.
Sent: 10 January 3105, 10:04

Hi Amit,

When you consider that we had exactly *three days'* notice to get this project off the ground, I think we did pretty well to get guns attached to arms at all. We had to strip the BJ-1s down to the frame to start fabricating new attachments for the RACs. My guys didn't have time to work out the weight tolerances for the frame, so if you wanted it to walk onto the field at all, it had to be with no armor and no secondary weapons. Don't even get me started on the state of the BJ-3 we found. That thing doesn't even have any room for ammo feeds to be run to the arms. It'll require a total reworking of the fire-control systems and new arm structures to get it working with any autocannon at all.

Regards,
Bill Knipe, R&D Engineering

* * *

To: Bill Knipe
From: Amit Schäfer
Subject: RE: RE: FW: Blackjack RAC product demo.
Sent: 10 January 3105, 14:05

Hi Bill,

I suppose there are some mitigating circumstances. I'll try to smooth things over with Calhoun and get us another chance to blow his socks off. Can't you just pull one of the BJ-5 prototypes from testing and refit that? Should be a simple drop in, right? One 2-class autocannon for another and all that.

Best regards,
Amit Schäfer, Marketing Manager, House Contracts

* * *

To: Amit Schäfer
From: Bill Knipe
Subject: RE: RE: RE: FW: Blackjack RAC product demo.
Sent: 10 January 3105, 15:31

Hi Amit,

No. That's not a simple drop in. The Mydron
Snipehunter cannons we're mounting in the new BJ-
5s are literally half the weight and a third the
volume of our Model RDs. It's just not possible to
cram them in there without removing something else,
and then we're back to stripping all the armor off.

Regards,
Bill Knipe, R&D Engineering

* * *

To: Amit Schäfer
From: Bill Knipe
Subject: RE: RE: RE: FW: Blackjack RAC product demo.
Sent: 10 January 3105, 15:48

Hi Amit,

Scratch that last, one of my techs said he
thinks we can probably do it if we strip out three
of the light PPCs.

Regards,
Bill Knipe, R&D Engineering

* * *

To: Bill Knipe
From: Amit Schäfer
Subject: Blackjack
Sent: 12 January 3105, 16:06

Hi Bill,

Can you fit the RACs into the torso of the BJ-3? It'd be a shame not to use it.

Best regards,
Amit Schäfer, Marketing Manager, House Contracts

* * *

To: Amit Schäfer
From: Bill Knipe
Subject: RE: Blackjack
Sent: 12 January 3105, 15:48

Hi Amit,

Sure we could do that, but half of what makes a *Blackjack* a *Blackjack* is the big guns in minimal arms. If the pilots can't flip the arms to address threats in all directions it'll probably be a hard sell.

Regards,
Bill Knipe, R&D Engineering

* * *

To: Bill Knipe
From: Amit Schäfer
Subject: RE: RE: Blackjack
Sent: 13 January 3105, 16:52

Hi Bill,

Okay, you know best. Just make sure to fit CASE to the side torso sections. I hear those old 'Mechs have problems with ammo storage. The next demo has to be perfect, so make sure your techs see my exact instructions.

Best regards,
Amit Schäfer, Marketing Manager, House Contracts

* * *

To: Amit
From: Bill Knipe
Subject: RE: RE: RE: Blackjack
Sent: 13 January 3105, 17:35

Hi Amit,

If you can reschedule for two weeks from today,
I can guarantee we will have something worth
showing the AFFS.

Regards,
Bill Knipe, R&D Engineering

* * *

To: All Staff, Kathil
From: Kathil Health and Safety Team
Subject: Incident on testing concourse
Sent: 19 January 3105, 14:11

Due to an ongoing safety emergency, all
nonessential staff are requested to evacuate the
area of the testing concourse until further notice.
Thank you for your cooperation.

Kathil Health and Safety Team

* * *

To: All Staff, Kathil
From: Conal Regnal
Subject: RE: Incident on testing concourse
Sent: 19 January 3105, 14:15

Why am I on this mailing list? Please remove me.

Best Wishes,
Conal Regnal, Printer Administrator

* * *

To: Bill Knipe
From: Amit Schäfer
Subject: FW: Hangar Safety Incident Report 30521-A
Sent: 19 January 3105, 16:06

Bill,

Why am I getting copied in on this report?
Did you blow up a 'Mech by setting off the
ammunition? How?

Best regards,
Amit Schäfer, Marketing Manager, House Contracts

* * *

To: Amit Schäfer
From: Bill Knipe
Subject: RE: FW: Hangar Safety Incident
    Report 30521-A
Sent: 20 January 3105, 09:35

Hi Amit,

The team installed the CASE in the side torso
locations, following your instructions to the
letter. Unfortunately, the ammunition bins on the
BJ-1 model are in the *center* torso. When moving out
onto the range, the test pilot, Tessa Arnaud, didn't
spot a patch of spilled coolant on the concrete of
the ramp, and the 'Mech slipped. It landed badly
and caught the edge of the ramp, puncturing the
torso. Tessa was lucky the autoeject didn't fire
her into the range's backstop. She's fine by the
way, thanks for asking.
Going forward I've ensured that we move the
ammunition bin to the left torso and we're
installing CASE II instead of the more primitive
model. We are still on track for the 27 Jan demo
but we'll only have two prototypes able to display.

Regards,
Bill Knipe, R&D Engineering

* * *

To: Bill Knipe
From: Amit Schäfer
Subject: RE: RE: FW: Hangar Safety Incident
    Report 30521-A
Sent: 20 January 3105, 16:06

Bill,

See if you can pull a chassis from the BJ-5 line
to replace it. We need to get multiple prototypes
completed. I promised the AFFS this was nearly
done already.

Best regards,
Amit Schäfer, Marketing Manager, House Contracts

* * *

To: Amit Schäfer
From: Bill Knipe
Subject: RE: RE: RE: FW: Hangar Safety Incident
   Report 30521-A
Sent: 20 January 3105, 16:22

Hi Amit,

   I'll get the team on it. It'll add to the
overtime bill though.

Regards,
Bill Knipe, R&D Engineering

* * *

To: Bill Knipe
From: Amit Schäfer
Subject: Field Demonstration
Sent: 30 January 3105, 14:37

Hi Bill,

   It looks like the demonstration on the practice
range was a great success. Calhoun was effusive
with praise, but he wants to see how they do in a
simulated duel. Can you get some 'Mechs and pilots
to run them against soon? How long will it take?

Best regards,
Amit Schäfer, Marketing Manager, House Contracts

* * *

To: Amit Schäfer
From: Bill Knipe
Subject: RE: Field Demonstration
Sent: 30 January 3105, 14:41

Hi Amit,

   I'll check the schedule for the simulated dueling
range. It usually books up pretty far ahead of

time, so it might not be available for the next
month though.

Regards,
Bill Knipe, R&D Engineering

* * *

To: Amit Schäfer
From: Bill Knipe
Subject: RE: RE: Field Demonstration
Sent: 30 January 3105, 15:12

Hi Amit,

I've checked the schedule and there's nothing
available before 7 March, and March is filling up
fast too. I've attached a list of the available
days for you to pick from.

Regards,
Bill Knipe, R&D Engineering

* * *

To: Bill Knipe
From: Amit Schäfer
Subject: RE: RE: RE: Field Demonstration
Sent: 31 January 3105, 11:14

Hi Bill,

Let's book all of them out and we'll let the
AFFS pick which date suits them best. I'll get back
to you when they get back to me.

Best regards,
Amit Schäfer, Marketing Manager, House Contracts

* * *

To: Bill Knipe
From: Amit Schäfer
Subject: RE: RE: RE: RE: Field Demonstration
Sent: 3 February 3105, 09:35

Hi Bill,

Leftenant Colonel Calhoun has off-world obligations for the end of February, so the first date that works for all of us is 13 March. I trust this is enough time to get the *Blackjacks* fully finished and painted nicely.

Best regards,
Amit Schäfer, Marketing Manager, House Contracts

* * *

To: Amit Schäfer
From: Bill Knipe
Subject: RE: RE: RE: RE: RE: Field Demonstration
Sent: 3 February 3105, 09:42

Hi Amit,

That works fine for us. We'll get the 'Mechs in perfect condition for the 13th at 1000.

Regards,
Bill Knipe, R&D Engineering

* * *

To: Amit Schäfer
From: Bill Knipe
Subject: RE: RE: RE: RE: RE: Field Demonstration
Sent: 13 March 3105, 19:05

Amit, I have no idea how or why you decided it was a good idea to put nitrocellulose in the paint rounds for the autocannon, and I definitely do not understand why you decided not to mention the purpose of it to the supplies office so they could tell you how outright stupid it was. Leftenant Colonel Calhoun is incandescently pissed after what happened. Some stray AC rounds peppered the viewports of the observation bunker during the demonstration skirmish and it *appears* what happened is the low-powered medium lasers on the 'Mechs were enough to flash dry the nitrocellulose and light the damn windows on fire. Turns out Calhoun's aide was moved into a staff position after taking a rack of Cappie infernos to the cockpit at the tail end of the fighting on Jacson. Poor sap had a full-blown panic attack on the spot at seeing the flames through the armored glass. I'm just happy you weren't stupid enough to demand standard depleted-uranium rounds for the test. You better smooth this over fast.

Regards,
Bill Knipe, R&D Engineering

* * *

To: Bill Knipe
From: Amit Schäfer
Subject: drop it
Sent: 15 March 3105, 09:06

Bill,

Drop the project, it's not worth it anymore. Don't want to piss off Calhoun any further and risk souring the relationship with the AFFS.

Best regards,
Amit Schäfer, Marketing Manager, House Contracts

* * *

To: Amit Schäfer
From: Bill Knipe
Subject: RE: drop it
Sent: 15 March 3105, 09:11

Hi Amit,

Why the sudden change in direction? We've put a lot of blood, sweat, and tears into this and pulled way too much overtime not to get a 'Mech finished and production ready. Anyway, I thought the leftenant colonel was impressed with our work apart from that little snafu? The AFFS has nowhere else to go if they want *Blackjacks*, and the project is basically done at this point.

Regards,
Bill Knipe, R&D Engineering

* * *

To: Bill Knipe

From: Amit Schäfer
Subject: Heads-up
Sent: 21 March 3105, 18:47

Hey Bill,

Sorry to spring this on you so late in the day,
but I've had Geoff from Finance ask me who approved
the expenditure on this project. I had to name
names. I'm sorry, man.

Best regards,
Amit Schäfer, Marketing Manager, House Contracts

* * *

To: Bill Knipe
From: Group HR
Sent: 22 March 3105, 09:35
Subject: Disciplinary Issues

Hi Bill,

I've put an appointment into your calendar this
afternoon to discuss the *Blackjack* RAC project.
Amit has been in touch to raise some concerns
with regard to you overpromising and blowing
through the quarterly R&D project budget without
approval. There's also something about causing an
AFFS major to have PTSD flashbacks that I'm not
entirely clear on.

Thanks,
Valerie Garcia, HR Officer

* * *

To: Group HR
From: Bill Knipe
Sent: 22 March 3105, 09:36
Subject: Automatic reply: Disciplinary Issues

To whom it may concern,

I am out of office from now until FOREVER. If
your query has anything to do with the *Blackjack*
RAC project, then you can go ask Amit about it. He
can shove the project up his arse. I'm on a DropShip
bound for Galatea with half my shop techs anyway.

Gonna sign on with a merc outfit where we won't have
to deal with dipshit salesbros getting shitfaced at
the Christmas party and making ridiculous promises
on our behalf.

Regards,
Bill Knipe, R&D Engineering

* * *

As you can see from the above, this appears to be the result of a rogue marketing executive stepping outside his lane. The R&D team lead operated under the assumption that all their instructions had been cleared as part of the AFFS outreach marketing budget and acted mostly appropriately, with only a single instance of malicious compliance. They were only to learn that the project was, in fact, not at all approved in any sense once Mr. Knipe had been thrown under the bus. It was at this point his entire team quit in solidarity, and they made arrangements to leave the planet.

As regards the hole in the research budget, the two BJ-1s cost 3,808,142 pounds per unit, the BJ-3 cost 4,346,774 pounds, and the BJ-5 pulled from the line is projected to have a per unit cost of 7,129,411 pounds when it is released to the market next year, for a total of 19,092,469 pounds. The eight Mydron Model RD Rotary Autocannons used in the project cost 211,750 pounds per unit, for a total of 1,694,000.

It is difficult to assess the man-hour cost of this, since the project was not approved, so all the overtime Knipe's team pulled never got processed. The regular daily rate adds up, however, and the opportunity cost of the delay to the BJ-5 project is difficult to quantify. Recruiting replacement techs is still ongoing, and has amortized the cost across HR, IT, Security, etc. However, with the exception of the single chassis lost to the ammunition explosion described above, we have retained custody of all the physical assets diverted to this project, and it did produce a functional prototype.

The test-pilot evaluation reports are attached, but to summarize, the 'Mech performs as expected, although it has a low ammunition capacity for the rotaries. The ammunition is now mounted in the left torso and is protected by a Class-II CASE system, to prevent loss of the 'Mech. It runs hot up close, but nothing pilots can't manage with a little restraint. It may be a viable product line with a minimal amount of additional work.

Thus far, apart from Leftenant Colonel Calhoun and his aide, Major Brottsman, the reputational damage to General Motors is limited to employees and covered by standard NDAs. Given the acrimonious nature of how our wayward techs made their exit, as insurance I have tasked our direct-sales agents on Galatea to keep tabs on new arrivals looking for work. It may be possible to provide them with a financial incentive to keep quiet about this misadventure, or even entice them to return. The leftenant colonel was quite impressed with "how much 'dee-you' [*sic*] she can sling downrange," so if we decide not to proceed with production, he might be convinced to be discreet in return for a "gift" of one of the prototypes. Conveniently, Major Brottsman (formerly of the First Federated Suns Armored Cavalry, invalided due to injuries taken on Jacson) already wants to pretend it never happened.

Amit Schäfer's access to company systems has been frozen, pending the outcome of disciplinary proceedings. I recommend a round of refresher training for the rest of the Marketing Department on the importance of raising a ticket via the internal helpdesk to ensure internal coordination of future ad-hoc customer requests proceeds smoothly and according to established practice.

Please let me know how you wish to proceed.

Yours sincerely,
Torin Maher, Corporate Risk and Governance Officer

PLANET DIGEST: HEAN

ZAC SCHWARTZ

Star Type (Recharge Time): K1V (192 hours)
Position in System: 3 (of 8)
Time to Jump Point: 5.18 days
Number of Satellites: None
Surface Gravity: 0.8
Atm. Pressure: Standard (Breathable)
Equatorial Temperature: 31°C (Temperate)
Surface Water: 70 percent
Recharge Station: Nadir
HPG Class: B (3152)
Highest Native Life: Amphibians
Population: 52,571,000 (as of 3152)
Socio-Industrial Levels: B-C-C-B-B (3152)
Landmasses (Capital City): Chau, Dũng-Lạc, Luan, Nghiem, Taigoan (Caduceus), Truyen

In the nine centuries since humanity settled on Hean, nine flags have flown over its citizens' heads. While this is not particularly unusual in the region of space the planet occupies, few others have weathered so many transitions with so few scars.

Hean was first colonized by wealthy Vietnamese Catholics fleeing the violence between the Terran Alliance and the Separatist nations at the turn of the 23rd century. A lush world with a pleasant climate, the main drawback to living on Hean was its dangerous, almost universally poisonous native flora and fauna. In particular, many of the prolific amphibious lifeforms possessed various powerful neurotoxins

that aided in either predation or defense against such predators. This meant agriculture had to be carefully segregated from the environment in agrodomes, putting hard limits on how large a populace could be supported. Only a few decades after Hean was settled, to prevent unchecked population growth from making widespread famine inevitable, the government established a strict two-child policy. Over the centuries, they would add certain exceptions to this legislation, but it left Hean with a much smaller population than would be expected for such a long-settled world.

Initially disregarded by the Demarcation Declaration, Hean was acquired without resistance during the Terran Hegemony's second "campaign of persuasion": When a Hegemony fleet arrived in 2328, the parliament proactively sent a delegation to signal their intent to surrender. This would set the tone for Hean's future: immediate accession to whichever new master decided to put the planet in their crosshairs. It would prove to be a wise policy, sparing them the worst vicissitudes of war that wracked so many of their neighbors. A second layer of protection came during the golden years of the Star League. The unusual biochemistry of Hean's ecosystem brought the attention of the Star League Medical Association in the early 27th century, when a research team from the Saffel Medical Institute made a momentous discovery. The tank toad, a beachball-sized, six-legged amphibian armored with a thick and spiny hide on its back to deter pouncing predators, secreted several unique tryptamines with potent medicinal effects. They would prove valuable ingredients in some of the anti-aging drug cocktails that gave the citizens of the Star League their famed long lifespans and delayed senescence.

With investment from both the Hegemony and interested parties in the aristocracy of the Federated Suns, medical infrastructure on Hean was soon second only to worlds like Terra and Saffel. Medical tourism from across the Inner Sphere became a central component of the planetary economy. Even the Amaris Empire didn't engage in its typical heavy-handed oppression on Hean; in fact, their representative in the Hegemony Congress was one of the Usurper's eager backers. Like many future rulers, Amaris did not wish to disrupt the supply of synthesized tryptamines or his cronies' access to their top-flight clinics, and Hean was so cooperative he didn't even bother to station a garrison inside the planet's small Castle (known as Fort Poisonwood). When the Star League Defense Force's Nineteenth Army landed in October 2772, they faced no opposition.

When the Hegemony dissolved in the storm of postwar de-Amarisification of the early 2780s, even Hean couldn't avoid the consequences. The same Federated Suns financial interests that had enthusiastically backed the parliament and business leaders even during the war now helped extradite those leaders to ad hoc regional courts, where they were variously imprisoned or (more often) summarily executed for collaboration with the Usurper. With their government figuratively decapitated by this single stroke, no one on Hean was surprised when House Davion annexed the system in 2786. However, the Suns' clever, near-bloodless coup did not anticipate the outbreak of the Succession Wars.

In October 2787, Chancellor Barbara Liao dispatched Capellan Confederation forces to snip the Federated Suns' nascent Terran Corridor and form a common border with the Draconis Combine as part of her attempt at a military alliance. The infamously bloodthirsty Fourth Tikonov Lancers, balanced in temperament by the gentlemanly Fourth Liao Lancers, touched down outside Caduceus. The Federated Suns' Eighth Deneb Light Cavalry had been expecting a *Kuritan* attack, and were caught off guard by the sudden arrival of two Capellan regiments. The defenders dug in around Hean's pharmaceutical factories and health clinics, hoping to ward off the assault by forcing extreme caution on the attackers. With the Fourth Liao restraining the worst instincts of their sister Tikonovian regiment, the battle that followed in some ways eerily mirrored those seen under the aegis of the recently renounced but long ignored Ares Conventions, as the Capellans resorted to hit-and-run and harassment tactics that went out of their way to protect medical infrastructure and minimize battlefield losses (like the Conventions' requirement of nearly bloodless combat). The rapid maneuvering and superior positioning enabled by their greater numbers quickly checkmated the Eighth, who abandoned Hean in November. Due to Barbara's failed attempt at an alliance with the Combine, a decade later House Davion reveled in watching the Fifteenth Dieron Regulars jump to Hean and effortlessly destroy the meager Capellan garrison.

The system would trade hands twice more during the Succession Wars: first back to the Capellan Confederation during an offensive by Chancellor Laurelli Liao in 2841, who snatched it after the Combine removed the Fifteenth Dieron Regulars to counter a Davion drive against Mallory's World. It would then fall again to the Federated Suns during Field Marshal Jerome Hasek's opportunistic campaign into Capellan space in the late 2860s following the abdication of Chancellor Dainmar Liao. In each case, both sides fought with a level of circumspection and chivalry rarely observed in 29th-century warfare. In this way, Hean was again spared the damage wrought on so many other worlds, though it could not avoid the technological backslide of the era. With the science and machinery necessary to maintain Star League-era levels of production ebbing away, the economy relied on other local industries: namely, exotic animal export and high-quality furniture made from lightweight, durable Taigoan teak. Occasional raids and a failed 2996 Kuritan invasion would strike the planet over the course of the 30th century, but otherwise Hean experienced its longest peaceful period since its days under the auspices of the Terran Hegemony.

That peace ended abruptly when elements of the Word of Blake's Tenth Division assaulted the planet in August 3069. Unlike previous conquerors, the Word imposed its will directly on the populace, using conscription to rapidly build both a local Protectorate Militia division and a compliant gendarmerie, so the Tenth could progress to new targets. While the parliament capitulated immediately, as was their want, leading intellectuals protested the Blakists. The Word responded with swift brutality, imprisoning and executing countless doctors and academics to force compliance. With no experience of resisting an occupier, Hean's citizens hunkered down and hoped for liberation from the fanatics. That day would come eight years later at a bloody cost.

With the maintenance of Terran support paramount, Precentor Martial Cameron St. Jamais had ordered the construction of a multi-layered Space Defense System, part of his "Maginot Line" strategy. When a Coalition invasion force led by the *Fox*-class FSS *Indefatigable* materialized at the nadir jump point on 3 May 3077, they were rapidly overwhelmed by swarms of deadly drone assault DropShips and aerospace fighters. A pair of *Tiamat*-class assault DropShips, unfazed by the missile fire from the *Indefatigable*'s five escorting *Arondight*s, hulled the corvette with their heavy subcapital cannons. In the swirling chaos that ensued, the Coalition JumpShips equipped with lithium-fusion batteries managed to jump away, but many were less lucky, as the Fifteenth Arcturan Guards and Fox's Teeth suffered heavy casualties before their transports could escape. It was not until the end of May that the Coalition returned, this time with a naval flotilla led by Clan Nova Cat's vastly more durable and dangerous *Aegis*-class NCS *Path of Honor*. This time, the preponderance of firepower was on the Coalition's side, and despite further losses, the SDS drones were annihilated. The first assault force's survivors, reinforced by the Fifth Crucis Lancers and two Clusters from the Cats' Sigma Galaxy, dug out the entrenched Protectorate Militia by using heavy artillery and orbital strikes from the *Path of Honor* to obliterate most of the defenders at Fort Poisonwood before advancing and dealing with survivors.

Under the Republic, the damage sustained in the invasion was rebuilt, but Hean never quite recovered from the Blakist purges. Instead, they turned inward. The predominantly Catholic Heanese had seen gradual inroads made by the schismatic New Avalonian branch during two centuries of Davion rule. While in those years the New Avalon Catholics peaked at a quarter of the population, they had used the social-networking advantages this affiliation afforded to gain a disproportionate hold on power: Nearly two-thirds of the prominent positions in government, business, and academia belonged to members of the New Avalon Catholic Church laity. After Devlin Stone decreed the Resettlement Act of 3082, millions of Heanese were moved off-world, and many upper-class Avalonian Catholics were among them. Those who remained resented their loss of power, and over the decades the NACC clergy, along with elements of the Ministry of Information, Intelligence, and Operations, nurtured that resentment, burnishing their numbers with a renewed zeal for proselytizing and conversion.

Three years after Gray Monday, as the Republic's grip on their rimward prefectures collapsed, mass protests and unrest occurred across Caduceus. Avalonian Catholics, now a plurality on Hean, demanded the Republic Senate recall their governor, Amit Desai. Being Davion rebels, the Swordsworn soon arrived to enforce their will. Desai fled, and Duke Aaron Sandoval ennobled Bishop Francois Nguyen as Marquess of Hean. The non-Avalonian majority relied on the Dragon's Fury to resist the Swordsworn, and civil war erupted between the two factions. Agents of the Order of the Five Pillars assassinated Nguyen on Christmas 3135, but this did not prevent the planet's ultimate reincorporation into the Federated Suns, which placed Hean under military governorship. The fighting guttered out in 3143 as the Dragon's Fury dissolved following the defeat and capture of Katana Tormark, and the Swordsworn left soon after. But blood was in the water. Sharks began to circle.

Clan Sea Fox, ever on the hunt for new markets, saw opportunity both in Hean's turmoil and position. When Tiburon Khanate inked a deal with Julian Davion that traded three worlds in the Federated Suns for transporting Task Force Navarre, Hean was one of their selections. It sat at a nexus of borders that could be exploited by a neutral party like the Foxes. And after a lengthy recession driven by civil conflict and the Blackout, the Khanate was able to buy out the venerable pharmacorps at rock-bottom prices. From there, they began transforming Hean into the largest Sea Fox trading center in the Inner Sphere, constructing a sprawling commercial DropPort just outside Caduceus.

At present, with the advantages of Clan medtech and the resuscitation of the export economy, Hean is thriving. The one problem the Foxes still find difficult to solve is the simmering sectarianism. While it has not yet boiled back over, Tiburon Khanate has little experience with such matters, and has thus far elected to leave peacekeeping to local officials. However, the presence of a BattleMech lance from the Knights Defensor, who arrived in 3142 to help eject the last of the Dragon's Fury guerrillas, threatens to disrupt the tenuous peace. The Khanate has not yet decided how to handle the Knights: They are loath to disrupt either Hean's precarious status quo or diplomatic relations with the Federated Suns. The Knights have maintained a purely defensive position around the New Giao Phong Basilica in Caduceus, but justified or not, many in the city worry the Foxes may be too aloof to intervene if that stance changes from defense to offense.

TERRAIN TABLES

Hean's terrain and environment are as varied as Terra's, so any set of terrain tables can be used for battles set there.

VIOLENT INCEPTION

RUSSELL ZIMMERMAN

PART 4 (OF 4)

GROUNDED *TRIUMPH*-CLASS DROPSHIP *BONNEVILLE*
ROCK 32
BROCCHI'S CLUSTER
ALBIERO PREFECTURE
PESHT MILITARY DISTRICT
DRACONIS COMBINE
12 JUNE 3050

Major Rachel Fox paced back and forth on the *Bonnie*'s bridge. She passed her officers as she did so: DropShip Captain Almase Munene, with her dark skin and tremendous intellect; Leftenant Nolan, "Doc," their veteran, Taurian-trained combat medic; Chief Tech Ash Kol, child and grandchild of Kol technicians working for Mountain Wolf BattleMechs; and young, untested Hannah Rippon-Hart. Her employer's granddaughter. The future Duchess of Vendrell, Rachel's own homeworld. Her XO. A tremendous asset, but also a tremendous responsibility.

The lot of them were waiting on, of all things, savage invaders from beyond the Inner Sphere to contact them. They were waiting to politely fight technologically superior, brutally savage foes, to put up an honorable defense of the ore-rich moon Metals of Earth called Rock 32. They were waiting—and then the call came through.

"The Smoke Jaguars claim this moon!" a deep voice boomed as soon as Munene's junior officer accepted the inbound transmission. Even as the audio echoed in the bridge, a stunningly warlike figure appeared on the viewscreen; muscles rippling beneath pale skin and dark leathers, broad-shouldered and with black hair shaved high on the sides until little more than a mohawk remained, his face decorated with sharp-edged, pitch-black tattoos. "Identify what paltry forces defend it, so that we may know upon whom we pounce!"

Off to one side, Hannah giggled nervously, despite herself. Fox shot the girl a look as brutal as a PPC shot, then faced the screen. "I am Major Rachel Fox, of the Mountain Wolves..." She faltered at the look of sheer hatred that suddenly twisted the bizarre invader's features.

"Bah, *Wolves*," he said, and spat. Actually, literally spat.

That's the deck of your DropShip that'll need cleaning, not mine, buddy.

"I..." Fox spoke carefully. The Smoke Jaguars had recently annihilated a city just for offending them. Fox knew she'd just managed to offend this one, somehow. "I don't understand how I've insulted you, or wh—"

"You do not understand how to keep filthy freebirth chatter from pouring from your filthy freebirth mouth, either," the Jaguar said with a sneer. "If you will speak to me at all, you will speak *properly*!"

"I don't..." Fox slowed, then saw the man's eyes narrow even at *that*. "I...*do not* understand?"

Listen to how he talks. No contractions?

"Better," he said, lip still half-curled in disgust.

Fox nodded pointedly to her fellow officers. *No contractions.*

"I *do not* know what insult I offered with our name, but I also *do not* know what to call you, or how to continue," Rachel said, meticulously, carefully.

"I am Star Captain Gabriel Furey of Trinary Assault! Sixth Jaguar Dragoons, the Wolf Slayers, pride of Alpha Galaxy, of Clan Smoke Jaguar," he said, proudly, just like it wasn't absolute gibberish.

Every word makes sense. Just not...put together like that. Fox nodded slowly to the viewscreen with what she hoped was a respectful look. *Err, wait, did he say "Wolf Slayers"? What was that about? What the hell is... Focus. Do the job.*

"I don't—I *do not*—understand your traditions well and I will not pretend to, but we *are* the Mountain Wolves. I did not, Star Captain, offer that name to mock you. May I ask how..." She pursed her lips for a second. Painstakingly speaking in this stilted, formal manner was harder than she thought it would be. "May I ask how all this works?"

Furey's eyes narrowed in something like suspicion, something like curiosity. "The *batchall*?"

"I...believe that is what this is called, yes." Fox tried to show her sincerity. All she wanted to do was go through the motions and put forth an honest, earnest defense of Rock 32. She refused to invite more war crimes by playing their game poorly or refusing entirely. She just wanted to do her job, then get the hell away from these lunatics.

"Please, Star Captain. I mean no disrespect, I just want to know what exactly is supposed to happen next. I want to know what I need to do to protect the people of Rock 32."

"Hmph," he grunted skeptically. "The 'people' of your Rock 32? Some are beyond your protection. Yesterday, I offered a challenge and it was accepted, on the far side of this moon. Yesterday, I shattered their paltry BattleMechs, including those they sought to ambush me with. Yesterday, my fangs tasted blood, yet still I thirst. Be warned! I am light on patience and entirely out of mercy where broken *batchalls* are concerned."

The pirates, Fox knew. She didn't take her eyes from the man, as though he *were* a jaguar, some great beast who would pounce if she gave him the opening. *The pirates we were hired to hunt down. It doesn't sound like they played by the rules. Or like he went easy on them.*

"But what is *supposed* to happen, little Fox, is a Trial of Possession. I announce to you my identity and what we seek, as I have already done. I tell you I claim this entire Rock 32 of yours, and I await your answer, where you supply me with data on the forces that dare to stand in opposition."

Rachel nodded slowly, hungry to show she was paying attention, keeping up, and trying to be respectful of their...traditions.

"With that information," Furey continued, "you are free to communicate to me your chosen battlefield, as well."

"You are...Trinary Assault, Sixth Jaguar Dragoons, Alpha Galaxy." She repeated it all with just the barest of glances off to one side, as Captain Munene mouthed the words in time with her and nodded along. "We are the Mountain Wolves, and we defend with one company of BattleMechs. My people will broadcast you the details."

She gave a little nod off to one side.

"Tchk," His little sound of disgust made it clear, again, that she had somehow disappointed him. "Only one company? Fine. I will seize this pathetic rock from you with only my command Star."

A..."Star"?

"I don't—er, I *do not*, understand. What is a Star?"

"Five OmniMechs," he said with supreme confidence and clearly thinning patience.

Well, shit, only five? Fox blinked. *Maybe we're actually still in this. I guess that depends on exactly what an OmniMech is, but...*

"I have heard your, er, 'OmniMechs' are...superior...to our BattleMechs, in some ways." Fox spoke more carefully than she ever had in her life, especially now that she had some tattered shred of hope held in front of her. *But maybe we can take five of them.*

"They are superior in every way," the Star Captain said with a sneer, but offered only certainty, rather than details. "As are our MechWarriors."

"Am I allowed to know more about these five of yours? So that I can…understand this tradition better? I do not wish to waste your time, Star Captain, or insult you, like the scum you fought yesterday. I would like to at least make a fight of it." She eyed him warily as she tried a little shift in tone. He narrowed his eyes, gauging her sincerity, but then he nodded to someone off-screen. A moment later Fox glanced over and saw Munene confer with Leftenant Goodman.

"It's their…TO&E, Major." The junior officer showed her.

"I do not expect the OmniMech designations to be familiar to you." Star Captain Furey shrugged. "Nor am I required to explain their every detail to you, such as their precise configurations. But I suspect even you can read their tonnage information, and allow me to savor your fear."

Oh. Shit. Fox looked down at the short list. *Maybe we're not still in this, after all.*

She didn't know what a *Dire Wolf* was, but it sounded bad, and so did an *Executioner*. She wasn't familiar with the pair of *Warhawk*s, either, but if Star Captain Furey piloted one, they likely weren't pushovers. Even a *Gargoyle* didn't sound friendly. Most worrying, though, was the column with their tonnage: 100, 95, 85, 85, 80.

The runt of their litter is bigger than anything we've got. And every ton of it is supposed to be better and badder.

"I…see." She looked up at him and swallowed.

Furey licked his lips from pleasure, not nerves. He had *savored* her fear.

"Thank you for explaining, and allowing me the opportunity to honor the…bat shall." She gave a respectful nod, trying her best. "As I said, we will face this Star with a company. The Mountain Wolves have nothing that rivals the might of the Sixth Jaguar Dragoons, but we will offer you fair combat for possession of Rock 32."

I might as well talk you up before you knock us down. Pricks. She licked her lips from nerves, not pleasure. *And I might as well get this over with.* "Let us say two hours from now?"

Before he could respond, Furey was distracted by a commotion off-screen. He looked away, head tilting incredulously, then glared back at her. "Do you mean to offer insult, or is this an attempt at deception?" he said, voice tight with anger. "Freebirth, I swear, I will paint my face with your blood if you are trying to trick me!"

"What?! Star Captain, I do not understand!" Fox glanced from officer to officer, and everyone looked as confused, as standing-on-a-landmine, as she felt. "How have I—"

"Tell me more about these '*Merlin*s' you claim to bring," he spoke slowly, as though to a very stupid child. But he also spoke angrily, with a barely contained rage, as though to a very stupid child he was about to drown with his bare hands. "And tell me who among you *dares* to call themself a Rippon?!"

As part of her name rang out, Hannah Rippon-Hart felt a sudden shock of nervousness, adrenaline, and absurdity, and didn't know whether to giggle, puke, or die trying to do both at once. Her body answered for her, and as every eye on the bridge turned her way—she hiccupped.

"That is my...junior officer," Hannah heard Major Fox answering as she looked desperately to her friend, Yoshi Goodman, looked to Doc and Kol, who knew everything, and to Captain Munene, who knew *everything*-everything. No luck. They all looked lost, too.

"Leftenant Hannah Rippon-Hart. Would you like to mee—"

"What I would *like*," a new, equally savage Clan warrior appeared on the screen, "is to tear the lying tongue from her mouth and eat it while she drowns in her own blood."

Um. Hannah gawked at a woman taller and more broad-shouldered than she was, or even athletic Tomoko Oga. She had slash-cut short hair, in a berserker's tight mohawk, over a face crisscrossed with geometric patterns that didn't quite look like tattoos. *A crazy lady wants to murder me and I don't even know why.*

"I...uh...sorry?" Hannah didn't mean to lean into the frame and speak up and was as horrified as anyone else when she realized she had done so.

"You!" the woman pointed, and Hannah sidestepped to stand more clearly in front of the screen even though her instinct was to duck away. Major Fox slid a step away, giving Hannah the spotlight as the Clanner continued. "Explain how it is that *you*, freebirth scum, dare to sully *my* name?"

"Sully your name?" Hannah felt very stupid and very scared all at once. "I don't even know—"

"I am Star Commander Monica Rippon, Bloodnamed. I have killed for this legacy. How do *you* claim it?"

"It's..." Hannah caught a wince from Major Fox, and fixed the abbreviation hurriedly. "It is just...my...name? I, um, I do not understand your question."

She knew how people screwing up simple things, like pronouns, could bother her. She prayed her own verbal stumbles bothered the Jaguars less. *They already seem bothered enough.*

"So you *do* claim to bear the mantle of David Rippon?"

"I..." Hannah stalled for time, wide-eyed, looking desperately from officer to officer, terrified that one wrong word was going to kill everyone anywhere nearby. She had been calm and collected when taking verbal exam after verbal exam at the War College of Buena. She had been angry, not afraid, staring down her own father and a military tribunal. But here, now, she was so *confused*, and these Jaguars were so *terrifying*, that she couldn't help but...but...

Wait, David *Rippon?* She startled slightly, then looked at Captain Munene. Just after it had fallen into place for Hannah, she saw the captain also make eager eye contact. *David Rippon!*

"Whatever it is, kid, they're already pissed," Major Fox whispered next to her, low and serious, "so shoot your shot."

Sometimes an officer has to say the hard thing, Fox had taught her.

"David Rippon," Hannah squeaked, then cleared her throat and started over, "David Rippon, the...do you mean the MechWarrior?"

Munene held up one finger on each hand, "one" and "one" side by side, and Hannah nodded as the rest of the trivial family history fell into place. *Of course* Captain Munene knew it, too.

"David Rippon, of the Eleventh Royal BattleMech Division?" Hannah looked excitedly at the viewscreen as she dredged up old lessons that tutors had drilled into her mind for half her life. "And *Sling* test pilot for Mountain Wolf BattleMechs?"

Monica Rippon, Bloodnamed, looked apoplectic enough Hannah knew she was right.

"Then...I...lay claim? I lay claim, yes!" She pressed on when Fox nodded at her to continue. "I can trace my lineage all the way back." *Thank you, stuffy Lyran nobility.* "House Rippon married into—"

"How. *Dare.* You!" Star Commander Monica Rippon snarled. "How *dare* you even speak his name, and prattle off some...some...*factoid*, you freebirth cur, about Mountain Wolf BattleMechs, as though you know!"

"Them, too!" Hannah interjected. Without meaning to, she'd put her feet beneath her for a well-balanced, combat-ready stance. She was surprised to notice her hands at her sides had balled into fists. "Major Fox told you! We *are* the Mountain Wolves, and we are part of *the* Mountain Wolf BattleMechs! My family owns the company, so, er, I claim that, too, along with the Rippon name. It will be mine someday."

Major Fox shrugged and nodded to her. Hannah had no idea what was happening, but *something* was. This crazy space lady was clearly furious about something, or maybe just looking for an excuse to be furious, and Hannah felt like that had fallen on her, somehow. The major had *said* their plan was to go through the motions of a challenge and put on a good show, right?

Oh!

"And I claim Mountain Wolf's *Merlin!*" Hannah added excitedly. "You, er, Star Captain Furey, you asked what a *Merlin* is? Well, a *Merlin* is a BattleMech. A *Mountain Wolf BattleMechs* BattleMech. You can see how many of them we are bringing to the fight, MLN-1A models, heavy 'Mechs, sixty tons of anti-pirate guardian, designed by my grandfather, Brandon O'Leary and Cassandra Fox, Major Fox, here? Her own mother! Brandon O'Leary owns the company and the rights, though. So...I...say *that's mine, too.* I claim the Rippon name, Mountain Wolf BattleMechs, and the *Merlin*. They are *mine.*"

She was picking up steam. Her beloved uncle Cameron, the only biological child of Brandon O'Leary and her Gran Gran, was the crown prince of Mountain Wolf BattleMechs. He had been on Alpheratz overseeing the operation for years. But Hannah *was* in line. And, she was surprised to find, she *meant* it. This wasn't some ruse. Here, life or death, under pressure, she was nervous, yes, but she was sincere.

I am *the future of House Rippon-Hart, of our planet, Vendrell, and of the company, Mountain Wolf BattleMechs. And I'm not afraid to say so. Not to you or anyone else.*

"Star Captain," Monica Rippon snarled, "I demand a Trial of Grievance against this freebirth scum who dares—"

"A proper Trial of Grievance requires the Clan Council, or as you are Bloodnamed and she, in a clumsy way, seems to lay claim such as well, in fact the *Grand* Council, to—"

"Star Captain, I demand a Trial of *Possession*," Monica Rippon tried again immediately, furiously, hungrily. "Allow me to claim data on this *Merlin*, and a shattered example of one to add to our *touman*, and in exchange allow me to wipe clean the stain of this Spheroid that dares to—"

"*Tchk*, against just a barbarian? Truly?" The Star Captain made that disgusted little noise he liked so much, as though challenging Hannah was complimenting her. "Fine. Major Fox! Has your subordinate leave to answer this new *batchall*? A *Trial of Possession*, separate from the one we wage over this planet, a bit of sport for the enjoyment of our troops? For the *Merlin*."

Hannah wouldn't pretend to understand half of what was happening, but it sure felt like the other Rippon had been overstepping in some way with everything else she'd been demanding. Monica would just have to live with only the *Merlin* being up for grabs—the *Merlin* and the chance to take a few shots at Hannah.

Fox gave Hannah a long sideways look, and Hannah imagined she could see gears turning. "We, well, we actually *do* have a spare *Merlin*, in mint condition," Major Fox spoke confidently up at the viewscreen, as though she'd grown up with these Clan rules. "Since it sounds like you would rather have that than merely some technical data."

Both Jaguars nodded; Furey eager for a prize, Rippon for blood.

"However," Major Fox dared to continue, "if Hannah fights this duel, I will be down a MechWarrior. One of my highest ranked!" Hannah couldn't help but notice she didn't say 'one of my best,' but Hannah also knew that was entirely fair. "If I remove her from our roster for the purposes of *our* Trial of Possession, I think it is only fair that I ask that you remove one MechWarrior from your proposed force as well."

Hannah could tell Fox was back to something she understood on a fundamental level, haggling.

Furey stared at the screen as though he didn't believe his ears. "It is impertinent to remove one-fifth of my force for *one-twelfth* of yours, while also implying that one freebirth MechWarrior is the equal to even our scrawniest *sibkin* kit, much less a Bloodnamed Star Commander!" Then, perhaps worst of all so far, he smiled. It was terrifying. "But it is bold of you to ask! I take it as an attempt at honoring our traditions. I accept your lessened bid, Fox, and I reciprocate. Our *Gargoyle* will not deploy!"

Hannah thought she could hear a disappointed cry from a Smoke Jaguar MechWarrior somewhere off-screen.

"You, Hannah! You will fight in this *Merlin* of yours? Of sixty tons? Which you claim is made by Mountain Wolf BattleMechs?" Star Commander Rippon snarled.

The Rippon family BattleMaster *is back on Vendrell, so...yeah.*

Hannah nodded. "I will."

"Then I will engage you in a *Mist Lynx*," Monica said confidently. "As I am a child of David Rippon, I will ride into battle in the child of his *Sling*!"

"Major Fox!" the Star Commander spoke up again. "Choose, then, the site of our battles. Let us commence in two hours. Duel first, then slaughter."

"Do you know the map designations the locals use? The plains-crater of Zone Delta Seven," Fox said. The core facility of Rock 32 was in what they'd called Zone Alpha Two, kilometers away. Hannah knew the major mostly only cared about keeping the fight a safe distance from the civilians.

"The *surat* we destroyed shared maps with us. Delta Seven, the crater there. Yes." Furey nodded with an air of finality, just like Fox should know what the hell a *surat* was. "Well bargained and done!"

Hannah saw Monica Rippon sneering at her, directly at her, just before the call went dead. She let out a long, low breath as the officers around her burst into motion.

"Doc," Major Fox said immediately, "Contact Director Chang. Tell him we're doing what we can, and to proceed with the groupings we discussed. We fill that cargo hold space with ore, or with people. Win or lose, we're taking *some* of Rock 32 away with us and keeping it out of these bastards' hands."

"On it, Major," the Taurian nodded. As a Mountain Wolf officer without any of his people in the fight or prepping 'Mechs for it, he was eager to help however he could. As a medical expert, he was the best qualified to realistically appraise their refugee-cargo capacity.

"Major," Hannah began, "I'm sorry, it just felt like—"

"You got them focused, and focused is how we wanted them." Fox replied grimly. "But you *did* just sign up to fight a duel."

"It felt like..." Hannah sighed and shrugged. "It felt like it was better for her to be mad at *me*, than for *all of them* to be mad at *all of us*."

Fox gave her an appraising look. "You're putting a lot on the line, but your gut check was probably right." She reached out and clapped Hannah's arm, giving her a little squeeze. "Your grandma would be proud, kid. Let's just make sure we get you back to her, okay?"

Hannah nodded.

"Worst case scenario, if you're careful?" Fox said. "You're losing one 'Mech, and Bran can replace it. So you put on a good fight, but you stay ready to punch out, you hear me? You just let 'em have it...and then... let 'em keep it." She gave Hannah a warm smile. "A *Merlin* can hold its own, no matter what monster they throw at you."

That's... Hannah squinted at her *Merlin*'s sensors. *That's not a monster.*

The Mountain Wolves had their gathered 'Mechs arrayed near the rim of Delta Seven's massive crater. There wasn't much *to* Rock 32, and the crater simply existing made it something of a regional landmark; the whole mineral-rich moon was nothing but prefab buildings slapped together near where industrial machines clawed into barren rocks to drag out ores, all blanketed by a thin, but technically breathable, atmosphere. Rock 32 itself felt temporary, and likely was. But right now it had people on it, too many to just *give* to the Smoke Jaguars to slaughter. People had made even one of the Brocchi Cluster's weird little moons into a *home*. People made it a place worth fighting over.

There they waited, all the Mountain Wolves. Major Fox in her blocky *Archer*, their heaviest 'Mech and heaviest hitter, poor Shotaro on the other end of the spectrum, lean and quick in their tiny *Locust*, Sergeant Brownpants in his *Shadow Hawk*—the hips and legs painted a muddy brown, the rest of his 'Mech fitting Mountain Wolf paint regulations—and then their long line of *Merlin*s. The pride and joy of Mountain Wolf BattleMechs, machines these bizarre invaders had apparently never seen before, broad-shouldered, all painted a wolfish gray and trimmed here and there with broad stripes of eye-catching blaze orange. Sentries, bristling with guns, waiting, each cockpit filling with fear or excitement or nerves...then watching a sleek, powerful Smoke Jaguar DropShip descend.

As the Smoke Jaguars expertly and, in fact, almost *gracefully* disembarked from their DropShip, only one of the 'Mechs didn't fit the tonnage classifications Hannah expected. She scanned her sensors' basic data, flicking the computer's attention from one to the next. They were absolute *beasts*, assault 'Mechs, but while they moved slowly, they showcased a crisp parade-formation precision that would've been the envy of any parade-marching MechWarrior outfit in the Inner Sphere. The machines were huge, titans of angular armor, purring engines, and lethal guns.

Except one. One of them was clearly not usually in service to a Trinary *Assault* (whatever exactly a Trinary was). It was tiny, especially compared to the other four.

Hannah's date.

She was, absurdly, hit with a memory from the War College of Buena. All of fifteen years old, new to calling herself Hannah instead of her old name, she'd gotten a spring formal invitation from handsome Cadet Goodman—no relation to Mountain Wolf's Yoshi Goodman—and had let herself be *thrilled*. Foolishly. She had arrived, eagerly, to find another girl on his arm, and to hear him laughing at her for believing he'd meant it. Worse, he'd encouraged their classmates, their peers, to laugh at her; stupid, lonely Hannah, all dressed up, all alone. She didn't remember exactly what he'd said, but his cruel remarks hadn't compared to just the joke of it all.

And invitation had turned to insult...and this challenge felt the same.

The *Mist Lynx* looked like a joke, all paltry 25 tons of it. It was almost as light as Shotaro's *Locust*! It was a silly little thing compared to the looming war gods of the Sixth Jaguar Dragoons, or even to the Mountain Wolves and their *Merlin*s. Like the Mountain Wolves' machines, the Jaguars had painted their 'Mechs gray. Instead of the Wolves' clean lines of blaze-orange highlights, though, the Dragoons' 'Mechs broke the gray up with jaguar spots painted here and there, along with other occasional feline markers—painted-on fangs, cats eyes, or swaths of synthetic fur—making them all look especially monstrous, especially predatory.

Except the *Mist Lynx*. It almost looked...adorably ugly?

For its size, it had a boxy chest reminiscent of Major Fox's *Archer*, but without any weapons mounted there. Instead, its spindly arms ended in comically overburdened-looking forearm weapon pods. It was ungainly, and it wasn't even half the weight of Hannah's *Merlin*. The *Mist Lynx* was puny. The second smallest 'Mech on this moon. Just for her. While the rest of the Wolves had to square off with alien assault 'Mechs covered in thick, angular panels and carrying massive, lethal weaponry, Hannah faced...that.

Why do I feel insulted again? Why does this shame feel worse than the fear?

Given her date was with a "child of the *Sling*," she hadn't been expecting an *Atlas* or something, but... Hannah cast an eye to her comms display, half prepared to hear laughter over it.

"You've got this, Hannah," Major Fox said instead over a tight-beam frequency. "Brawl with her, kid, you hear me? You've learned plenty of kicks from Oga and Kanezaka. Believe in them, believe in yourself. Do it. Trust your armor, get in close, and *hit* her."

Hannah flicked a confirmation-green light when she didn't trust her voice to return the major's advice.

Allah, please, Hannah prayed as the weird little *Mist Lynx* strode forward, outpacing the looming, fearsome war machines behind it. A Rippon sat at the controls, apparently. A Rippon who wanted very badly to kill her. A Rippon who wanted her dead, and Hannah had no idea why.

Let me make my family proud.

Just as she throttled forward in her big, broad *Merlin*, it hit her, though.

"Wait!" she said in the emptiness of her neurohelmet, then toggled on a broad-spectrum comms blast, coupled with external speakers for good measure. "Er, wait!"

Her *Merlin* kicked up dirt and stone as it skidded to an awkward stop. The *Mist Lynx* stopped on a dime, incredulous.

"Your cowardice will not save you now, *pretender*," Monica Rippon snarled. "We are committed. I will *not* be denied your throat in my teeth."

"I don't want—er, I *do not* want to quit! I am not asking...that! I just..." Hannah lifted her *Merlin*'s arms, bulky, blocky things, ending in the barrels of medium lasers instead of hands. She hoped that pointing them skyward relayed a nonthreatening gesture to these angry Jaguars.

She finally managed to collect herself. "What are the rules of the fight? Not the trial, not the bat shawl, though, *this*? I mean, Star Commander Monica Rippon, with respect, I am asking: are there rules to this *actual fight*?"

The *Mist Lynx* held very still, then its shoulders slumped slightly as its weapons lowered. In disappointment? Exasperation?

The Jaguar answered, though, and used her words. Not violence. "First, I say your warriors and mine stay where they have already stopped," Monica growled the words grudgingly. "They form our Circle of Equals, and let neither of us leave it on pain of death."

Hannah saw that as both sides had slowed their approaches, they had left over half a kilometer between them to create this "Circle of Equals." It wasn't much space, but it was enough. There'd be no cat and mouse games between them. No hunting, just fighting.

Painfully aware of the *Merlin*'s integrated, almost motionless cockpit, and of how awkwardly she piloted compared to this Smoke Jaguar, Hannah bobbed her 'Mech's upper torso forward and back in something like a bow or a nod. A terrible, ridiculous nod.

"Second, I say let *none* interfere, on pain of death and dishonor," Monica continued. "Freebirth, if even *one* other warrior of your 'Mountain Wolves' attacks me, I swear we will wipe this stone clean of all life, starting with yours."

Hannah shifted her 'Mech's weight again, showing another nod as best she could.

"And third, finally, I say we both vow that neither of us will tarnish our honor by lowering ourselves to physical attacks," the Smoke Jaguar finished. "We wield our weapons, we fire our guns, as David Rippon would have wanted."

Hannah's *Merlin* froze.

No kicks or punches? She felt very stupid and very hopeless, all at the same time. *Those physical attacks were my best chance at maybe winning this thing...*

"Let us not shame Founder Rippon's legacy by simply clashing 'Mech to 'Mech," Monica continued, filling the silence, "clumsily smashing against one another. Let skill decide this, not brawn!"

Hannah took a long moment and marveled at the absurd hypocrisy.

You...you keep talking about teeth and throats, you threatened to rip my tongue out and eat it, you're saying you're willing to wipe out Rock 32 right after you Smoke Jaguars glassed a whole city, and... somehow...'Mech-on-'Mech contact is a bridge too far?

She saw a blinking comms light from Major Fox flashing on her board. Yellow for caution, but to continue.

You're bringing 100-ton assault 'Mechs stuffed to the gills with superior weapons and armor, knowing we've got no choice but to fight back as best we can, and you claim "skill," not brawn, will decide this?!

She saw a green light blinking as well. Encouragement from Tomoko.

Hannah got herself under control and took a breath.

"I understand and I promise, no physical attacks," Hannah said, her confidence diminished at the removal of a tried-and-true combat staple where her *Merlin*'s size would be a major advantage, but she was determined to give it a go. "I am ready."

The moment she spoke, the *Mist Lynx* began her way, so she throttled up her *Merlin* and lumbered forward to meet it.

As she drew closer, her battle computer told her more about her opponent. The *Mist Lynx* was bristling with missile ports, yes, just like an old Mountain Wolf *Sling* would have been. Looking for the similarity in design, Hannah *did* see how the *Sling* could have been an inspiration, but there were differences, too. *Sling*s had been infamous for, if anything, their fragile, sleek chassis carrying only long-range missiles, three LRM-5 launchers. The *Mist Lynx* carried an LRM-10 and what appeared to be an SRM-4—so it had shorter range, fewer missiles, but heavier warheads. Its bulbous arm also bristled with machine guns, high caliber for anti-infantry work, but almost laughably low caliber for anti-'Mech work. More irritating than dangerous, as long as Hannah's armor held.

I can...I can do this? she half marveled as the gap closed. She knew she had lost more one-on-one 'Mech fights than she had won, in both the *Bonneville*'s simulators and in training exercises at the War College of Buena. But, if she played it smart...

Take stock, Hannah.

Their close-support weapons balanced out. Her *Merlin* had a machine gun, too, coupled with a similarly short-range, anti-infantry flamer. In medium range, her pair of Martell Model 5 medium lasers should more than match the SRM-4. Most importantly, while her single Holly LRM-5 lagged behind with missile firepower, her *Merlin* was built around a massive Magna Hellstar PPC. The particle projection cannon was a brutal, long-range energy weapon that would more than make up for the difference in the LRMs' firepower.

As small as the enemy 'Mech was, as heavily armed and fast, it couldn't be carrying much armor. If Hannah's internal calculations, extrapolations, and best guesses were correct, there was probably nowhere the *Mist Lynx* could take a PPC shot without suffering at least an armor breach. It seemed to be some sort of recon 'Mech and was armored appropriately...and the *Merlin* very much wasn't.

I can do this!

And, of course, Mountain Wolf's *Merlin* was a 60-ton beast, a burly, broad-chested workhorse. The profile was meant to intimidate Periphery pirates as much as fight them, and it showed. While the size of her *Merlin* might not rattle this Smoke Jaguar's confidence, it bolstered Hannah's. A *Merlin* was a proven, trusted design, even if these Jaguar people had never heard of it. Most importantly, Hannah was protected—*thank you, Grandpa Bran!*—by over ten tons of armor. If Hannah's math was right, the *Mist Lynx* likely didn't have half that!

What'd Tomi call that, a boxer's chance, right? All I have to do is hit *this thing!*

The first handful of the Jaguar's missiles scattered damage across her *Merlin*, and she returned fire, feeling calmer. It was simple math. She had the armor and the biggest gun in play, and even if she didn't land a knockout PPC shot, she *would* win a battle of attrition. *Every* battle was a battle of attrition, when you got down to it.

Her first blue-white beam of PPC fire flashed just by the nimble little 'Mech, blasting a divot in the dull gray stone of Rock 32.

PLOG19

Damn. Gotta connect! Hannah angled off to one side, figuring they would both circle. It made sense to circle. The *Mist Lynx*'s biggest weapon was its LRM-10, so the Jaguar should really, really want to circle. Circling maximized their range and kept the *Merlin*'s lasers out of play.

They didn't circle.

Well, *Hannah* circled, but Monica didn't. She charged. The *Mist Lynx*'s engine hurled it forward suddenly, closing at well over 100 kilometers an hour, jinking as it came.

The frak?!

Hannah rushed her second shot, and her PPC seared the air in a narrow miss just as her next volley of missiles kicked up dirt in the *Mist Lynx*'s wake. Monica's LRMs unerringly splashed a fresh wave of damage across Hannah's *Merlin*, and a flurry of SRMs punched into the *Merlin* an instant later. The *Mist Lynx* had gotten so close so fast its knife-fighting weapons were already in range. Hannah backpedaled to even out her firing angles, drew a bead, and slashed her targeting reticule across the smaller 'Mech while firing both lasers.

Her twin beams of energy gouged Rock 32's harsh surface, another disappointing volley, so Hannah stomped the controls for her jump jets to lift herself out of machine-gun range, safely past her opponent. Her trusty Pitban LFT 50s screamed, her *Merlin* shuddered, and she took to the skies in an awkward, heavy leap away. She landed, then turned to face the Jaguar across the crater.

The pair of Rippons began a dangerous, lopsided dance. A graceless ballet. A leaping contest, firing as they went, for pass after pass.

Like jousters, they would close the gap, attack one another as they clashed while riding flaring jump jets, pass each other, then circle and roar in once more. When the gap widened, Hannah snapped off hurried shots with her PPC and her LRMs, struggling to draw a clean bead at the edges of her weapons' ideal targeting ranges. At medium range, Monica hammered Hannah again and again with missiles, both large and small. When the gap closed, they prodded one another with machine guns and fiery gouts from the *Merlin*'s flamer.

But every time, those flurries of *Mist Lynx* missiles gnawed at the *Merlin*'s armor. The LRMs didn't seem to care how close or far away their target was, and those SRMs, Hannah swore, simply *didn't miss*, ever. Every time the quartet of missile ports flared with an attack, every one of the missiles punched into her *Merlin* somewhere, cratering the armor, rocking her in her harness, and updating her wireframe display to show more and more damage.

Allah, how much longer do I do this? Hannah panted in the heat of her cockpit.

The joust-ballet continued. Running, jumping, crisscrossing one another. Hannah was *losing*, there was no denying it. Armor be damned, bulk be damned, logic be damned, she was losing this battle of attrition. She just couldn't seem to land clean shots, and the other Rippon couldn't seem to miss. She leaped, she turned, she fired, and over and over, she lost armor.

How much longer do I keep this up, before I ca—

Something in the belly of her *Merlin* shuddered beneath another storm of missiles, and a fresh wave of heat rolled into her cockpit. Warning lights blazed, alerting her to a hit on her fusion engine's shielding. Her PPC threatened to spike her heat level to dangerous heights now, especially with the jump jets blazing and lasers flashing so eagerly.

Hannah interrupted their dance, not straining her engine with jump jets on their next pass. The heat was getting untenable, and she merely wanted to conserve energy, but...she broke the pattern. The change in rhythm, the unexpected move, caught the Clan warrior off guard as the *Mist Lynx* lifted off.

Hannah, still and stable as any firing platform could hope to be, scored a clean hit with both lasers, raking them across the *Mist Lynx*'s chest as it sailed by overhead. For the first time in the duel, she marked her opponent solidly, leaving a glowing X across its chest. She saw a puff of spraying gas that told of a ruptured heat sink, and her thermal sensors registered a mild increase in the Smoke Jaguar's heat levels for the first time in their entire duel.

Finally!

Even so, the *Mist Lynx* returned fire viciously. Caught in mid-air, the Smoke Jaguar still feathered her jump jets just so, spinning, twisting to maintain her aim as she leaped over and past Hannah's *Merlin*, bracketing the heavier 'Mech. Fresh warning lights blazed in Hannah's cockpit, new alerts about yet more lost armor, yet more myomer musculature and steel skeleton damage.

Worse, the impact of this latest missile volley threatened to bowl her *Merlin* right over. Half in a panic, Hannah *did* have to slam her feet into the jump-jet pedals after all, riding on pillars of plasma to keep herself upright, lunging into the air to keep from slamming to the ground. Her cockpit turned into an oven and took her breath away as her engine strained.

But this time, she took off just as the *Mist Lynx* was descending.

In front of her, *below* her now, Star Commander Monica Rippon's *Mist Lynx* was stuck half landing and half turning, its slow, almost-still clawed feet gouging Rock 32's surface for grip and stability. The Jaguar was right under her.

Right under her, as Hannah's Pitban jump jets fought to keep 60 tons of steel aloft.

Time slowed down.

I could do it.

The attack was called a death from above, the oldest jump-jet trick in the book, the most brutal, most desperate, most popular on Solaris (despite Tomoko's fondness for spinning backfists). All you had to do was jump on top of someone, throw your 'Mech at them, and you tested the sturdy feet of your 'Mech against the fragile top of theirs. A vicious enough MechWarrior just had to gamble that their leg armor would take the beating better than their opponent's arms, or shoulders, or especially cockpit, and *any* fight could be turned around in an instant.

A *Merlin* landing atop a *Mist Lynx* would be grotesque, like a professional wrestler climbing the ropes and diving onto an elementary schoolgirl. The fight would be over. Brutally. In that hanging, crawling moment, as gravity seduced Hannah to crush her opponent, the fight was as one-sided as the Smoke Jaguar WarShip pummeling Edo off the map had been. In that moment, the Star Commander was as vulnerable as that poor, doomed city.

Hannah could more than survive this, she could *win* this!

All she had to do was...let it happen. All she had to do was *let* her *Merlin's* huge, reinforced legs fall and touch the scrawny *Mist Lynx's* cockpit just below her. All she had to do was let gravity finish the fight for her.

Allah, forgive me, she thought.

Grandmother forgive me.

Gravity reached out and pulled her ungainly *Merlin* down.

Major, forgive me...

She began to drop down onto the smaller 'Mech—

I can't! Hannah stomped onto her jump-jet pedals again, suddenly. She flailed and lost control of both legs as the jump jets—in each of those swinging legs—flared and roared and fought to, only just barely, keep from smashing the tiny *Mist Lynx*.

I promised.

Hannah desperately, artlessly scissor-kicked in the air, her jump jets screaming and scorching the *Mist Lynx*'s paint and only, oh-so-narrowly avoiding a lethal drop onto the Star Commander's cockpit. Instead, Hannah's *Merlin* fell to the harsh stone of Rock 32 with agonizing, embarrassing clumsiness, its shock-absorbing legs splayed wide and angled all wrong, 60 tons of metal falling like a carelessly dropped toy.

Her outstretched left leg hit the ground with a crash and nearly snapped off, hip joint screaming as metal sheared through metal. The upper half of her *Merlin* followed it and hit Rock 32 like a felled tree. The impact slammed her around the cockpit mercilessly. Her life was saved—however briefly—by her harness, but her face still smashed against the interior of her neurohelmet, and her laser-arm, trying pathetically to stop the fall, still got mangled from the effort. She still saw her console light up with armor breach alerts. She still hit the ground, and the world went dark with the impact as she blacked out.

Hannah gulped in air and a mouthful of blood as she came to. Damningly, emergency warnings about critical damage to her PPC lit up. In the fall, her *Merlin* had crushed its biggest, most crucial gun.

Joke's on you... I couldn't fire the PPC without cooking myself anyways.

She spit blood inside her neurohelmet. Heat warnings blared at her even as sweat and blood flash-dried from her clothes and skin. Her engine was even *more* damaged after the fall, her heat climbing and climbing.

It had taken every bit of Hannah's piloting ability to flop her ungainly *Merlin* onto its broken back and stare up at the unblinking stars of Brocchi's Cluster.

Her view was interrupted by Rippon's *Mist Lynx* striding over to her, looking down at her. *Aiming* down at her. It lined up the paired machine guns and that murderously accurate SRM-4, all straight at her already-cracked cockpit canopy. All straight at *her*.

At the edge of her vision, she saw Tomoko Oga's blue sensor blip move forward just a few meters...then stop before she got them all killed.

Hannah was certain she was going to die. She squeezed her triggers in a last, desperate attempt at survival, hoping her tertiary weapons—the flamer and machine gun—might do *something* to the scarred, lightly armored *Mist Lynx*, and perhaps her torso-mounted support weaponry could somehow save the day. Or at least she would look proud and defiant. Like Grandmother, or Aunt Fatima.

Right?

Nothing happened. None of her weapons fired. Hannah blinked slowly past her concussion and saw yet more red lights. Broken. *Everything is broken.* She wanted to cry. She didn't.

"*Ashahadu an la ilaha illa Allah*," Hannah prayed as best she could despite the blood refilling her mouth. She didn't look away. *There is no god but Allah.* She was as ready to die as she would ever be.

Savoring the murderous moment, the *Mist Lynx*'s hand tightened into a fist, nimble widget-fingers all tucked safely out of the line of fire, guns pointed right at Hannah. Then...it didn't shoot.

"I know why you fell," Star Commander Monica's electronically enhanced voice said, slowly, almost painfully as she decided Hannah's fate. "I know what you could have done."

Hannah reeled.

"You fought with honor. I say, enough. I offer you..." Monica said grudgingly, and even past her concussion, Hannah could tell the Jaguar hated saying what she was saying. "The opportunity to surrender. Yield! I will take your *Merlin* before I must damage it more. Yield, acknowledge your defeat. Save me from destroying the cockpit of my pathetic prize, and you with it."

Wh...what? Hannah blinked slowly, swallowed a mouthful of blood, and tried to make sense of what she was hearing. *These people are all crazy.*

"Because you did not take my life, freebirth, I give you yours. I offer you safe retreat, much as I hate doing so. Leave this circle with your honor intact." She spoke slowly, as though Hannah were hard of hearing, not battered, concussed, and ignorant. The offer was being broadcast on the same wide-band, short-range channel everyone else, Mountain Wolves and Smoke Jaguars alike, would hear.

"Yield," Monica repeated, as though she were giving a subordinate an order. "You have failed, but have not shamed Founder Rippon. You fought, you lost. That is all."

It sounded better than the alternative.

"I..." Hannah coughed and tried again. "I yield."

The instant Rippon-Hart's *Merlin* cracked open its cockpit hatch, Fox figured the duel was over, and gave the go-order to Kanezaka to get her clear.

His *Locust* was already moving before she finished speaking. As Rippon's *Mist Lynx* was leaving Hannah behind, Shotaro's *Locust* darted up. Fox zoomed in and saw Hannah climbing out with the agonizing slowness of a drunk or a walking wounded.

There was no answering motion from the Smoke Jaguar line. Were they busy arguing about Oga's little stutter-step and near intrusion? Appraising the duel? Making fun of Rippon for not butchering Rippon-Hart when she'd had the chance? What mattered was they weren't taking the *Locust*'s arrival as a threat. Rippon arrogantly kept her back to Kanezaka's 'Mech, either confident in the Mountain Wolves' honor, or confident in her ability to survive a backstab.

Kanezaka deployed his rope ladder. It flapped like a tail as he slowed near Hannah's downed 'Mech. He maneuvered his *Locust*—moving with grace more like the *Mist Lynx* than the *Merlin* had—and crouched slightly, literally bumping Hannah with the hanging ladder. Hannah, battered, neurohelmet under one arm, stumbled like she was drunk and tangled herself up in the rungs. The *Locust* lifted gingerly, and once Kanezaka was satisfied the leftenant wasn't going to fall, it strode away while doing what it could to move smoothly, crouching weirdly as it went, its torso held steady rather than bobbing and jerking, keeping its precious cargo safe despite the flimsiness of the ladder.

Fox's sensors confirmed he was making a beeline for quadrant Alpha Two, just outside Rock 32's headquarters, where the *Bonneville* waited. Like he'd been ordered, before the duel. She'd never *really* planned for him to fight. Fox would've loved to have him in a *Grand Dragon*, fighting sim-pod to sim-pod with these assholes. But that wasn't what the *Locust* was for.

No matter what happens, I'm not letting the future Duchess of Vendrell die out here, on my watch. I'm not losing Bran's granddaughter.

Fox allowed herself a relieved sigh as the *Locust*'s blue sensor blip slid farther and farther off to the edges of her RCA Instatrac's effective range. Before she lost visual completely, she zoomed enough to see Hannah clambering up the ladder to the *Locust*'s cockpit.

Good luck fitting in there, kiddo, sorry about the cramped quarters. Fox smiled softly. *Kanezaka can barely cram himself and his ego into that damned thing, and he brought his stupid katana, like he and Oga always do. I doubt there's much room left for a passenger.*

The *Mist Lynx* had continued strolling away rather than watching the *Locust* leave with its prey, making a beeline for its own DropShip. The moment the light 'Mech passed the waiting war titans of Trinary Assault, one of the angular, predatory OmniMechs took a single step forward. A *Warhawk*, according to Fox's computer. This had to be Furey.

I guess it's our turn. Fox nodded to herself, adjusting her grip on her *Archer*'s controls.

"Major Fox," said the Star Captain's voice. His 'Mech was a boxy, ugly thing, just a weapon with legs. It had gun-arms like a *Merlin* or a *Warhammer*, but wickedly lethal and double-barreled, each arm a pair of PPCs. Terrible, powerful Clan weapons, specifically singled out in warnings from even the hurried, chaotic report Major Fox has received. Almost an afterthought, a missile launcher sat atop its squared-off torso. Its legs canted backward like a bird's or a *Locust*'s. The Clan 'Mechs were brutally crafted, ungainly things. They were meant to evoke predators, not people.

Fox stretched her fingers and resettled them back on her controls.

"Perhaps you need a moment to straighten your formation. Are you ready to begin? *Aff* or *neg*?" Furey asked.

Aff or neg. *Affirmative or negative? Huh.* Fox made a face inside her neurohelmet. This bastard was so damned cocky he wasn't even calling out Oga's aborted little rescue charge; he was just chalking it up to a mistake at the controls from a clumsy pilot. Hannah's performance really hadn't impressed them.

"*Aff*," Fox broadcast, "We're rea—"

Furey's gun-arms flared, and twin beams of supercharged particles lanced out from each barrel and crossed the empty field, spearing perfectly dead center into the heart of Dunbar's *Merlin* just in front of Fox. The Lyran vet's ammo went off, his belly full of missiles and machine-gun rounds fireballing the 'Mech from the inside out. Even though she was standing right behind Dunbar, she didn't see an ejection plume. She only saw the explosion, saw the blue light on her sensors flash and then suddenly then blink out. She only saw him die, and his cored-out *Merlin* fell into her path.

Holy hell!

"Wolves, charge!" she snarled.

Damn it. Fox throttled up and swerved wide around Dunbar's remains, moving forward to get her missiles in range. Furey's heat spiked from that demonstration of firepower, but that was cold consolation for losing Dunbar and his *Merlin*. Fox rechecked her sensors and her frown deepened. That had been a long, *long* shot, and right at the most heavily armored part of the 'Mech. *The bastard made that look easy!*

Her sensor board lit up as battle was joined—every Clanner firing first, either faster on the draw, firing longer-ranged weapons, or both—as the Mountain Wolves surged forward.

"Hold the line," she said over team-band comms. "Scuff 'em up. Take a few hits. Make it—"

The other *Warhawk* fired. With a supersonic crack, a Gauss rifle slug cut the head right off of Lincoln's *Merlin*, to Fox's left. She got the briefest of updates from her lancemate's mildly lagging damage readout, saw the 'Mech go from wholly unharmed to headless in the blink of a few pixels, and a sad little noise caught in her throat.

At least he never felt a thing. Hell, he probably never even saw it coming. I sure didn't.

PPC beams—Mountain Wolf's looking diminished in comparison, weaker, unfocused, ragged around the edges instead of killer-precise—began to crisscross the field in earnest.

Make it look good, she had wanted to say.

Play their game. Now two Wolves were already dead.

Put on a good show. More damage readouts on her company-command sensors lit up, green to yellow to red, penetrated savagely in the blink of an eye.

What was I thinking? How do we make this even look like a fight*?!*

Standing opposite the looming *Executioner* and broad *Dire Wolf*, Ishihara and Stringer were both still alive, somehow, while both of their *Merlin*s had been raked with fire. "Taco" Ishihara punched out after the savage volley. Stringer wobbled and almost fell, but stubbornly stayed on her feet with both her *Merlin*'s arms missing, blasting away with her PPC. That PPC paled in comparison to the cruelly powerful ones mounted in the *Warhawk* and *Dire Wolf*, perhaps, but it was still the heaviest weapon a *Merlin* carried...

Wait.

Stringer had customized her ride, bullying and cajoling her techs during their long journey across the Sphere. She had opted for additional heat sinks in lieu of her machine gun or her five-tube LRM launcher and their associated ammunition bins. And Stringer was still upright, still fighting.

Ammo!

"Dump ammo," Fox ordered. The *Merlin*'s machine guns weren't going to make the difference here, their LRM-5s weren't going to be what scored any kills. All the Mountain Wolves were doing was sitting on bombs. "All Mountain Wolves, ammo drop! Now!"

A waterfall of bullets and missiles rained down from the rear of each *Merlin*. Not Fox's own *Archer*, though. She had other plans for her missiles.

Affirmative lights flashed across her console, then another storm of PPC bolts flashed everywhere else in the whole damned world. Star Captain Furey had found himself another target. A single arm had fired again. Brownpants' *Shadow Hawk* lit up emergency lights on Fox's display. The only other non-*Merlin* in the company was running hot enough to show Brownpants had been firing plenty, and a heat spike from an engine hit meant he'd clearly already drawn some fire back.

"Well, shit," the old ranch hand drawled as his left arm sloughed off, streaming sparks. His damage readout updated to show Fox that his PPC had been destroyed along with the rest of that left shoulder.

That was all his SHD-2K carried: a PPC and his own LRM-5. He'd followed her order and dumped ammo, *then* he'd lost his only other weapon. He was truly helpless.

"Boss," he began, apologetically, "Boss, ain't much I can—"

"Shut up," Fox cut him off. "Get going, Brownie."

His *Shadow Hawk*'s cockpit burst open, and her unit's senior noncommissioned officer flew out, launched like a rocket in his ejection chair. Before the blown-open canopy could even finish falling to the ground, another brutal, pinpoint-accurate pair of PPC shots from Furey's *Warhawk* blasted out the heart of his 'Mech.

A twist of the knife just because Furey could. Just to show he didn't want to keep the 'Mech. Just to show he didn't care if she and her Wolves lived or died.

Methodically, one by one, he was picking a target and tearing it apart. So, it seemed, were the rest of the Sixth Jaguar Dragoons. And they were doing it effortlessly.

Fox glanced and saw Stringer, too, finally sailing away on an ejection plume. Wachowski's *Merlin* lost both legs to the looming *Executioner* in two volleys, a Gauss slug taking off one and twin, surgically precise lasers amputating the other. Another volley tore into the prone, helpless 'Mech after it fell, aimed high, and tore Wachowski's cockpit apart.

The Wolves' Andurien, Noodles, managed to get the nearby Gauss rifle-toting *Warhawk*'s attention with an accurate alpha strike that left the assault 'Mech limping and one leg trailing sparks, then was instantly punished for it as a gleaming silver round punched into his 'Mech's belly. A Singh—*forgive me, boys, I can't see which of you that was!*—went down under the savage fury of the massive *Dire Wolf*, next. Something went terribly wrong, and the *Merlin*'s cockpit blasted open by auto-ejectors only *after* the 'Mech fell prone. The still-filled ejection seat skipped like a stone across Rock 32, shattered corpse spiraling crazily away.

Please, she thought, to no one in particular. She knew no one in particular would answer. *I was wrong. We can't do this.*

Bile filled her throat. They weren't play-acting, this wasn't a game or, hell, even really a fight. It was butchery. Fox's console was lit up too brightly, too many yellow, orange, and red lights blinking. They needed her guns. They needed her *Archer*. There was no "commanding" her way out of a mess like this. She, in what felt like slow motion, had finally maneuvered into her own weapons' range.

"Let's go, you bastard." She aimed her targeting reticule and thumbed both firing studs. Thirty missiles arced through the air from her ARC-2K and battered against Furey's massive *Warhawk*.

I just have to do some damage. I just have to hurt them, hurt them enough there's no shame in it. I just have to stand up to them enough they decide these people get to live. Shoot, overheat, punch out. It's what Mom would do.

Fox's *Archer* never stopped running forward, heat be damned, and she reached out with fingers of large laser fire, slashing at Furey's too-thick armor as soon as she could. The *Warhawk* finally turned her way, head-on, as the heat spiked in Fox's cockpit.

That's right, bastard. Shoot at me, *not them!*

Fox fought heat-twisting myomers to stomp her feet into a stable firing stance and triggered an alpha strike. She filled the air between them with another volley of missiles and another pair of laser beams as stifling heat took her breath away and threatened the stability of her ammunition. Furey's *Warhawk* seemed undaunted, he merely lifted an arm slightly in response. Fox snarled and triggered override shutdowns to keep her *Archer* in the fight.

One more volley, then *I punch out while I overheat. I'm not ejecting until I do more than scuff up your paint, you weird son of a—*

"Oh." Hannah saw Major Fox's icon wink out on Shotaro's console. "Oh, no."

Moments earlier, she had bandaged herself up as awkwardly and clumsily as anyone had ever bandaged anything. Contorting and twisting and squeezing herself like someone trying to change clothes in a phone booth, she had, at least, dragged some stinging wipes across her cuts, then put a bandage or two on the worst of them.

Locusts were infamous for their tiny cockpits, and Shotaro Kanezaka *alone* didn't belong in one. Shotaro, with his silly damned katana lashed against the seat? Shotaro, with Hannah wedged in behind him, the hatch unable to even close around the both of them? She could barely breathe.

And then, as Major Fox's icon simply blinked away, she found she couldn't breathe at all.

The speakers in the cockpit crackled to life with distress calls, wails of pain, emergency retrieval beacons, and screams about losing the major. The comm lines, choking on desperation, rang out in the tiny, cramped space. The Mountain Wolves weren't just in trouble. They weren't just fighting hard. They weren't just losing. They had already lost.

And Major Fox was gone. And Brownpants was gone. And Hannah was out of the fight. No one was left leading them.

"Stop." Hannah's hands tightened like claws on Shotaro's broad shoulders.

The *Locust*'s claws matched her grasp and gouged the stone of Rock 32 as it slewed to a halt.

"Back or *Bonnie*?" Shotaro said, his 'Mech in a low-crouch, ready to run either direction.

Hannah reeled, dizzy as she tried to focus past her concussion, tried to literally focus past Shotaro's bulk, tried to make sense of the impossible, terrible madness of what the sensors were showing.

"Back or *Bonnie*, Leftenant?!" he asked again, louder, impatient to either flee or fall.

"Back," she said, and barely held on as the recon 'Mech spun and sprinted.

"At least we'll die with everyone else," Shotaro said, sounding genuinely relieved that he would go down next to the only family he had ever known.

"Maybe." Hannah bruised her ribs on his stupid katana while lunging past him and to reach for the backup comms gear meant for when neurohelmets failed. She held her breath to squeeze in far enough to reach the controls and ignored his complaints as she punched in a commcode. "But maybe not."

"*Bonneville*, this is Hannah." She wriggled enough to take a breath, then corrected herself. "I mean, this is Leftenant Rippon-Hart. Major Fox is—"

"KIA," Captain Munene finished for her, *confirmed* for her. The sensors aboard the *Bonneville* were designed to scour the empty darkness of the night sky, and Munene and Goodman were two of the best operators the Mountain Wolves had. Interference from Rock 32's magnetic anomalies weren't stopping them from doing everything they could to monitor the fight. Hannah had been about to optimistically say "out of contact," but Munene had taken that from her.

"You are in command of all remaining Mountain Wolf forces," Munene continued, her voice clipped, precise, certain. Neutral. Like always. "What are your orders?"

Hannah felt dizzy, and didn't know if it was from the head wound, the jostling in an impossibly cramped *Locust*, the head-spinning loss of Major Fox—*Allah, how so quickly? And in an* Archer*?!*—or the crushing responsibility she just had dumped on her by the most clinical, dispassionate, and standoffish woman she had ever known.

That's enough, girl. She heard her grandmother's voice, always harsh, always right.

"Enough," she said to herself, tasting blood. *You have trained for this, Hannah.* She had to say something. She had to *do* something. She had to command.

She thumbed the comm back to life.

"*Bonneville,* relay to Director Chang that we accept Refugee Group Alpha," she said, voice firm and level. "Board them immediately, an hour or less."

It was the right thing to do. The *Bonneville* could leave Rock 32 following the letter of a prior contract, cargo hold full of ore, carrying out the ongoing industrials needs of Mountain Wolf BattleMech...*or* it could fly away, saving lives much more directly. It could leave, laden with people who would otherwise be helpless before the claws of these savage Smoke Jaguars.

The old. The young. The ones in the infirmary. The ones who weren't essential Rock 32 facility personnel. The ones that, she hoped, the Smoke Jaguars wouldn't miss enough to come after.

"Roger that, Group Alpha, one hour," was all Munene said.

"And boost my comms," Hannah said, "broad-spectrum, so all remaining Mountain Wolves and Smoke Jaguars can pick me up. Do it."

A moment later, the *Locust*, Shotaro's neurohelmet, and Hannah's handheld all squawked with static backwash and bolstered signals.

Sometimes an officer has to say the hard thing, Major Fox had taught her.

Hannah stared down at the vanishingly few remaining blue sensor blips. She saw the ones marked for Oga and Burke moving, side by side, desperately charging straight at Star Captain Furey's wickedly lethal *Warhawk.*

Please let this work. Hannah took a deep breath and thumbed the transmission button. *If not, I've got nothing left to try.*

"We yield!" she shouted, trying to be loud without her voice breaking, to be urgent without sounding desperate. *That's what she'd called it, right?*

"This is Leftenant Rippon-Hart, ranking officer of the Mountain Wolves! Cease fire! We yield!" she shouted into the handpiece as she stared at Shotaro's sensors.

Allah, please! Hannah watched Burke and Oga's icons draw closer to the Star Captain's.

"We give! We yield!" she shouted again, an increasingly desperate plea for mercy from the merciless Clan who had glassed a city and broadcast the footage for the galaxy to see.

"We fought by your rules, you won! We lost! We..." She choked on her words.

Burke's icon flashed, then dimmed. Tomoko's moved closer to Furey, right on him. Then Tomoko Oga's icon flared and winked out. Hannah didn't fall to her knees, but only because there wasn't room to do so.

Allah, no!

Hannah's stomach roiled as she stared down at the dimming spot where Tomoko's *Merlin* had been, its icon overlapping with the *Warhawk*. Shotaro's *Locust*, somehow, throttled up even faster. He leaned into the controls, racing against time, refusing to acknowledge Tomoko's death while desperate to die with her.

Hannah couldn't stop staring at the place Tomoko's *Merlin* should have been lighting up the console. She wanted desperately to throw up. *Puke later. Save lives now.* She didn't have time. Hannah choked down a mouthful of sick as, finally, she got an answer.

"Enough!" the radio screamed back at her in Star Captain Furey's voice, bloodlust finally sated after a few last kills. Hannah knew, in her heart of hearts, she'd hear that voice in her nightmares...if she survived to ever sleep again. "They see they are beaten! Sixth Jaguar Dragoons, stand down!"

Hannah took in what remained as, finally, Furey was satisfied. One Mountain Wolf icon remained in the circle. Just one. The Jaguar had decided to stop his troops, but only just barely. To offer mercy, but only technically.

"We offer you *hegira*, Leftenant," the Star Captain said, almost sarcastically. "Those who are able may return to your vessel and depart."

Hannah's brow furrowed and she, for a split second, was distracted by this new Smoke Jaguar turn of phrase. She knew the *Hijra* from her grandmother's studies, but hadn't expected to hear it from...

Focus!

"The moon is yours, we...we will be ready to depart in...an hour?" She tried to gather herself. She *had* to gather herself. She had to gather, more literally, her people. "Star Captain, is that okay? Our staff will collect our fallen from the, from the Circle of Equals, and then we will be off-world as quickly as possible. Thank y—"

"*Neg*. From within this Circle, you will collect *nothing*. Your salvage is ours. Your dead are ours. Any Wolf or *Merlin* that cannot leave of its own volition is ours. All that remains in the Circle is in the Jaguar's maw. Pick up only whatever cowardly survivors were scattered by our fury. You have your one hour, Hannah, and not a breath longer."

His voice was as hard as the mineral deposits of Rock 32.

"Know this!" he proclaimed. "It is only rarely the Smoke Jaguars' custom to grant *hegira*. You Mountain Wolves were pathetic! But..."

Hannah stared down at the cold, dark display where Oga and Burke's *Merlins* had been, lifetimes ago.

"You answered our *batchall*," Furey continued, "you spoke with what dignity you could muster, and you fought with honor, if not ability. Take this rarest of gifts, the Jaguar's mercy."

He said "mercy" like an insult, like he was spitting out a mouthful of poison.

"Take it knowing that if ever you stand in my way again, I will kill you all."

They took it. Doc's people sent their fastest vehicles. The Mountain Wolves recovered who they could, from where they could, as quickly and desperately as possible.

They rescued one Singh, Daveed, piloting the last *Merlin* still able to limp out of the crater, but they found only the shattered corpse of his brother. Their Andurien hotshot, Noodles, whose *Merlin* was untouched save the ruined gyro that had forced an ejection, was fireman-carrying the unconscious, smoldering Brownpants. They found Stringer with a broken arm wrapped in hurried air bandages and curses. They picked up Burke, ejected, out cold, and bloody, almost a klick away. Just Burke. Tomoko's body stayed in the Circle with her *Merlin*, Major Fox, and the others.

They left. Hannah oversaw it all on autopilot.

Grieve later. Work now. Command. Say the hard things and get them out of here.

Hannah consoled herself. Alongside their injured, they also left with a belly full of Kuritan citizens, old and young, sick and injured, desperate and aimless. The *Bonnie*'s cargo hold turned into a refugee camp. They were doing the hard thing. The right thing.

With nowhere else to go, with Jaguars nipping at their heels, the *Bonneville* flew rimward. Galactic "south."

Toward Luthien, the heart of the Dragon.

Hannah couldn't think of anyplace better to go. They had to move desperately, simply, *away*. The Smoke Jaguars weren't stopping, and Hannah couldn't imagine anything that would change that. Luthien would have the most traffic coming and going, it would be their best shot of finding available portage on a JumpShip, it would be the safest place—if anywhere was—to deliver Rock 32's shattered survivors.

She didn't have time to grieve Tomoko, didn't have time to reel at the loss of Major Fox, didn't have time to dwell on the Mountain Wolves she was leaving behind. Hannah didn't have time to wonder how the hell someone named Rippon had fallen in with these Smoke Jaguars, much *less* time to wonder who or what the Smoke Jaguars were. She didn't have time to worry about the rest of the Inner Sphere, about her stern father, her beloved grandmother, her Grandpa Bran, CEO of Mountain Wolf, or to worry about his company.

The *Bonneville* and the Mountain Wolves were her whole galaxy.

She was in command now.

Ready or not.

EPILOGUE

ROCK 32 ADMINISTRATIVE HQ
BROCCHI'S CLUSTER
SMOKE JAGUAR OCCUPATION ZONE
12 JUNE 3050

The retreating, tail-tucked "Mountain Wolves" were a diminishing streak across the mad sky of Brocchi's Cluster.

"*Tchk.*" Star Captain Furey stood over the corpse of Rock 32's Director Chang. No Jaguar had touched him. They had found him dead, having gutted himself, the way so many Kuritans did.

Vanessa, a member of the merchant caste, fidgeted nearby.

"Find his assistant," Furey snarled at her. "Promote them. Maintain this facility's productivity after our technicians see to the necessary upgrades. Mine this pathetic rock hollow. But!"

He sighed, resenting any sort of restraint, especially on a day where he had already shown such remarkable softness.

"But follow the ilKhan's new instructions. Coddle them, as we are commanded. House these *isorla* together by caste. Pay them if they behave well, punish them if they do not. Cluster their bunks near the most dangerous chemicals and machinery, let their sleeping bodies be our armor against sabotage. We will not suffer rebels here. I will not have another Tarnby."

The Sixth Jaguar Dragoons had taken that world as expertly as predicted. They had been let down by their garrison Clusters, however, and the duplicity of Spheroid barbarians, in the months since. Tarnby rebels had overtaken the planet's spaceport and boarded the Smoke Jaguar DropShips stationed there. Aerospace fighters had been forced to destroy them from overhead to prevent their takeoff, burning a swath of destruction across a spaceport that should have been theirs, a world that should have known it was conquered. The loss of materiel was galling, and their ilKhan had issued new directives that were designed to prevent future rebellions. Furey would not be responsible for the *next* such failure.

He waved the merchant on her way, then strode down Rock 32's rough surface toward his waiting OmniMechs. Star Commander Monica Rippon fell into pace beside him. Ever so slightly, his mood improved. Just as, Furey knew, letting Rippon fight her pathetic, distant, freebirth cousin had improved *her* mood. The Sixth had been aching for combat, and Rock 32, of all places, had given them a little taste of blood.

"Status?" he said, raising an eyebrow at her. He was still somewhere between amused and surprised she had not slain her opposite in their duel.

"The Elemental sweep of the...'town'...is done," Monica replied, all business. "Point Commander Rita reports zero resistance. With their children gone and their old and worthless hauled off like trash, only the workers remain to be fed. A fine day for the Jaguar!"

"Salvage?" Furey stopped at the foot of his *Warhawk*. He pointedly ignored the cratered armor, refusing to acknowledge the damage he had taken. He thought only of his still-warm guns and the glory they had found.

"Collected, but...unimpressive," she frowned. "These *Merlin*s are..."

"Unremarkable, save for their novelty." He nodded. "We will report their *existence* to our commanders, but will combine that knowledge with our disappointment. Do what you will with yours. They are newly built, but that is all. Mountain Wolf BattleMechs..."

He snorted.

"Is not as innovative as it once was, nor as proud."

"Indeed, not," she agreed, sounding faintly disappointed. "Nor as dangerous."

"The battle unfolded the only way it could. We *are* the Wolf Slayers," he said with a slight smile. "Whether they are Trueborn Wolves or freebirth Mountain Wolves, our victory over such curs is inevitable."

"*Aff.*" She smiled and nodded. Their moods *had* improved. He thought they might couple later.

"And the other matter?" he asked. Now, he could not help but glance up at the state of his *Warhawk*. The cockpit smoldered from a direct PPC hit, but the well-armored canopy had held. Barely. The armor near the cockpit—*dangerously* near it—was battered, dented by the muzzle-fisted arm of a *Merlin* whose MechWarrior had resorted to physical combat.

If the spinning backfist—of all things!—had hit a meter higher, he would be no more, and his Dragoons would have drowned Rock 32 in blood. It had been a close thing. A close, close thing.

"The MechWarrior killed one technician and took the arm off another, the first two into the cockpit for recovery." Monica shook her head ruefully, amused rather than furious. "We then executed a third for refusing to follow. It took Point Commander Rita to claw it open and fetch our prize."

"Hah! Killed one, maimed another?" Furey raised an eyebrow, almost impressed.

"With a katana, of all things," Monica nodded.

"*Tchk.*" He made a face. "*Merlin*s must have wastefully spacious cockpits."

"Inner Sphere decadence," she said with a wry smile. "Apparently they have room for *most* of three people at once."

He snorted. She *was* in a good mood.

"Well then, we have one more bondsman...and one we will not waste here on Rock 32," he said with certainty. IlKhan's orders be damned, not *all* the civilians would serve as laborers in perpetuity.

"She is, according to Mountain Wolf files, a qualified technician," Monica offered.

"She wanted to win more than to obey, follow the rules, or even live." He nodded, satisfied. "Then, in defeat, she desired blood more than rescue."

The Jaguar allowed himself a smile.

"Perhaps this Tomoko will make a bondsman worthy of our proud Clan."

UNIT DIGEST: SHARPE REDEMPTION

LORCAN NAGLE

Name: Special Operations Company, First Battalion, Fifth Sian Dragoons
Nickname: Sharpe Redemption
Affiliation: Capellan Confederation
CO: *Shàng-wèi* Cian Scattergood
Average Experience: Regular/Fanatical
Force Composition: 1 Medium BattleMech Company
Unit Abilities: All units must have a Walking MP of 5+ or a Jumping MP of 4+. All units gain the Terrain Master SPA (see p. 81, *Campaign Operations* or pp. 100–101, *Alpha Strike: Commander's Edition*); the player may choose the terrain type after the game table is set up, but before deployment.
Parade Scheme: The company uses the parade colors of the Fifth Sian Dragoons: red torsos with forest-green limbs and alternating yellow accents. The company's insignia is the regimental patch of the Sharpe Rifles, which each 'Mech wears on the left side of the chest.

UNIT HISTORY

The Scattergood MechWarrior family of Gan Singh had a lengthy history of military service to the Capellan Confederation. While the family didn't formally own a BattleMech and pass it from parent to child until after the chaos of the First Succession War, members of the lineage have served in the Capellan Confederation Armed Forces going back to the Age of War.

However, during the Fourth Succession War, Commander Albert Scattergood was captured by the Armed Forces of the Federated Suns during the invasion of Algol. A condition of his ransom was that he would retire as a MechWarrior, send his children to a Federated Suns military academy, and they would serve in the newly formed Federated Commonwealth RCTs. A second generation of the family had begun FedCom service when the Sarna March disintegrated. And while they could retain ties to their ancestral home, as the world was part of the Styk Commonality, when the Capellans were invited back to take control in the face of Blakist aggression, the family had to sever all contact with their off-world relatives to maintain a position in *Xin Sheng*'s new world order.

All this would change again with the end of the Jihad. Captain Mina Scattergood of the Sixth Crucis Lancers repatriated to the Republic with her wife, her children, and her *Vindicator*. Gan Singh was captured by the Republic Armed Forces during the fighting with the Capellans in the nation's early years, and Mina took the opportunity to reconnect with her wider family. She requested and received an exemption from the Military Materiel Redemption Program, and her son Erik would serve in the RAF. Obsessed with Capellan culture and their military history from a young age, Erik's grandson Cian, however, discovered a distant ancestor was one of the Sharpe Rifles' last commanders in the Second Succession War and fixated on that regiment's history. He

signed up for military service with the CCAF soon after Gan Singh's pacification in 3134, graduated from the Capella War College in 3138, and was assigned to the Fifth Sian Dragoons, where he took part in the invasion of Tikonov in late 3144. He gained a reputation for zeal and aggression in combat, volunteering for many of the most dangerous missions the regiment faced.

The Fifth Dragoons specialize in siege warfare, and during refit and reorganization in advance of their deployment to the former Republic in 3145, one company was reassigned to Special Operations, designed to take advantage of any breach in enemy lines the rest of the regiment could create, to move fast and strike with maximum aggression. Naturally, newly promoted *Shàng-wèi* Scattergood took the chance to command the company. Scattergood's well-known interest in the Sharpe Rifles and his zealous desire to prove his value to the Confederation have given rise to their nickname of Sharpe Redemption. The lack of action during their landing on Keid and more recent damage to the regiment by sabotage have frustrated the unit, which is eager to prove their mettle in combat.

While the Dragoons wait for the Fortress Wall to fail or be breached, they have engaged in training exercises and war games. As an aggressor unit in these exercises, the company has excelled at their stated purpose so far. Most notably, during a simulation where Third Battalion defended a fortified structure against First and Second, Scattergood's unit left the main body as they moved to invest the fortification and engage Third Battalion's pickets in a rolling battle. This allowed a team of combat engineers to slip past the Third's defenders and breach the fortification's walls. Conversely, when First Battalion took their turn as the defender, Scattergood's company accepted the roving picket role supported by two hovertank lances. They were able to blunt probing attacks by Second and Third Battalion's battle lances, who were unable to easily contend with the Redemption's faster units and aggressive fighting style. These victories have bolstered the company's morale.

While he was able to choose most of his unit, Scattergood was not given total freedom on this front. *Shào-wèi* Christine Feng, the commander of his fire lance and executive officer of the company, is in fact a Maskirovka agent assigned to continually assess the *shàng-wèi*'s loyalty to the Confederation. The Strategios recognize the propaganda coup of an enemy MechWarrior family's scion fighting on the front lines, but they have been especially wary of defectors since the Justin Xiang Allard debacle during the Fourth Succession War. As such, Feng has been tasked with keeping a very close eye on the unit overall and Scattergood in particular. She is no political appointee, however. She graduated from the Sian Center for Martial Disciplines in the top ten percent of her class and is an accomplished MechWarrior. She was recruited by the Maskirovka while at the Center, and cut her teeth observing her classmates for any indiscretions. Since being assigned to the Sian Dragoons, she has been watching more for politically incorrect thought rather than personal failings.

By comparison Aaron Medvedev, commander of the recon lance, was a constant thorn in his last company commander's side. There is no question of his loyalty, but he rankled at the limited sort of recon missions one can undertake while attacking a fixed position, which led to many clashes with his superiors during war games and training exercises. He joined the regiment after the assault on Tikonov, and was highly critical of how recon elements of the Dragoons operated in that battle—he found them to be overly cautious and gun shy—but his last company commander was one of the senior recon lance commanders prior to their promotion to company command. As a result, transferring him to Scattergood's new company was seen as a win-win. Medvedev gets to engage in his more aggressive style of warfare, and his old commander has a more agreeable subordinate.

COMPOSITION

At present, the unit is a single BattleMech company with no permanently attached support elements. *Shàng-wèi* Scattergood's command lance is the literal tip of the unit's spear, composed entirely of fast-moving units armed with physical weapons. Scattergood commands the unit from the cockpit of a TSG-9DDC *Ti Ts'ang*, with a pennant showing the Sharpe Rifles' regimental insignia flying from the 'Mech's lance. The company's fire lance comprises medium 'Mechs with stealth armor and at least some LRM capacity such as *Shào-wèi* Feng's HUR-WO-R4N *Huron Warrior*, while their recon lance consists of typical Capellan scout 'Mechs centered around *Shào-wèi* Medvedev's *Raven II*.

Shàng-wèi Scattergood has recognized the utility of integral support following their initial war game on Keid and has been pushing for closer relations between his company and the fast strike elements of the Fifty-Fifth Grand Base Lancers, the armor regiment attached to the Dragoons. He was particularly impressed when he saw a platoon of Fa Shih battle armor deploy from a lance of Saladin hovertanks at high speed. This has not led to an interest in switching to augmented lances, however: the company is assigned to the *Union*-class DropShip *Rhyme of the Heavens*, and they have been training closely with the crew on rapid deployments and orbital drops, so permanently adding units that can't fit into one ship or be dropped easily would reduce their operational flexibility.

TACTICS

Scattergood lives by a maxim of preparedness. He pays special attention to the terrain his unit will be operating in, poring over maps to ensure he and his troops are intimately familiar with the area. This is the key to his aggressive, maneuver-based style of combat. In exercises, he has successfully surprised opponents both by ambush and by moving through rough terrain at speeds the enemy thought impossible. Broadly, the recon lance will locate and harass the opponent, the fire lance will pin them in place, and then the command lance will charge into the middle of them sowing confusion and chaos, allowing the company to select vulnerable targets and take them down piecemeal.

As befits the title of "Special Operations," the unit is using more varied modes of deployment and fighting within the Fifth's overall specialization. As noted above, they have drilled in orbital drops recently, and the recon lance has been training in long-term observation of targets to call in artillery fire. *Shàng-wèi* Scattergood intends for the company to be more than just shock troops by the time they hit Terra.

LAND OF THE FREE

ERIC SALZMAN

> How was it possible for Malthus Gambling Unlimited to avoid paying taxes for decades? Simple. They set up their casinos in the free zones. "No laws" covers tax codes, too.
>
> —Agent Zach Simonson,
> Lyran Organized Crime Unit (OCU), 3152

It is held as an article of faith on many Lyran worlds that their planetary crime rates are held artificially low by the presence of "free zones." In these regions, no laws apply, and criminals can attack anyone stupid enough to venture in without consequence. The OCU has gone on the record calling for these zones to be closed and for law and order to be restored, but local politicians and lobbying groups overrule us every time.

Our analysts' reports (not to mention basic logic) prove the zones don't work as advertised: drawing all the street thieves, looters, and homicidal maniacs to an apocalyptic free-fire zone, allowing the rest of the planet to live in peace. In my experience, street gangs are too paranoid to relocate to a "commit crime here" area—an obvious trap. Likewise, such criminals need victims—things to steal, people to shake down, and so on. Once a zone is designated "free," everybody not having a death wish (outside of a few heavily armed vigilantes) will steer well clear.

So what's the real deal with the zones?

WHERE'D THEY COME FROM?

It goes back to 2908, when Archon Eric Steiner amended the Military Disaster Act to expand conscription and extended mandatory military terms of service. People rioted, and lots of businesses suffered from the resulting labor shortages, but the fact that the Draconis Combine continued to nibble away at under-defended Tamar Pact worlds got the nobility to back Eric's reforms.

Training tankers, gunners, and grunts to be more than cannon fodder took time, and the Armored Corps, Infantry Corps, and Artillery Corps were already down to 70 percent strength, on average. They needed trained personnel immediately to keep from losing even more worlds. So, where was the Lyran Commonwealth Armed Forces to get a bunch of people who knew their way around firearms and field discipline? The police. Civilian police forces from dozens of worlds were stripped to the bone to furnish the first wave of recruits under the expanded Military Disaster Act.

The consequences were obvious and immediate: Skeleton-crew police departments couldn't keep up with an opportunistic surge in street crime, especially on worlds where anti-conscription rioting was consuming their attention. Donegal was the first planetary government to propose concentrating criminals in a controllable area in 2910, designating a decrepit industrial slum on the outskirts of Marsdenville as a "free zone." Thanks to House Doons' evangelizing of the concept, dozens of other worlds followed Donegal's lead.

Of course, the crime waves subsided as the five-year terms of service ended and the dragooned cops returned to their homeworlds. However, as far as the public and the politicos were concerned, it was their "free zone" concept that had gotten the job done. Meanwhile, outside Marsdenville, House Doons' massive new Nashan Diversified complex was under construction in the free zone, without any regulatory oversight or permits. A few individuals of the criminal persuasion attempted to extort the construction crews and set up a protection racket. They simply disappeared, courtesy of Nashan's "Black Guards."

CORPORATE HAVENS AND VICE DENS

Corporate districts within the zones played host to a variety of industries, attracted by the significantly lower operating costs. Some unfortunate incidents with heavy pollution (acid rain, salt storms, contaminated aquifers, toxic smog, permanent underground fires, etc.) damaging nearby settlements created enough public outcry that industrially oriented free zones were relegated to barren areas, far from population centers.

Galatea, for example, designated an area on its scorching-hot equator as a free zone, far from the major settlements at the poles, and was rewarded when anonymous investors built a spaceport and recreational facilities under a climate dome. On Konstance (prior to the Combine's invasion), as surging greenhouse-effect temperatures forced the populace to withdraw to the cooler poles, the government designated the uninhabitable Juranias and Tiburia continents as free zones to entice development.

The lure of "walking on the wild side" attracted many Lyran citizens to venture to the free zones. Rather than the smog-ridden industrial sites, however, they frequented upwind districts where glitzy casinos towered above fortified perimeter walls, and all manner of illicit substances and morally questionable pleasures were on offer. The lack of law enforcement meant pleasure palaces had to invest in powerful private   security forces, and most visitors came wearing a mix of nightclub chic and advanced tactical gear, setting fashion trends on some worlds.

Some criminal syndicates, Internal Security Force cells, and SAFE-backed "Liberation Units" began to operate under the misunderstanding that the free zones would be safe havens for exporting illegal substances, engaging in human trafficking, and staging insurrectionist campaigns. They failed to understand Lyran Intelligence Corps monitoring was extensive, and the laws prohibiting extrajudicial executions by Lohengrin teams were likewise suspended. If any free-zone activity appeared to pose an imminent threat to the Lyran people, its perpetrators were brutally eradicated as object warnings.

Likewise, smuggling was kept under control via aggressive customs patrols, intercepting inbound and outbound DropShips for thorough inspections. Though operating costs were kept low in the zones, parent corporations were frequently audited to ensure they paid appropriate taxes on free-zone activity. Only Malthus Gambling Unlimited   evaded such scrutiny by   establishing the entirety of their operations within free zones. They even used their control of Dustball's government to declare the entire planet an official free zone.

FEDERATED COMMONWEALTH

Following the formation of the Federated Commonwealth alliance, groups like the Citizens for Davion Purity spread lurid stories about the free zones, claiming they were used for illegal human experimentation and slave labor, and were breeding grounds for drug addiction and the moral degradation of the Lyran populace. They warned that every world in the Federated Suns would be forced to host free zones as part of the FedCom alliance, conveniently ignoring the fact the Federated Suns charter already granted all member worlds significant autonomy and prohibited central government interference in planetary affairs. In fact, Lyrans pointed out that Outback worlds like Sabanillas were already planet-wide "free zones" in all but name. The furor over House Davion "selling us out to Lyran criminals" even led to sporadic anti-alliance riots throughout the Federated Suns—most notably on Mararn and Errai (where the Lyran Casimir Family was trying to establish a foothold).

THE CLANS

Whereas the Federated Commonwealth had taken a "hands off" approach to the free zones, the Clans saw them as prime examples of the Great Houses' moral degradation. Following their first waves of conquest, Clan Jade Falcon was alerted to the presence of bandit caste enclaves in its new holdings. Whereas most bandit encampments in the Homeworlds were small and transient, many of the conquered free zones were as large as Katyusha City, the Clans' capital on Strana Mechty. Star Admiral Adrian Malthus advocated using them for WarShip target practice, since bandits in the Homeworlds were rarely so obliging as to concentrate themselves in such numbers and operate so brazenly. Moreover, such an annihilation would eliminate the "*dezgra* scum" of the Malthus Syndicate, whose very existence was a stain on the honor of the Malthus Bloodhouse.

Two factors precluded Adrian's plan to turn every free zone in their territory into a smoking stain: (1) the Smoke Jaguars' eradication of the densely populated city of Edo on Turtle Bay and other Clans' subsequent decision to bid away naval assets and (2) the massive debts the Falcons had incurred in contracting the Free Guilds for logistical support. Each Clan can only have a certain amount of kerenskies in circulation, based on their enclaves' economic output. Until their occupation zone holdings became productive parts of the Clan economy, the Falcons could not legally produce the necessary kerenskies to pay their debts. Instead, saKhan Timur Malthus proposed the idea of transferring the bandit caste populace of the free zones to the guilds as a fresh labor pool. Rather than conducting mass evacuations of the zones, the Falcons simply designated them Free Guild enclaves, placing the citizenry there under guild rule. Timur mandated the guilds should work Malthus Syndicate members to death, but his Bloodhouse's disgrace at Twycross shortly thereafter meant the Jade Falcons failed to enforce this edict.

The Clans' disregard for the Free Guilds was coupled with a lack of oversight, allowing flexible guildmasters to turn their zones into active smuggling and espionage hubs, regularly frequented by criminal cartels, underground resistance cells, and intelligence agents.

THE HINTERLANDS

Free zones in former Jade Falcon territories largely continue to operate as Free Guild enclaves. Most have significant industrial capacity, sprawling ports, and large populations. Having relied on Clan protection, many were left defenseless. Raiders have hit several, inflicting grievous harm. Others have managed to arm themselves, some working in tandem with the post-Clan planetary government, others declaring open rebellion against any outside authority seeking to assert control. Those free zones controlled by Free Guilds associated with the Malthus Confederation are heavily armed, bustling centers of trade, thriving in the surrounding chaos.

THE PROMISE

BRIAN F. KENNY

LAKELAND
KENDALL
FORMER FREE WORLDS LEAGUE
22 MARCH 3095

Marcus didn't want to get out of the cab. More than anything, he wanted to leave this place, this planet. The neat rows of dwellings had a comfortable domesticity to them, the smell of flowers and freshly cut grass contrasting with the lingering tang of 'Mech coolant and sweat that came off his olive drab jumpsuit. He didn't belong here. The fatigues with the shoulder patch of the Third Marik Protectors seemed out of place, but he needed help, and this was the only place he might get it.

With a deep breath, he stepped out and started toward a house across the street. The front door opened as he started up the drive, and a teenage girl almost as tall as him bounced out, followed by an older man.

"Hi, Marcus!" she called out with a smile.

"Hey, Sarah, where you off to?"

"Soccer practice! We're trying for the championship this year."

"Nice! Hey, Pierce."

"Hi, Marcus." Sarah's father nodded a greeting as he stepped around the ground car and waved at the open door. "Emma's in the kitchen if you want to head on in."

"Thanks. Kick ass, kiddo." Marcus grinned as he walked past, earning him an identical look from the young girl.

Stepping into the house, he gently closed the door behind him and went to the kitchen at the back, where a small woman with shoulder-length, dirty-blond hair stood beside a sink full of suds and dishes. She glanced up with a look of mock annoyance as he entered. "If you're looking to beg some dinner, you're too late."

"Dodged a bullet there, then," Emma's former commander shot back, earning him a flick of soapy bubbles in the face.

"When did Sarah get so big? What are you feeding her?" he asked in amazement.

"She's fifteen now. If you were around more often, you might've noticed she's growing up."

Marcus shrugged. "I get bounced around a lot. Lot of people need the Protectors right now."

"Always do," Emma replied softly, wiping at a plate. "So what brings you here, if it's not my cooking?"

"I found the kid."

The plate stopped in mid-air, the four words changing the whole conversation. Emma slowly lowered the plate onto the drying rack, not looking at Marcus.

"Where?"

"Reykavis, in the Hegemony. He was sold at a slave auction there a couple of months ago."

"How did you find him?"

"I've been working with a group that helps locate people taken in pirate raids. They trace them and try to get them back. Sometimes they buy them, sometimes they mount ops to get them out. They have a network in the Hegemony that monitors the slave trade."

Slowly, Emma continued washing the dishes, head down, her whole body tensed like a spring as she took it all in, Marcus said nothing, but simply waited.

"You're going after him." It wasn't a question.

"Officially, no. *Un*officially..."

"Alone?"

"The Nenge brothers are tagging along, and the old man put me in touch with an independent ship captain. *Union*-class DropShip, couple of aerojocks too, still got a berth left, though."

"You asked Neena?"

"She's on assignment near the Magistracy, can't make it back in time."

"What about Tito?"

"Tito's dead."

Emma's head snapped up, and she looked at him in shock; he held her gaze for a moment before looking at the floor.

"He came in off a patrol a couple of weeks ago, signed off his paperwork, went back to his quarters, took out his service pistol, and..." Marcus shrugged, the gesture heavy with grief. Emma turned back to the sink and squeezed her eyes shut against the tears that threatened to run loose.

She sniffed. "I guess he never really got over Alexander's death."

"Did any of us?"

The two stood there in silence for a long time before Marcus slowly straightened.

"I'm not asking you to come," he said softly. "You've a good life here, Em, and you've more than earned the happiness you've got. If you decide to come, the *Queen* is waiting in the hangar at the base for you. If you don't, I'm okay with that, too. I'll let you know how it turns out. We'll be boosting in three days."

With that, he turned and left.

It was late. Pierce was working the night shift at the hospital, and Emma was sitting on the couch with a glass of wine. On the floor next to her was a metal ammunition box filled with photos, trinkets, and memories. A noise made her look up, and she saw her daughter come down the stairs and duck into the kitchen. She heard the refrigerator door open and close before she emerged with a glass of milk in her hand.

"You're up late," she said.

"Can't sleep, too wired from practice," the teenager muttered, slumping next to her mother. "What's all this? Is that you?" she asked, looking at the photograph in Emma's hand, a group shot of men and women in habitual MechWarrior cooling vest and shorts.

"Yeah, that's me," Emma murmured with a smile as she pointed at each of the faces in the photo. "There's Marcus, Tito, Alexander, Neena..."

"Who's that?" Her daughter pointed at a skinny, red-haired young man who couldn't have been older than nineteen.

Emma considered telling a lie, but found she didn't want to.

"That's who we used to call the Kid."

SEVEN YEARS EARLIER

Emma watched the fresh-faced young man as Marcus gave him the same talk he gave to all new recruits. She couldn't hear what he was saying over the sounds of the techs working on Alexander's *Rifleman*, but she didn't need to: she'd heard it herself a long time ago.

MechWarrior Cadet Matteo Farinelli was tall and skinny; that was the only way to describe him. You couldn't even be polite and call him rangy: he was skinny, and had the beaming pride only teenagers who think they are going to be heroes could possibly have. Marcus finished up, and the kid saluted so crisply Emma half expected to hear the air snap before he gave an equally crisp about-face and headed out of the 'Mech hangar.

Marcus turned to her and frowned at her expression. "Don't start on me, Emma. Everyone gets a greenie now and then. This is our turn."

She snorted in disgust. "That one's so green I don't know where his fatigues finish and he begins." "What choice do we have? The League's gone, and with it our pipeline for replacements. We either take any volunteers we can get, or we go out short a body next time. Which do you prefer?"

"We go out with that kid, and a body's what we'll get." She sighed, holding her head in her hands.

Unfortunately, Marcus was right.

"Any idea what you're going to do with him?" she finally asked, looking up.

"We got a couple replacement chassis as well. I'm thinking we move Tito over to that new *Thunderbolt* and give the kid his *Apollo.* That way we can keep him at the back on fire support until we get a better idea of what he can handle."

"That could work. Tito's been wanting to move up to something bigger anyway."

THE PRESENT

"And it did work," Emma said to her daughter as they sat on the couch. "For five years he was our mascot, always smiling and optimistic, even when everything else was going to hell. We taught him everything we could and made him into a MechWarrior, a Marik Protector, and he was so proud of what he was doing you couldn't help but feel the same."

"What happened to him?" Sarah asked in a small voice.

TWO YEARS EARLIER

Sweat ran down Emma's neck as she pushed *Fashion Queen* to its maximum speed. It wasn't the sweat she normally built up in combat, but the clammy stink of fear as she and the other ten 'Mechs of the abbreviated company raced back to the refinery across the uneven ground.

The pirates had suckered the Marik Protectors company by dressing up a half-dozen AgroMechs to look like actual BattleMechs and sending them off to attack a nearby town. The ruse had fooled the panicked locals and forced the Protectors to respond, leaving just a pair of 'Mechs and a company of local militia armor to defend the petrochemical refinery that was the pirates' actual target. Now those tanks and infantry, along with the kid's *Apollo* and Alexander's *Rifleman*, were trying to hold off twice their numbers in 'Mechs, tanks, and infantry while Emma, Marcus, and the rest were racing to get back after demolishing the fake attackers.

"There's too many of them!" the kid yelled over the radio in panic.

"Hang in there, kid, we're coming," Marcus replied, trying to steady him. "Keep moving. Don't let them pin any of you down. Don't try to take them down, just stay alive, we're coming."

"Yes, sir, I...I'll try."

"What 'Mechs are we looking at?" Marcus asked. He was obviously trying to get the kid to focus and keep the panic at bay.

"I...I count, uh, eleven. I got a *Warhammer*, a *Lineholder*, and a *Panther* closing."

"Concentrate on the *Warhammer*. Give it two volleys and then fall back. If you can make it hesitate, the others will too."

"Yes, sir."

For long minutes, that was how it went, Marcus giving the kid instructions while Emma and the rest tried to eke a micron more speed out of their 'Mechs, but it wasn't enough.

"Alexander's down!" the kid cried out followed by "I'm Winchester," indicating the *Apollo*'s LRM racks had run dry.

"Just keep moving!" Emma called out in frustration.

"Don't give up," she heard Marcus call. "Keep moving. We're coming. We'll find you. I promise."

More explosions could be heard over the comm, along with the young MechWarrior's cries of pain before one final call.

"I'm going down! Ejecting."

THE PRESENT

"What happened to him?" Sarah asked.

"By the time we got there, there was no sign of him. Alexander was comatose from neurofeedback after both light Gauss rifles on his *Rifleman* had exploded. We found out from one of the survivors that the Kid ejected, but was picked up by the pirates and taken away with a bunch of civilians. For a long time, we thought he'd been killed. Turns out he was sold as a slave to some landholder in the Marian Hegemony."

"That's why Marcus was here today, wasn't it? He wants you to help get him back, doesn't he?"

"He didn't ask, he just told me what he was doing. He knows you're more important, and I promised you I wasn't going to leave again."

For a long moment Sarah said nothing, just stared at the photo in Emma's lap while resting her head against her mother's shoulder. Finally she spoke words that Emma never thought she would hear.

"You should go."

"*What?* Sarah, I..."

"They told us what happens in the Hegemony in school, the way they treat slaves. You can't leave him there, you can't leave any of them there."

"Sarah, I made a promise to you..."

Her daughter looked Emma hard in the eye.

"You made a promise to him, too."

REYKAVIS
MARIAN HEGEMONY
7 MAY 3095

Where the hell are they? Marcus cursed inwardly.

The insertion had gone like clockwork, the DropShip swooping in under the planetary radar and dropping the rescue team and his 'Mech lance off a couple of kilometers from the estate, or latifundium, as the Marians referred to it, that was the target.

Then it went sideways, as usual.

The pair of aerospace fighters they had brought along was tangled up with a squadron of conventional fighters no one had expected, but they had managed to spot a group of 'Mechs nearby before the dogfight started. Close enough to the estate that once the shooting started they were bound to see and hear the weapons fire and come running.

Marcus had split off with the 'Mech lance to try and intercept the newcomers, but the area was all low hills and trees that, combined with the predawn dark, limited them to sensors that were struggling with interference.

A distant *thump* picked up by his external mics told him the assault had started, which meant they had only about a minute to find their targets or this whole operation was going to turn into a bloodbath. Still, his sensors showed nothing but trees overlaid with rough static that shouldn't have been there. Was there something in the environment? Then his brain finally kicked in, and he bit back a curse and keyed the radio.

"Red Group, hostiles are running ECM! Stand by, I'm countering."

His *Marauder* had been an original MAD-4X prototype produced during the technological renaissance before the Clans' arrival, and its specifications had been ahead of its time. Mothballed in a storage warehouse for decades, it had been dug out during the Jihad, a time when any 'Mech was badly needed. Refitted to the more modern -9M2 configuration, it sported a Guardian ECM system Marcus had used to keep his lance hidden from Hegemony sensors, a system their quarry also had and was using in exactly the same way.

Time for that to change.

Fingers flew over the controls as Marcus flipped his ECM over to ECCM mode, blasting out a wave of electronic noise designed to cancel out the other system. Within seconds, the static cleared, and five blips flashed on radar moving parallel to the Marik lance and almost past them.

"Four o'clock, two hundred meters. Go! Go!"

Slamming his throttle forward, Marcus yanked the *Marauder* around and charged through a copse of thin trees and up over a small rise. Plunging down the back slope without even knowing if the others were with him, he found himself staring at a line of five Marian 'Mechs moving from his left to his right. Smack in the middle of the column strode the source of the ECM interference: a *Toyama*, a 'Mech equal to Marcus' in size. But it wasn't the shock of seeing a Word of Blake 'Mech in front of him that made him go cold.

To his right, second in line, walked a *Firestarter*. The 'Mech was a walking atrocity against infantry, and if it got to the estate, the assault team wouldn't have a prayer. Even as he thrust his *Marauder*'s arms forward and loosed both heavy PPCs at the *Toyama*, he knew the lighter 'Mech had to go at all costs.

"Red Three and Four. Stop that *Firestarter*, I don't care what it takes."

"Copy."

The two *Wraith*s piloted by the Nenge brothers blasted skyward on their jump jets as their target accelerated into the woods, along with a *Wolfhound* that had probably been around longer than Marcus. *Fashion Queen*, Emma's *Bandersnatch*, appeared to his right, her PPC and Ultra-series autocannon throwing thunder and lightning downrange at an *Ostroc*.

"Gonna be outnumbered here, Red Lead," she noted with a hint of irritation.

"Can't be helped, Two," he replied. "Let's dance!"

Years fell away as the two heavy 'Mechs moved together like the well-oiled machine they had been for so long. The close quarters played havoc with the *Toyama*'s LRM battery, but it had plenty of other guns to bring to bear. Marcus' heavy PPCs had issues up close as well, but he'd had years of practice getting the best out of them, and he had killed plenty of *Toyama*s before. *Fashion Queen* stayed close as the pair kept up a constant weaving among trees and between 'Mechs, snapping off shots at whatever targets presented themselves.

Flights of long-range missiles from a trailing *Trebuchet* fell among them, as dangerous to the other Marians as the two Protectors, while the heat in Marcus's cockpit crept up as his PPCs snapped out bolt after bolt. The 'Mech's Streak SRM-6s were firing as fast as the autoloader could cycle, each one blowing chunks off whatever target was unfortunate enough to end up under his sights. But the damage wasn't all one way. The *Marauder*'s armor-status monitor shifted from green to yellow to amber as lasers, missiles, and autocannon shells scored across its carapace, arms, and legs.

"Watch the *Ostroc*, Red Leader."

Emma's warning came as the flicker of motion on his right drew Marcus' attention. The 60-tonner was swinging wide, angling to get behind them. The 'Mech's barrel-chest was studded with missile ports he knew were one-shot rocket launchers that could put a horrific number of missiles into the air in a single volley.

Marcus twisted the *Marauder* back to the right, canting the big 'Mech so far over its gyro screamed in protest, but the whine failed to drown out the more important tone of a missile lock. Pulling the trigger, he ripple-fired both Streak SRM-6 packs at the *Ostroc* just as Emma swung the *Fashion Queen*'s left arm out and let loose both the arm-mounted medium lasers and a double burst from the *Bandersnatch*'s Ultra autocannon. One of the lasers missed high, but the other and the stream of high-explosive shells blasted the *Ostroc*'s left arm and torso, causing the 'Mech to twist left, a twist that turned into a full-on spin as the wave of SRMs slammed into its right side. The entire 'Mech staggered drunkenly all the way around before stumbling and falling flat on its face.

Something slammed into the *Marauder*'s left side, the force of the impact, combined with the heavy tilt, almost sent the 75-ton war machine over as a finger-sized chunk of metal spalled off the side of the cockpit. It skimmed across Marcus' forearm before driving through his cooling vest, the ballistic weave slowing it just enough that it lodged halfway into his left side rather than eviscerating him. His sense of balance let him turn the hard shove into an ugly but effective spin that stumbled the *Marauder* almost completely around and facing the triumphant-looking *Trebuchet*.

Son of a... Eat this!

His crosshairs locked gold, and Marcus pulled the triggers in a full alpha strike. Almost everything hit center mass and, like a scene from *Immortal Warrior*, the impacts picked up the *Trebuchet* and sent it sprawling back into the trees.

The *Marauder*'s cockpit was a sauna. Flashing indicators showed damaged heat sinks, and the shutdown alarm flickered, but what Marcus saw on his display sent a chill down his spine. Emma was hammering the *Toyama*, but the *Ostroc* was getting back to its feet, lining up for a killing shot at her back. Desperately he tried to turn, but his 'Mech was still too hot, too slow.

Two pillars of flame descended from the heavens and unleashed a torrent of fire that lashed into the *Ostroc*'s back. Whether by reflex or panic, the pilot cut loose all their rocket launchers, but the missiles flew wide as the 'Mech spasmed and fell in the limp way that spoke of a shattered gyro.

"What kept you two?" Marcus asked with a trace of sarcasm.

"Sorry, One. Our two friends took a little bit of time to finish off."

The two *Wraith*s had scoring from laser fire and scorch marks indicative of the *Firestarter*'s flamers, but both were obviously still good. Emma's *Bandersnatch* fell back toward the group with heat rippling off its torn armor in waves.

"Status of the *Toyama*?" Marcus asked her.

"Heading home. They've had enough. You okay?"

He shifted carefully in his command couch and felt the splinter in his side poke into him, but not deeply. A glance at the medical monitor that received data from the sensors on his arms and legs told him his heart rate, pulse, and oxygen levels were stable.

"Just another nick to add to the collection," he grunted.

"Let's get over to the target and see if they need a hand."

The sun had climbed over the horizon by the time the four 'Mechs were stomping across the plowed fields surrounding an elaborate Romanesque palātium house. Smoke was rising from a half-dozen outbuildings and a pair of burning vehicles. A large group of men, women, and children in rough, dirty smocks huddled around several long wooden huts while members of the infantry force moved among them.

Slowing to a halt as they rounded the front of the palātium, Marcus noticed a row of crude scaffolds along the gravel driveway as a man in combat armor approached the *Marauder*'s feet. Captain Mathi was the former Gurkha who had contacted Marcus and brought him into the operation.

"What's the situation, Captain?" he asked over the *Marauder*'s external speakers.

"Compound is secure and DropShip is four minutes out. We've got six dead, eleven wounded, but that's not counting the prisoners. The landowner here wasn't a kind master, and most of them have been badly abused. The man managed to lock himself in a panic room inside the main building before we could get to him, and it's too heavily armored for us to crack. You look like you ran into problems yourself."

"Nothing we couldn't handle. They won't be bothering us."

"Oh, god!"

Marcus turned to Emma. Her battered *Bandersnatch* was standing immobile before the scaffolds, and the shock and pain in her voice filled Marcus with dread as he looked down. The scaffolds were merely two I beams that had been hammered into the ground in an X configuration, and tied to each one was a human figure. None of them were moving, and all showed up as horribly cold under the 'Mech's thermal imaging. Several members of the rescue force were gently cutting the bodies down and carefully placing them in body bags.

"Punishment examples the master of the house liked to display," Mathi shouted up to him, but Marcus barely heard him, his attention drawn to the second figure they were cutting down.

The man's long limbs were reduced from their former skinny state to those of a stick figure. The face was a gaunt death mask Marcus desperately wanted to believe he didn't recognize, but the hair that hung lank and lifeless was still the same vibrant red he remembered.

"Captain, where's that panic room?" Marcus snarled as a burning rage filled him.

The infantry commander pointed and led him to the far end of the building and pointed up at the first floor. Marcus flipped his primary monitor over to thermal imaging and noticed a number of orange blobs clustered next to a darker square area, a thermal dead zone cooler than the rest of the building.

"Get everyone out of the building, *now*!"

Mathi turned and yelled into his commlink, waving frantically at the other members of the strike team, who scattered as if sensing the rage coming off the big 'Mech.

Somehow Marcus managed to keep control long enough for everyone to get clear as he centered his crosshairs over the dead zone and squeezed the trigger. The right-arm heavy PPC discharged and blasted chunks of ferrocrete away from the mansion's facade with a crack like thunder. A cloud of dust slowly parted to reveal a gaping hole backed by a sheet of dull gray 'Mech armor that was glowing faintly from the heat of the impact.

The left-arm PPC discharged. The cerulean beam lashed at the metal, which for a moment stubbornly held before caving in. More smoke came from within as the ready light blinked green on the right-arm weapon. Marcus pulled the trigger again and watched the artificial lightning shoot through the hole and into the room, incinerating everyone and everything inside. The fourth bolt was unnecessary, as was the fifth and the sixth.

Another PPC blast, as well as a long stream of high-explosive shells, slammed into the building from the left as Emma's *Bandersnatch* unleashed volley after volley into the structure, the two 'Mechs reducing the entire house to ruin in a minute.

Emma found him in the small storage compartment where the DropShip crew had stowed the bodies. He was sitting on a storage locker with his head in his hands before the neatly arranged row of black body bags, his coveralls half open despite the chill of the makeshift morgue. Carefully, she sat down beside him, making sure not to bump his wounds.

Marcus lifted his head and looked at her with all the *what if*s she knew were going through his head, written on his face. "I let him down, Em. I made him a promise, and I couldn't keep it."

Silence stretched between the two friends for a long minute before Emma found the words she wanted to share with him.

"Do you know why he was killed?"

Marcus frowned and shook his head, puzzled.

"The estate owner took an interest in one of the slaves, a thirteen-year-old girl. The other slaves decided to hide her from him and try to get her out. When the owner learned Matteo was one of the ones involved, he tortured him. They worked on him for three days, and he never gave them anything, even when they tied him to that scaffold and left him to die."

"How did...?"

"The survivors told me. We rescued fifty-two people from that place, including the girl Matteo gave his life for. You may not have been able to keep your promise to the Kid, but you were able to keep a different promise we both made, a promise he made, too. To stand on a line and protect people from tyrants and sadists and all the other evils in this universe, whatever the price. He believed in that promise, and he gave his life for it. That's the only promise that matters."

Emma rose and extended her hand to her friend and captain.

"Come on. There are some people who would like to say thank you."

CHAOS CAMPAIGN SCENARIO: PARTING SHOTS

MARC FOLLIN

"Well, there are a few more Falcons present than we expected, but that does not change the mission. Galaxy Commander Chistu has granted us safcon, and I intend to meet her on the field. I want payback, and I see the same fury in your eyes. I want all of you on your guard though, Chistu feels different, but the Falcons torched sibkos and crèches on Arc-Royal. If they fight with honor, then so will we, and we will prove that Wolves are better than Falcons any day of the week."

—GALAXY COMMANDER ANNIE WARD, BRONZE KESHIK, 3148

The months following the loss of Arc-Royal to the Jade Falcons and the relocation to Donegal were some of the lowest for the Exiled Wolves. Before the major defeat, they were already spread thin over nine Clusters, in many ways a paper tiger holding the line against the Falcons. The First Wolf Legion sold itself completely to buy time for the evacuation, and the losses in warriors, equipment, and infrastructure were heavy across the remainder of the *touman*.

The Exiles spent their time on Donegal not only expanding the capabilities of Assault Tech industries with what infrastructure they had managed to save from Arc-Royal, but also consolidating what remained of their *sibkos* and crèches. Anger and low morale permeated the entire Clan, even across caste boundaries. A daring raid on Timkovichi produced a boost in morale Khan Miriam Shaw decided to capitalize on. Giving her Clan the prospect of a counteroffensive to galvanize them, they rebuilt and planned an attack on a trio of Falcon-held worlds.

The offensive saw early successes on Upano and Incukalns, with the final target being Pobeda. The successes on the first two worlds caused Khan Malvina Hazen to redirect Galaxy Commander Stephanie Chistu to reinforce the area. Chistu and her First Falcon Striker Cluster arrived in-system shortly before Galaxy Commander Annie Ward entered with the Bronze Keshik. Wary of Falcon treachery, Ward nevertheless trusted Chistu's actions and her own instincts, and accepted Chistu's offer to conduct an honorable fight for the planet.

TOUCHPOINT: TWO BIRDS, ONE WOLF

This scenario can be played as a stand-alone game or incorporated into a longer campaign using the *Chaos Campaign* rules (available as a free download from https://store.catalystgamelabs.com/products/battletech-chaos-campaign-succession-wars).

For flexibility of play, this track contains rules for *Total Warfare* (*TW*), with *Alpha Strike: Commander's Edition* (*AS* or *AS:CE*) rules noted in parentheses, allowing the battle to be played with either rule set.

> *Galaxy Commander Annie Ward tucked her* Cygnus *behind a multi-story office building so she could focus on her subordinates' reports. The warriors of her command Star performed their duty and picked up the slack, increasing their efforts to retaliate against the Falcons and give her a moment of respite amid the battle.*
>
> *"Sender, your scouts have verified the newcomers from the DropShips, quiaff?"*
>
> *"Aff, Galaxy Commander. They appear to be the Fifth Battle Cluster. They show signs of damage and hastily applied armor patches, but they have cut off our route to the DropShips."*
>
> *Ward failed to silence the frustrated growl that escaped her throat. None of this had gone like it was supposed to go, and now they could not even escape to their DropShips. "I am sending new coordinates. Make an orderly withdrawal to the Black Valley at that location. We will concentrate and wait for an opportunity to break through to the DropShips."*
>
> *Ward started to return her focus to the battle and her own fight and the retreat ahead, but hesitated, then opened a channel to the DropShips. "Captain, send a message to one of the JumpShips. Give them as much as you can of the current situation, and tell them to jump back to Upano. Request reinforcements."*

SITUATION

POBEDA
JADE FALCON OCCUPATION ZONE
24 APRIL 3148

The Bronze Keshik and First Falcon Striker Cluster engaged in an honorable fight for Pobeda in the fields outside the spaceport where the Bronze Keshik made planetfall. Despite the Bronze Keshik's desire to get revenge on the Jade Falcons for Arc-Royal, the ferocity of the First Falcon Striker's attack inflicted heavy casualties. By the time Galaxy Commander Annie Ward could rein in her forces' bloodlust, she had few options but to retreat toward her waiting DropShips. However, additional Falcon forces returning from the assault on Coventry joined the fray, cutting off Ward's route to the spaceport. With few options left, she ordered a retreat to the nearby Black Valley and dispatched one of her JumpShips to request reinforcements.

GAME SETUP

Recommended Terrain: Light Urban, Grasslands

The mapsheets should be arranged so that half are light urban and half are grasslands. The edge of the light urban terrain mapsheets will be the Defender's home edge. The opposite edge, on the grasslands mapsheets, will be the Attacker's home edge. The Attacker must then select one of the short edges of the light urban mapsheets as the entrance point for the Fifth Battle Cluster.

Attacker

Recommended Forces: First Falcon Striker Cluster and Fifth Battle Cluster, Jade Falcon Delta Galaxy (Gyrfalcon Galaxy)

The Attacker consists of elements of the First Falcon Striker Cluster, with reinforcements from the Fifth Battle Cluster; 60 percent of the Falcon forces are part of the First Falcon Strikers, and the remaining 40 percent are drawn from the arriving Fifth Battle Cluster. Use the random assignment tables in *Tamar Rising* (pp. 122–124). The First Falcon Striker Cluster may shift the roll up or down by 1 after seeing the result, to represent the greater choice in equipment afforded to the warriors of the Command Cluster. Once the units for the Fifth Battle Cluster are determined, the owner must roll a number of 5-point damage clusters prior to the start of the game to represent existing damage. Roll 1 cluster for light units, 2 clusters for medium units, 3 clusters for heavy units, and 4 clusters for assault units. Reroll any to-hit rolls that result in damage to the head.

The Attacker deploys their forces from the Defender's home edge and from the edge selected for the Fifth Battle Cluster. The First Falcon Striker Cluster enters the battlefield from the Defender's home edge during the movement phase of Turn 2. The Fifth Battle Cluster will enter from their selected edge during the movement phase of Turn 3. Attacking units may only exit the map via their starting edge; exiting from any other edge counts as unit destruction.

Defender

Recommended Forces: Bronze Keshik, Clan Wolf (in-Exile) Omega Galaxy (Guardians of the Lair)

The Defender consists of elements of the Bronze Keshik composed of forces from Donegal; 60 percent of the units should be drawn from forces produced by Assault Tech Industries on Donegal: the *Jaguar*, *Jaguar 2*, *Adder*, *Sojourner*, *Ice Ferret*, and *Linebacker*. The remainder may be selected using the random assignment tables for the Lyran Commonwealth (pp. 117–118, 120, *Tamar Rising*); add a +2 to the roll to represent better access to technology.

The Defender enters from their home edge at the start of the track. Defending units may only exit the map via the Attacker's home edge; exiting from any other edge counts as unit destruction.

WARCHEST
Track Cost: 400

Optional Bonuses

+200 Shoddy Repair Job (Defender Only): Add an additional 5-point damage cluster to all the Attacker's units, including the First Falcon Striker Cluster. The Falcons entered the field from a major offensive on Coventry with little time to repair.

+200 Wide Maneuvers (Attacker Only): The Fifth Battle Cluster may arrive from the short edge of the grasslands map in addition to the light urban map. The Fifth swung deeper into the Bronze Keshik's retreat path before initiating their flanking maneuver.

OBJECTIVES

Hammer: Destroy or Cripple half of the opponent's force. **[300]**

Gauntlet (Defender Only): Exit at least half of the player's force through the Attacker's home edge. **[300]**

Honorable Warriors (Attacker Only): For every unit that follows Clan Honor rules at Honor Level 1 (pp. 273–275, *TW*) for the entirety of the track. **[60 per unit]**

SPECIAL RULES

Forced Withdrawal

All units adhere to the Forced Withdrawal rules (p. 258, *TW* or pp. 126–127, *AS:CE*).

Track End

The track ends after the end of any turn where at least one side has no units in play, or after the end of Turn 10.

AFTERMATH

Within hours of sending a message for reinforcements, the Wolf-in-Exile Cluster was overwhelmed by the combined forces of both Jade Falcon Clusters. The honorable conduct of the warriors in Stephanie Chistu's command was surprising to the Wolf warriors, as they did not fight with the Mongol tactics the Wolves had grown used to, but with the old Jade Falcons' tactics. Chistu's actions allowed Galaxy Commander Ward to look past her own wariness of the Falcons and accept the lifeline provided by her opponent. Chistu offered the Bronze Keshik *hegira* while making it abundantly clear she did not conduct herself or her command like Malvina Hazen.

A NIGHT TO FORGET
(A DEATH KANGAROOS STORY)

MICHAEL A. STACKPOLE

I

PEDRO'S GRANDE PIG AND WHIST
GALATEAN CITY
GALATEA
GALATEAN LEAGUE
2 FEBRUARY 3146

Scrambled eggs, if you listen to the experts, are a work of art. Eggs—on most worlds from birds or small mammals—are whipped to a froth, then poured into a blazing hot, lightly oiled stainless steel pan. They bubble up immediately with a rumble of distant thunder. Gently teased around the pan; chased, in fact, by a spatula, the curd solidifies into the color of sunshine. All light and fluffy, still glistening, they slide from the pan onto a plate, where an anointing of parsley—and, for the daring, a dusting of lemon zest—completes the heavenly concoction.

A miracle in which minimalism and technique create a divine offering.

Huevos Volcanus is pretty much the opposite of that. It starts with eggs roughly beaten with most of the shells plucked out. Whatever peppers are on hand get chopped up and scraped into them. The griddle jockey adds some other fluid roughly the viscosity of old motor oil, and then they usually toss in whatever crusty bits are tucked in the kitchen's corners just to add that crunchy surprise. Splashed into a pan last cleaned about the time the Clans came back to the Inner Sphere, it gets chucked into an oven. Cook knows it's done when the smoke coming from where it boils over sets off the fire alarm. After that the eggs just crawl onto what passes for a plate and the server who drew the short straw wrestles with them until plunking them down on the table.

That's when I usually drive a steak knife through 'em and start adding salt until the eggs just kinda quiver.

Oh, and toast.

So I'm sitting there, about to tuck into this masterpiece belching out steam that will melt eyebrows, when I hear, "Captain Hamilton, a word, if we may?"

Now on Galatea, if you look at the morbidity and mortality statistics, disturbing me at breakfast is solidly in the top ten causes of sudden death. And the words, offered softly, came in a voice I most commonly heard in nightmares.

I didn't even bother to look back over my shoulder because part of my breakfast was trying to twitch its way to freedom. "Got my money?"

"This is what we wish to speak with you about."

I recovered my knife and turned my chair a quarter of the way around. I wanted to keep an eye on *them* and my breakfast—I wasn't sure which one I distrusted most.

Mykaellie, turned out, had chosen a stylish suit of roughly the same gold-green hue as my eggs, with gloves, shoes, and—new for them—a snap-brimmed fedora to match. White shirt beneath, with an opalescent ascot that injected a little color into their pale skin tone. Hair hadn't grown much since last I saw them, but the fluorescent green had me thinking it was most likely a wig.

Even odds that I would have driven my knife straight through them, but standing there behind their shoulder was Lanie Chase, my cousin and pretty much the only decent person with Hamilton blood running through their veins. Brown hair and brown eyes, Lanie had an easy smile and an air about her suggesting she was an innocent young woman from the sticks visiting Galatean City for the very first time. Easy to like, definitely, but a demon driving a *Firestarter*. Plus she could have polished off every bottle back of the bar at Pedro's Grande Pig and Whist and would have been more sober than what passes as judges here.

I lowered the knife. "This better be good."

Lanie came around and sat across from me. She glanced at my meal, then gave Pedro the high sign. "Me too, but make it hot."

I growled and pointed Mykaellie to the seat beside my cousin. "It better be *really* good."

I wasn't sure what was worse: having my breakfast disturbed or having the two of them grinning at each other like school girls sharing a secret. Mykaellie I wouldn't have trusted to carry a dirty plate back to the kitchen, and Lanie usually had more sense than to fall for their line of patter—whatever it was this time. The fact they seemed thick as thieves now meant trouble, and even *if* Mykaellie was able to come across with my money, I'd have earned it yet one more time.

Lanie gave me her best grin—which wasn't fair, since she knew it would work. "I'm down Deep last night getting *Black Agnes* ready for some fun and games, and Mykaellie comes walking up. I don't immediately recognize them because it's a different look from when they were Missy at the Kentares Club. But they lead some people over to me and say, 'And you simply *must* meet Lanie Chase. This woman is amazing, puts on an incredible show, and is a sharp businesswoman. You'll be intent on wrangling up a group of MechWarriors who can follow orders and have the sort of equipment you need. She is definitely your girl.'"

I cut a tentacle off my eggs and started chewing on it before it congealed too much. "And?"

"So, they're a group of trideo producers scouting Galatean City for locations for a new trideo. And you'll never guess who is going to star." Lanie leaned in and lowered her voice. "Duncan Treat!"

Didn't ring a bell. Didn't even make a dead-body thump. "Who?"

Mykaellie shook their head. "Duncan Treat is simply the most bankable action star of this generation. His trideos have raked in more than the Capellan Confederation's Gross National Product this year or last. He is coming to Galatean City because he wants to remake and relaunch a seminal series of 'Mech-based trideo dramas. They will pour a lot of money into the local economy, and as the trideos spread throughout the Inner Sphere, the tourist economy will boom. It is not inconceivable that the publicity might even transform Galatea into a new Solaris VII."

I swallowed hard, trying to keep that bit of egg from clawing its way back up to freedom. "Save that pitch for suckers like Wheeler. Yeah, I know you're somehow working him to invest in this moving holo show, with you getting a cut going in and coming out."

"That's the point, Cousin." Lanie sat back as Pedro delivered her breakfast and it took one last, vengeful swipe at him. "Mykaellie's the one who got Wheeler and some of the other Kentares Clubbers to buy in, which is why the producers came all the way down the gravity well to scout things out. There's enough money on this rock willing to back this thing that the studio will see a profit before it ever gets shown anywhere."

"Too much money, too little sense." I covered a little burp. "'Nuff of that in evidence at the club. So, how are you planning to ruin my life with this?"

Lanie broke eye contact.

Mykaellie refused to meet my gaze as well, but kept the business edge in their voice. "Mr. Treat will write, direct, and star in the trivids. He is a Method actor who inhabits his characters fully. Moreover, he uses a modified version of the Method to research and write his holoplays."

I shoved my plate in Mykaellie's direction, but the eggs had cooled enough that they only twitched at my nemesis. "You want me to babysit some self-important, self-centered guy who plays 'Let's Pretend' to make a living? And having him happy and liking Galatean City is critical to your project getting off the ground? Have you met me? There is absolutely no way I would ever be so stupid as to agree to something like that."

You know how it is when, sometimes, you say something with concrete conviction and the half second it's out of your mouth you know someone else will shove it right back down your throat? Yeah.

So Mykaellie smiles and I know I'm doomed, but I'm not going down without a fight.

I pointed at them. "And I don't care how much my money is going to be quintupled or whatever with this deal. That's only money."

Mykaellie's smile broadened. "Do you really want us to let you continue? We have more rope here, but we think you've got quite enough to hang yourself already."

My eyes became slits. "You can't buy me."

"Oh, Quarrel, such a sweet summer child, Quarrel. Lanie told us money would never tempt you—confirming what we had seen in our association with you." They rested an elbow on the table, the treacle in their tone causing the *Huevos Volcanus* to slide to my side of the plate. "We only have your best interest at heart, dearest."

I closed my eyes. "Get it over with."

Mykaellie giggled. "Our friend, Mr. Wheeler, is not just investing *money* in the trideo. He's going to let us use the *Hatchetman*. And after the recording, we have a plan to make that *Hatchetman* yours."

I ran a hand over my chin. Ephram Wheeler, owner of one of the largest food conglomerates on Galatea, had hired me to get his youngest out of a spot of trouble. Doing that included the destruction of one of Wheeler's legion of homes, which would have been a blow to anyone's budget. However, during the mayhem, Wheeler managed to lay claim to a vintage *Hatchetman* which, by all laws of salvage, should have been mine.

"Are you sure? You guarantee it?" I leaned in, resting both elbows on the table. "I got a pretty good plan already myself, but if you guarantee it."

Mykaellie nodded once. "Guaranteed. It's as good as yours."

Despite that chill creeping bone by bone up my spine, I returned the nod. "Okay, you got yourself a babysitter. Now tell me exactly how bad it's going to be."

II

Anyone with half a brain cell would have used the week Treat was taking to get dirtside to watch some of his trideos. I'd get to know the client, could tailor my approach to him so I could stretch out the gig. But they were all streaming behind a paywall and Savannah, my resident computer genius, was off destabilizing a government somewhere, so I would've had to pay. That pissed me off. And it wasn't much to pay, but when your credit score and the average winter temp are interchangeable, well, that pissed me off more.

Then there was my feeling I'd been trapped into this thing by Mykaellie using Lanie against me, and that I *still* didn't have my money, and their dangling that damned *Hatchetman*—which should have been *mine*—in front of me, well, I was about to tell Duncan Treat where he could shove that 'Mech and I'd toss in a helping of *Huevos Volcanus* on me.

So I'd pretty much done everything I could do to forget he existed when this guy comes walking into the repair shop where I was rethreading myomer fibers on a hip actuator. Delicate business, especially if you want to come away with all of your fingers. The surgical arc suture you use to fuse fibers can cause the artificial muscles to contract. You only goof up like that once, then you're spending the rest of your life with folks calling you "Lefty."

"Mr. Hamilton..."

I didn't even look in his direction. "One more word, one step closer, and they'll be dragging you out of here in a body bag."

The man stood stock still.

My little cauterizer arced blue. Something popped—something tiny, not a finger—and a little puff of smoke curled up. I blew it away and couldn't even see a scar. I smiled because I still had the touch.

I wriggled back out of 'Mech's groin and sat up. I pulled off my welding goggles and looked at the guy. I opened my mouth, but he raised a hand to stop me.

"One more word, one step closer, and they'll be dragging you out of here in a body bag." His brows furrowed and he shook his head. "One more *word,* one more *step*... no, no. Can you give me the line again?"

"What?"

"Say it again, the way you did. Menace, but frustration and exhaustion worked in there. Not a straight threat, more of a warning, but clearly backed up." The clean-shaven man smiled easily, but concentration still wrinkled his forehead. "One more time."

I hesitated, then shrugged. "One more word, one step closer, and they'll be dragging you out of here in a body bag."

"Good, good, yeah, almost there." The man nodded, then interlaced his fingers and bridged them, stretching his arms out. "Okay, here goes: One more word, *one* step closer, and they'll be dragging you out of here in a body bag." He smiled infectiously, his blue eyes bright. "Nailed it."

"Huh." I tugged off my work gloves and chucked them aside. "You're the actor, then?"

He offered me his hand, and didn't even flinch when my mitt entombed his. "Duncan Treat. Mykaellie told me where to find you."

I shook his hand and didn't let go. "You know Mykaellie is using you to make a fortune for themself."

Treat chuckled. "Mr. Hamilton, I'm in the entertainment business. *Everybody* is out to make a fortune off me. If I couldn't spot them by now, I'd still be doing magic tricks at kiddie birthday parties and performing in community theater on the weekends."

"Okay." I released his hand. "What was it you were doing there?"

"Repeating what you said?" He scratched at his throat. "That probably did look a little odd. Fact is, I'm here to watch you, study you. This vid we're going to do, it's a remake of Constantine Fisk's *I, MechWarrior*, but it's more. I'll be the MechWarrior, and I want my portrayal to be realistic and gritty. So, what you said, that was a MechWarrior telling me to back off, and I wanted to remember what you said, but more importantly, *how* you said it. Then I internalize it, and I can deliver it in a way that will play as authentic in the trideo."

I grunted.

"And if I use that line, I'll get you a credit. Clearly already will, of course."

"Uh-huh." I stood up and towered over him by forty-five centimeters.

He craned his head back, and when I smiled, his complexion drained of most color. "And you will be paid for this consultation."

"Got it." I ran a hand over my unshaven jaw. "So, you want to follow me around for a day? Or do you want to know what really makes a MechWarrior tick?"

"Whatever will let me inhabit a MechWarrior's skin and reveal his internal emotional struggle to the waiting world."

"Oh, is that all?" I looked down at him and read an earnestness in his eyes one didn't much see down this end of Galatean City. I could blow this clown off and it wouldn't affect my immediate life much at all. But if I went along, *if* things happened the way Mykaellie said they would, life could get better for a number of people.

And I'll get my Hatchetman.

"I'll really appreciate whatever you choose to share with me, Mr. Hamilton."

"If we're working together, call me Quarrel." I pointed him toward the repair shop's door. "So the first thing we gotta do is start you off with a proper MechWarrior's breakfast."

"Thanks, but I've already eaten."

"Good for you. I haven't." I shrugged on a jacket. "Then we can work on that internal struggle stuff you want. And don't worry. I'll make it real for ya—all the real you can handle."

III

After breakfast, Duncan Treat, wearing a cap and some sunglasses to hide his identity, paused at the foot of the stairs and looked up. Blue eyes studied the place, measuring it. I figured for angles for the vid, not measuring what it really meant. He took it all in and, given the confidence on his mug, figured he could shoot it to convey everything from hope to dread.

"I don't believe it."

I paused halfway up the stairs. "I'm not big on believing either, but here we are."

He jogged up beside me. "Didn't have going to church on my list of things I figured you would do."

I could have told him that this was because he was seeing me through a societal lens that cast me as a mercenary, which meant I was without scruples, morals, or any sense of decency. In seeing me thusly, he was perpetuating the oligarchic stereotype that wholly justified the neo-feudalism that governs the Inner Sphere. Moreover, it equated lack of money with a lack of virtue, making it easy for men like Ephram Wheeler to not only see himself as economically superior to me, but likewise morally superior. It allowed Wheeler to forgive any crimes he might commit simply because if they were truly crimes—and therefore amoral—he would not be allowed to profit from them. Because he was rich, he was moral—with all the immorality trickling down to the lower classes.

I didn't say that because it might start Treat thinking other things, and that just would not do.

So I grunted. "MechWarriors are full of surprises." I kept my voice barely above a growl, and tossed some challenge into my comment.

On cue, he paused and mouthed the words. He continued, silently, until he smiled to himself, then met me at the cathedral's door. "The Cathedral of Saint Michael—patron saint of warriors."

I let a hand rest on the *Hermes* carved from the cathedral's stone flesh. "He's the biggie. Saint Martin, Saint George for those fighting the Dracs, Saint Barbara for missile boats, but Sebastian for *Archer* pilots; something for everyone here."

Treat removed his sunglasses. "They say there's no atheists in foxholes."

"Nor in a burned-out 'Mech cockpit."

I held the door open, then entered behind him. The door slowly closed, strangling the sunlight and leaving us in reverential darkness. I dipped my fingers and crossed myself. Treat caught the last of that and made a move to repeat what I'd done. Not in imitation of me, but out of half-forgotten reflex. He also pulled his cap off, and ducked his head as if half expecting to be smacked for having been so slow to do that.

"This is Saint Mike's. Lotta mercs buried here. Or listed."

"Listed?"

"Get your ticket punched with a headshot, and there'll be maybe a teaspoon of you left to bury." I wandered down the central aisle, genuflected near the altar, then hooked a right. Didn't know if he was following me and didn't care. I walked over to the ornate stone-scroll memorial built into the wall, with names engraved and highlighted in gold. Those were the dead of the Kell Hounds. Long list, but I didn't linger.

Instead, I stopped a few steps on, before a more modest display. Looked like the tablets Moses got from a burning bush. Had lots of names on it—primarily first initial and last name, but a few had paid for having their call signs worked in there. No unit name because they'd all been true mercenaries. They worked for themselves, doing the jobs units like the Hounds or the Light Horse wouldn't.

And about the only good stuff in their contracts was a clause that had their employers agreeing to see to it they'd have their names carved into one of those tablets.

Treat kept his voice respectful. "Did you know many of them?"

"These folks, no, don't think so." I stared for a moment longer, then shook my head. "It just reminds you that sometimes, having your name scratched on a rock is all you're ever gonna get in life. And you sure as hell don't want your mistake to be the reason a friend has their name scrawled here."

Treat glanced up at me. "But you don't mind causing someone else to have *their* name 'scratched on a rock' if it means a friend doesn't, right?"

I let my hands curl into white-knuckled fists. "There's no virtue in smearing someone else into a paste. No honor. Maybe some relief because you're not paste. The whole romance of combat and MechWarriors is bullshit."

"It's fantasy."

"It's why those names are there." I pressed my right hand against the tablets. "Because of what you do, because of some novelist churning out suspense stories to thrill bored commuters, a fantasy that should have died long ago just gallops forward. You know, somewhere out there, there's some teenage girl finding a 'Mech in a jungle and suddenly realizing her calling is to be a MechWarrior. She wants to help people. And maybe she does. Once. Twice. Finds some other folks who have the same dream. Great, gallant career going, then some Clan Khan sends troops stumbling in their direction. One terrible, swift firefight later, and a guy's here chiseling more names on this rock."

The actor's expression slackened for a moment, then he glanced down, his voice soft. "I don't want you to think I'm glorifying war..."

"I don't care."

"Then what?"

"You missed my point." I traced a thumb over one of the names. "A merc always knows someone just like him was behind that name. Hopes. Dreams. Good times. Bad times. The worst times. You never forget. You can try, but you can never forget."

"It's a burden."

"It's a *debt*. One can never pay it off. It's with you always." My hand fell to my side. "You always remember they're human. They're *you*. And you do for them as you'd have them do for you."

Treat turned away and slid into one of the pews. He lowered the kneeler and dropped to his knees. He even crossed himself and bent his head in prayer. At least, I'm pretty sure that's what he was doing. If he was just playacting, he should have been making better films and winning awards, because this audience of one bought the sincerity.

While he did his thing, I returned to the entrance and lit a few candles. Always lit one more than the list of folks I could remember, just in case someone slipped my mind. In case I *had* somehow forgotten. Wasn't that I believed in the candles' magic, but they had. Most of them, anyway. Those who hadn't would appreciate the irony.

I was just standing there watching flames dance when Treat joined me. "You need more time?"

I shook my head.

"A somber lesson, Quarrel." He frowned. "One I won't forget."

I turned and pushed the door open, sunlight and street sounds desecrating the church. I held the door for him, letting the sun burn the chill out of my soul.

He smiled and pulled his cap back on. "Where to now?"

I shrugged. "New lesson. Old warrior from Terra, some guy from Corsica, once said 'Armies march on their stomachs.'"

"Food, now?" Treat's eyes widened. "Your breakfast, those, ah, *volcano eggs*, you can't possibly be hungry again so soon."

"Think like a merc. You think I want those to be my last meal?"

"No. No, I suppose not."

"Right answer. A merc never refuses food, especially a *free* meal."

The actor arched an eyebrow. "And it's a free meal because I'm paying?"

"Again, think like a merc, man." I settled a heavy hand on the back of his neck. "You're a merc. Your patron covers your expenses."

"And that would be?"

I squeezed my hand just a little. "Ephram Wheeler. Give him a call. I'm sure he'd love to see how things are going with his new investment."

IV

Wheeler looks like the love child of Gluttony and Hubris. He's secure in the belief that he's smarter than he really is. The man's an ethical shark in the body of a goldfish, and he knows he's at the top of the food chain. On Galatea, he's khan of all he surveyed, but sitting in the Wok and Locust, he had the whole fish-out-of-water thing going. And he was doing his best to pretend it didn't bother him at all.

Treat called him and suggested we get together for lunch. Though I couldn't hear the other side of the conversation, I knew how it would go. Wheeler would first protest he couldn't come on such short notice, then would suggest lunch at his club or some swanky place. Treat must have anticipated him, because he neatly parried that second thrust, saying, "That won't do. I'm researching my character. We need a fitting place." Then he looked at me.

I gave him a thumbs up and suggested the Wok and Locust.

Treat convinced Wheeler no other place would do, so Wheeler agreed to humble himself within an hour.

I don't know what Wok and Locust was originally, other than a run-down incubation facility for *E. coli*, but back around the time Saint Mike's had been little more than a chapel, someone with a serious love for the venerable *Locust* decided to open a restaurant. Some folks say it was an old 'Mech driver who started selling food to earn enough to refurb the family's *Locust*. Better cook than she was a pilot, she built up a clientele who would sit and eat in the shadow of the *Locust* that still stands on the lot's corner. Local legend has it starving MechWarriors would sabotage the *Locust* just so she wouldn't leave.

Everyone also knew if you were a *Locust* pilot down on your luck—which is pretty much the description of *any Locust* pilot—you could always catch a free meal there. Pilots kept the place alive, brought in mementos of battles from all over the Inner Sphere. Some folks painted murals, others built models and dioramas of *Locust*s and dropped them off for safekeeping. Over half the tables had wooden *Locust*s as bases, with old windscreens repurposed as tabletops.

The food...well, as I said, the original owner had been a better cook than driver. And she must have been a *really* bad driver. Over the years the quality had risen, or so I'm told. What that means is that real basic food—bland sausages, watery beans, and boiled burgers on semi-stale buns—got drowned in every spicy sauce known to man. I always ordered my food with "CapCon and a splash of Scorcher," just to keep things balanced.

Wheeler, total white bread, ordered his Tharkad Gravy on the side, then never even glanced at it. Treat got a bit more adventurous, going for Hair of the Dragon, but then he ruined it by asking for a salad. They tossed a wilted leaf of a kale-ish thing over his lunch, and I began wondering if I'd ever be able to show my face in the place again.

Wheeler wanted to be the boss-man, but Duncan Treat was the big entertainment star. Wheeler did make it known that I worked for him—or had worked for him. He called me "Captain Hamilton," and once—only once—called me by my first name. My scowl cut off that line of inquiry, and Treat took it all in. From the start, he pegged Wheeler as a guy who was proud of everything he had accomplished in life, but who desperately wanted to be like either one of us.

Treat gave Wheeler a dazzling smile. "I'm so glad you were able to join us, Ephram."

"Yes, yes, me too." The large man sighed. "And I'm sure the staff can pack for me without supervision. Want to get out of town early, beat the weekend traffic, you understand."

"Completely."

"So you have to answer a question for me, Duncan." Wheeler wanted to sit back, but wasn't sure he could trust the chair surviving such an assault. "All the preliminary negotiations, no one ever mentioned why you came to Galatea, and why you want to remake *I, MechWarrior*. I mean, there are so many vids you could have chosen."

"Ephram, you see through things, don't you?" Duncan patted the prosperous grocery merchant on the arm. "I knew that about you. It's obvious. You see that too, don't you, Quarrel?"

I looked Wheeler up and down. "I've always been amazed at our friend's perception."

Wheeler tried to look sly. "Well, I will admit—"

"It's this way, Ephram." Treat cut him off so easily Wheeler hardly noticed. "When I was a boy, things were not always good. Not a lot of money. I'd retreat into a world of fantasy. Graphic novels. Regular novels. And trideo. I fell in love with the dramas Constantine Fisk made, so I read up about him. Fascinating man. Aside from his *MechWarrior* series reimagining and reshaping adventure trideo, he was more than an actor. Director, sure. Writer, sure. He did his own stunts, too; and in all those dramas *he drove his own 'Mechs*. To get the content right, he even spent time out here as part of a mercenary-bandit group."

Wheeler blinked. "I didn't know that."

"Nobody does, really. Some say he even ran up against Prince Ian Davion and was there when the Kell Hounds were founded. All fragments of stories, most of them buried by Quintus Allard when he was running the Federated Suns' intelligence apparatus. Some of the stories even have hints of murder and treasure—very much the legendary stuff that Fisk clearly fed back into his work."

Treat spread his arms. "That is why I'm here. I grew up with Constantine Fisk saving my life, making me believe in dreams. Now that I've achieved my dream, it's time to repay the man who led me here. And, because he shot vids on location here, we've returned to revisit those locations. It's a labor of love, and I can't thank the both of you enough for making it a reality."

Wheeler beamed as if Treat had just thanked him for curing the scourge of crotch-rot. "I know something about having dreams come true, too. That's why I'm going to contribute more than just money here—and, of course, take care of all your catering needs during the shoot. As Captain Hamilton knows, I've recently acquired and refurbished a *Hatchetman*, which you'll be free to use in the production. It's a beauty, isn't it, Captain?"

'Cept for the fact that I'd already finished my lunch, I'd have drowned that smug prick in Scorch. I counted to ten—and aborted that effort at about three. "Oh, yes, I remember a little something about that. It was *special*."

Treat squeezed Wheeler's forearm and the purest note of sincerity slid like a dagger into his voice. "Ephram, I know the only way we'll succeed in making our production is with your support. Thank you, my friend."

"I'll do all I can do."

"I know you will." Treat nodded solemnly. "Unfortunately, that means you're going to have to excuse the two of us. Quarrel has a lot more to teach me. This man...well, you already know how invaluable he is."

"Absolutely. He's a lifesaver." Wheeler rose from the table. "We will have to do this again, next week, when I'm back in town."

"I can't wait. Just have your people call mine."

"Done. And, Captain Hamilton, please convey my best wishes to Mykaellie. They've been very helpful in this deal." Wheeler flashed teeth. "In fact, if you're not careful, I might just hire them away from your Death Kangaroos."

I tossed Wheeler a wink. "Just remember, I know where you live." I added a smile, which generally makes crocodiles look good by comparison, but kept my voice flat. Joke or threat, who's to know? *Until it's too late.*

Treat watched Wheeler disappear into the mid-afternoon sunshine, then turned to me. "He really doesn't have a clue, does he?"

"He's the smartest cow in the herd." I shrugged. "Long as I'm smart enough to get milk and cheese without shedding blood, I don't care if he thinks he's King Genius of Galatea."

"'Smartest cow in the herd.' I like that." Duncan Treat slowly nodded. "So, how about you show me where the wolves hide out on this rock."

"Thought you'd never ask." I stood, almost banging my head on a *Locust* model hanging down from the ceiling in a DFA pose. "It's time we go Deep."

V

Treat probably figured I meant we'd have a soul-baring conversation where I'd reveal the traumas of my life that explained why I am who I am today. That would have taken some heavy lifting, since I've never done that, and don't see how it would do me any good. Knowing how and why I'd gotten to my place in life wouldn't do a damned thing to change where I was. And despite what a lot of folks told themselves, it wouldn't point me to a way to change things.

Not everything broken can be set right again.

So no sense in delving into all of that with someone who was going to take whatever I gave him and display it for billions in his vid. My life wasn't the stuff someone could make into beautiful interpretive dance, so no reason to get his hopes up. I could spoon-feed him all he needed to know to do his job, and I didn't feel terribly motivated to do much more than that.

The *Hatchetman* notwithstanding.

Dusk was coming on a bit early, aided by thunderclouds heading our way. I got Treat back to the shop before any storms broke, rigged a jump seat in the *Commando*'s cockpit, and got him all strapped in. "There you go. Comfy?"

"Jump seats aren't usually in light 'Mech cockpits, are they?"

"I do a lot of kids' birthday parties—'first 'Mech ride,' that kind of thing."

He pointed toward the cockpit canopy. "But if you have to eject..."

"Explosive bolts will blow the screen out." I didn't add that he'd probably leave an arm or a leg behind as we scraped through the opening, but then the chances of us punching out hovered around the same as Mykaellie ever fully paying me my money. "Just hang on if that happens."

I buckled myself in, then handed him a pair of refurbed virtual reality goggles. They spliced into the targeting system, so he'd see exactly what I did when I fired up the combat sensor array. I pulled on the neurohelmet, settling it on the insufficiently padded collar of my cooling vest, and snapped the leads into the plugs at its throat. They led to sensor pads on my arms and legs. Once clipped together, they let the computers use my sense of balance to adjust the 'Mech's gyro, which is critical to keeping the *Commando* upright.

"Shouldn't I have a cooling vest?"

"We're not gonna be running hot." I jerked a thumb at the footlocker strapped on top of my command couch's ejection jets. "Some shorts and a T-shirt in there, if you want to keep your clothes from getting damp."

"Yeah, let me think." His voice drifted off for a moment. "When you mentioned going Deep…"

"This ain't a confessional, and you're not a priest." I punched up the ignition code and my monitors sprang to life. This included a 160-degree holograph that gave me a full 360-degree view of the 'Mech's surroundings. I kept heat levels on the secondary monitor and my weapons status on the auxiliary monitor. The short-range missiles in the six-pack reported zero loads. The quad launchers had two loads of fireworks left over from Timmy Fujimori's birthday. The medium laser on the humanoid 'Mech's left forearm showed up in green, but reported it was set for 10 percent power.

"When I said 'going Deep,' I meant a place. The place your producers met Lanie."

"Why do you want me to see it?"

"Seeing isn't what it's about." I almost added, "You'll see," but that would have been me being clever. Not my strong suit. "Where do you think most MechWarriors get their rides?"

"Do a stint in the military and… No, wait." Treat grew silent as we left the shop and headed southwest, toward Deep and the incoming storm. "If you're serving in the military, any salvage you got would belong to the unit. If you're a merc, you'd own it…"

"…depending on your contract."

"Right. And even if you did get a 'Mech as salvage for an engagement, it's chicken and egg. Where did you get the 'Mech you were in to win the salvage?" Treat's voice faded. "Where did you get this *Commando*?"

I smiled because Treat couldn't see it. "This ride came off the Coventry Metal Works line in 2875. It's seen action in the Commonwealth and the Combine, even fought against the Clans. It's been blown to scrap at least twice and rebuilt at least three times. Last time was here, about fifty years ago. Woman who left it to be rebuilt never returned to the shop, never paid for the repairs, so my family took possession. My grandfather drove it until he traded up for something better. Now I use it."

"So you're saying they *inherit* their machines."

"'Mechs aren't things you just buy off the rack."

Treat shifted around in the jump seat as we headed out of town. Galatean City—like most large urban areas—had roads that could handle war machines and their little industrial cousins. Hovercar traffic kept to other, daintier roads—with the exception of the occasional moron that thought running a slalom course between a 'Mech's legs was a surefire way to get laid.

Route 417 similarly segregated traffic as it headed toward the mountains, so folks in Wheeler's class could get to their weekend homes with all necessary speed. Traffic soon became strings of gold and red lights heading this way or that while 'Mechs played pedestrian, trudging along on access roads. The occasional spur road headed south or west, directing traffic to their final destinations.

Deep used to be a thing known as Blackwood Mountain. When Galatea's mining magnates turned the world's *outie* into an *innie*, Galatean City decided to use the resulting void as a landfill. After a couple decades of fermenting, gas built up, exploded, and started the dump burning. Authorities have pretty much given up trying to put out the blaze, so folks built the place into their own amusement park. They themed it on Dante's Inferno. Down in the Ninth Circle, 'Mechs battled for pink slips. Somewhere up on the Fourth, a bunch of kids worshipped Lanie's *Black Agnes* as if the *Firestarter* was a brass incarnation of some cruel goddess.

"So your family has had this *Commando* for fifty years? But it's been in action for over two and a half centuries."

"There's many more that have been around for far longer. Handed down generation to generation. The new pilots know the history. They know the names of every one of their kin who died fighting in it. They know where it's fought. They see the worn spots, the dents, hear the creaks and groans, knowing their blood has experienced all the same things."

"Oh." The actor lapsed into silence again.

For a half second, I thought that was because the storm plowed into us right about then. The hiss of dust playing over the canopy lasted for a heartbeat, cutting normal visibility to nothing. Then sheeting rain lashed the *Commando*. I glanced at the canopy, happy to see the patch

I'd done on the seals wasn't going to fail immediately. Lightning flashed nearby, and the resulting thundercrack shook us.

Treat scratched at the back of his head. "So they'd know their family history. Who'd won medals, and who had been dishonored. They'd know who killed their kin. They'd want revenge, or at least to redeem the family name."

"Man, you're so close."

"Meaning?"

"Revenge. Redemption. Those are high-ticket items. The Kells have more money than God. They can afford those things. Most mercs find paying for a bowl at Wok and Locust to be a stretch. Remember, the person who wanted to have this 'Mech repaired never came back for it. The old owner died out there, somewhere, hoping to scratch together enough cash to get back where I'm sitting."

"I can see that, Quarrel, but grubbing around for scraps doesn't a very exciting vid make."

"That's what you're not getting, all due respect." I twisted around in the couch to look at him. "Why would anyone work for nothing to put together a war machine that could be blasted to bits in the blink of an eye?"

"Revenge. Redemption. Family. Honor." Treat pulled the VR goggles off and stared at me. "But we've already said a merc can't afford those things when they're just trying to survive. Which leads us back... It's a circle..."

"No, it's not. You just see it as a circle."

"I don't know how else to see it..."

Which is why you're an entertainer... Why you live through other people's lives... I couldn't decide how I wanted to deliver that news to him. Cold and cruel, he'd walk away no matter how much he thought he owed Constantine Fisk. Friendly, and he'd never believe what I was telling him.

And maybe it wasn't something that could even be told, but had to be lived.

Before I could begin to wrestle with that tangle, a massive lightning bolt burned silver-white off to the left. Thick as a city block, shooting off forks that stabbed there and there and there. The thunder bounced the *Commando* back a half step and, despite my having the neurohelmet on, started my ears ringing.

Then something exploded. Small, golden burst. Then another and another, like a belt of ammo lighting off. More explosions, this time with golden highlights. Another lightning spear stabbed down, and silver tentacles raced off it.

"What?!"

"Serious trouble." I punched up the cousins' frequency. "Lanie, you in *Aggie*?"

Even before she'd have a chance to reply, I brought the *Commando* around and headed toward the highway. I flicked on my external running lights—not because I needed them to see, but so others would know something big was incoming.

Treat grabbed my shoulder. "Talk to me, Quarrel."

I wasn't sure what good talking would do, since everything seemed obvious. "Put your goggles back on. Glance lower-right corner, change the view to IR—the little fire icon."

"Oh my God, everything's on fire."

Yeah, probably looks that way to the goggles. "Not everything, but plenty is."

"What are we going to do?"

Another vehicle exploded in the distance. "I, um, I...I have to drop you off first."

The hand on my shoulder squeezed. "No, man, just go. Fast as you can." No ghoulish glee in his voice, no fascinated gasping, just the right amount of horror and urgency. "So much fire..."

"It's a mess in there. I should—"

"No, Quarrel, two sets of eyes are better than one, right?"

"Sure. See anybody? Tell me."

"Headings on the top of the screen, range on the side."

"Right." I nodded as I kicked the 'Mech up to full speed. "Just stay on IR, look for silhouettes."

"Got it."

I flicked the holographic display over to vislight because of reasons. I shouldn't have, because it wouldn't help. I could only guess what had caused the flaming pileup, and that pegged the perp as one of those morons who figured *they* could drive just fine with zero visibility even if no one else could. Probably was late and had been pregaming, just to make things fun. They'd raced their hovercar into a pack of vehicles that had prudently slowed. The speeding car used a family sedan as a launching pad, crushing that vehicle and everyone in it. The hovercar flew about thirty meters, then arced down into a propane tanker that had cars clustered around it like goslings around the mother goose.

The explosion, the collisions, the static electricity building up, just teased that first bolt from the sky. Mangled vehicles, twisted as if giant hands had wrung all the life out of them, smoldered ten and twenty meters from the roadway. Fragments pinged off the *Commando* as more hovercars exploded. I headed toward the nearest intact vehicle, seeing a terrified child clutching a dog, their faces pressed to the window.

Then another lightning bolt and they evaporated.

That bolt fried my forward sensors. I stopped. I couldn't... Any place my *Commando*'s feet could land, I saw that kid and the dog just lying there and I'd... *Going in blind is...*

You won't be blind if you open your eyes.

I did. The lack of sensors didn't matter. The fire created enough light to lay the hellscape out in all its glory. People trapped in cars, bodies strewn over the roadway, one man stumbling naked through the storm, flames flickering and lightning slicing the night with silver. An explosion flipped a vehicle end over end like a coin. It landed, crushing the life out of another car as easily as if I'd stomped on them both.

I made it to the roadway and grabbed the first wrecked hovercar I could. Calling it a charred husk would have been generous. I had my *Commando* grab it by the nose. I would have tossed it aside, but I couldn't see that guy who'd been wandering around in the darkness. Instead I dragged it off the 417, clearing a path.

"Quarrel, over there." Treat leaned forward, pointing toward the right. "Thirty meters maybe. Family van, I think."

I brought the 'Mech around. Family van, back end jacked up onto the hood of the sporty model behind it. Couldn't see through the little car's cracked windscreen to assess how the passengers there were doing. The van had one adult in the front, a kid in a child's seat behind, and maybe a teenager in that row, too.

"Got it, but I don't see a way clear to it."

Treat came up out of the jump seat and stood in front of me. "Let me out."

"What, no, you can't."

"Quarrel, let me out. I can be your eyes down there. Take this thing down to a knee. I'll go out and help."

"Are you crazy? There's fire. Lightning!"

He just shook his head. "Not any better for them out there."

"I can't." I stared at him through the neurohelmet's little viewport. "You're my responsibility..."

"Quarrel, I do all my own stunts." He jerked a thumb at the windscreen. "I'll be on the ground, you do as I say."

I froze for a heartbeat, then nodded as best I could. "Radio in the locker behind me. Set it to tac two."

"Tac two, got you." He gently tapped me on the helmet. "We'll make this work."

I brought the *Commando* down to a knee. Treat, radio in hand, exited through the escape port on the neck and raced down to the 'Mech's wrist. From there he leaped to the ground and scrambled up an incline to the van.

"Okay, Quarrel, we've got three, two back seat. One in the front. But he's not driving so there's got to be someone behind the wheel."

"Okay. Give me a sec. Anything starts to go wrong, you tell me *immediately*, right?"

"Roger."

I had two choices. The first was to carry the van off the road. For the *Commando*, it would be roughly the same sort of burden as hauling a sack of potatoes. Problem was, it could also be a big bomb. Didn't matter what was fueling it—battery, hydrogen cell, or some kind of hydrocarbon—if it went up, it wasn't gonna do the passengers or my 'Mech any favors.

I opted for Plan B. I reached out with the 'Mech's right hand. With thumb and forefinger I pinched the front passenger door, crumpling it. That I slid back away from the road with a flick of the 'Mech's wrist, as if I was dealing cards. In the van's front seat a man with blood running freely from a scalp cut stared up at me. He tore at his seatbelt, then turned toward the driver's position, waving desperately with his right hand.

"What does he expect me to do, peel the roof off?"

"No, Quarrel, he's going for the driver. Don't worry. I got him."

Treat got the adult out of the van, had me take the back door off so they could free the kids, then Treat went back for the driver. Dragged him free and wrangled a few other folks to help, as the guy's leg looked pretty well shattered.

Soaking wet, Treat went from vehicle to vehicle, waving me over and telling me what had to be done. We went up and down the line, helping as best as we could.

Reinforcements arrived soon enough. Lanie and some of the other folks from Deep had started over even before I sent out that first call. Scrapyard 'Mechs driven by folks who demolished things for fun seemed pretty unlikely as a rescue crew, but as Lanie pointed out, all of them *did* have megatons of experience tearing things apart: "Making insides into outsides is what we do for fun."

Rain slacked off fairly fast, and emergency services vehicles got out to the site quickly enough. The local constabulary got a bit testy about my having moved vehicles around, as did a later horde of insurance adjusters. In fact, the local government would have been happy to cite all the Deep denizens who came to help out, and then confiscate their 'Mechs to satisfy claims for damages to the vehicles. Luckily, Duncan Treat had a word with Ephram Wheeler, who had a talk with his buddy, the governor of Galatea. Some Good Samaritan law got cited, so the various lawyers were left to fight among themselves, and for once, the defenders of the Golden Rule ruled in our favor.

That little favor Duncan Treat did was the only publicity he got out of the 417 Meltdown, as it became known. A few survivors swore he'd helped them, that they recognized him, but when folks told him he was Duncan Treat, he'd just smiled and said, "Thanks. I get that a lot, but he's much taller."

Those of us who knew didn't see any reason to contradict his denials.

The night of the meltdown, I'd dragged him back to town half-drowned. We didn't talk on the way back, and after changing into some drier duds at the shop, he vanished for a couple days. I didn't think about it much. Wouldn't let myself. *Done is done.*

When I did—in those two minutes brushing my teeth at night where running water reminded me—I figured Treat went somewhere to detox, dry out, or center himself—whatever celebrities do when they get a snootful of a world they didn't want to meet.

About a week later, I was at Pedro's, staring at a plate of Satan's Scrapple, trying to figure out what ungodly creature contributed the alleged protein, when he waltzes in. Looks pretty much the same, save he'd not shaved since I last saw. He'd slept more than I had—or his skin care regimen was better than mine—and gave me an easy smile.

He set a package on the table. "The stuff I borrowed. It's been laundered."

"First time for everything."

Treat laughed. "I wanted to see you before I left."

"Scrapping the *I, MechWarrior* remake in favor of the true-life drama of the Meltdown?"

"My people were in favor of that. They said we could shift it to Tharkad and turn it into an incident that got Phelan Kell kicked out of the Nagelring. They think there's some nostalgia for the Clan era, so we could do a series." He shook his head. "Clans are old news, and will stay that way until Terra falls—like that will ever happen."

I rapped knuckles on the table. "So if the Fisk remake is still going to happen, why are you leaving?"

"It's your fault, really."

I thrust a fist into the air. "And still the undefeated champion of screwing things up." Mykaellie wasn't going to be happy, but that's a them problem. Not like I didn't warn them about getting me involved.

"No, no, not that way." Treat sat forward, elbows on the table, hands clasped together. "You asked me if I wanted a 'day in the life', or if I really wanted to know what made a MechWarrior tick."

"And you think you got it? I mean, we did pack a lot into our day, but..."

"Not sure I got 'it' exactly, but I got a lot of things." He opened his hands and started counting things off on his fingers. "You made things clear—the life of the average merc is crap. You have a legion of ghosts haunting you. Friends you've lost, people you've killed, people you failed to save. That I got from the church. Then, from the 'Mechs themselves, you've got a pedigree where you're trying to keep up with what someone did a couple of centuries ago, or trying to redeem your family and your 'Mech from what they failed to do. You know you're constantly being judged, and you also know the likely best outcome of everything is that someone carves your name into the memorial at Saint Mike's."

I stabbed my scrapple with a fork just to pin it down. "Well, there you go."

"No." His blue eyes narrowed. "That's what everyone else would settle for, but it's a circle. You pointed that out, and I would have been stuck there wondering why the hell would anyone do this? Why would anyone endure grinding poverty just to walk into a battle where glory is a fantasy and pain is the payoff?"

"Mental illness is a popular answer to that question."

"A wrong one, though, I think."

"Read up on Wayne Waco."

The actor tapped a finger on the table. "You're glib. Irreverent. You growl a lot to keep people back and away. Convince yourself you don't care."

"Is this the part where you tell me that I do care for humanity, deep down, and I have a tender heart because I feel all the pain, but don't dare show it?" I shook my head. "Next you'll pull the doll out and ask me to point to where the bad man hurt me."

"No, Quarrel, because that's not you. You know who that is? That's every hero in every half-assed attempt at getting what you showed me." His hands curled down into fists, then he forced them open and flat against the table. "People who do that, who hide their pain, they're the ones who lash out when *they* get hurt; when their best friend gets hurt. It's a cliché that was old before Homer started writing down the *Odyssey*."

Treat looked me straight in the eye. "When that lightning hit, when those explosions started, you got angry, you lashed out, not because of some injustice done to you and yours, but because an injustice *was being done*. Your day might have been shit. Your life might be going to shit, but in that moment in time, if you acted, you could stop someone *else's* life from going to shit. And by doing that, you can tell all your ancestors and all your ghosts and anyone judging you that right then, right there, you're making life better for somebody.

"And for the love of God, I hope I'm right, otherwise you and every other mercenary out there is trapped in a hellish cycle I wouldn't wish on anyone, not even Stefan Amaris."

He didn't sit back as others would have done and asked me to grade him on his effort. His gaze flicked over my face, trying to read my reaction, but only for a heartbeat or three. Then he half smiled. "At least, that's what I got from you. I don't think it's everything…"

My hesitation in the cockpit burst back into my brain. *You know it's not everything.*

Treat studied me. If he got more than what he had, I couldn't tell. His smile broadened. "It's a lot. You gave me a lot to digest. You know, gotta try it on for size, and figure out how to make it work in a vid."

I nodded. "You got your work cut out for you."

"I do." He got up from his seat and pulled on his sunglasses. "Hey, ah, if I ever need to do more research?"

I looked him up and down, then nodded again. "You know where I live."

BATTLETECH ERAS

The *BattleTech* universe is a living, vibrant entity that grows each year as more sourcebooks and fiction are published. A dynamic universe, its setting and characters evolve over time within a highly detailed continuity framework, bringing everything to life in a way a static game universe cannot match.

To help quickly and easily convey the timeline of the universe—and to allow a player to easily "plug in" a given novel or sourcebook—we've divided *BattleTech* into eight major eras.

STAR LEAGUE
(Present–2780)

Ian Cameron, ruler of the Terran Hegemony, concludes decades of tireless effort with the creation of the Star League, a political and military alliance between all Great Houses and the Hegemony. Star League armed forces immediately launch the Reunification War, forcing the Periphery realms to join. For the next two centuries, humanity experiences a golden age across the thousand light-years of human-occupied space known as the Inner Sphere. It also sees the creation of the most powerful military in human history.

(This era also covers the centuries before the founding of the Star League in 2571, most notably the Age of War.)

SUCCESSION WARS
(2781–3049)

Every last member of First Lord Richard Cameron's family is killed during a coup launched by Stefan Amaris. Following the thirteen-year war to unseat him, the rulers of each of the five Great Houses disband the Star League. General Aleksandr Kerensky departs with eighty percent of the Star League Defense Force beyond known space and the Inner Sphere collapses into centuries of warfare known as the Succession Wars that will eventually result in a massive loss of technology across most worlds.

CLAN INVASION
(3050–3061)

A mysterious invading force strikes the coreward region of the Inner Sphere. The invaders, called the Clans, are descendants of Kerensky's SLDF troops, forged into a society dedicated to becoming the greatest fighting force in history. With vastly superior technology and warriors, the Clans conquer world after world. Eventually this outside threat will forge a new Star League, something hundreds of years of warfare failed to accomplish. In addition, the Clans will act as a catalyst for a technological renaissance.

CIVIL WAR
(3062–3067)

The Clan threat is eventually lessened with the complete destruction of a Clan. With that massive external threat apparently neutralized, internal conflicts explode around the Inner Sphere. House Liao conquers its former Commonality, the St. Ives Compact; a rebellion of military units belonging to House Kurita sparks a war with their powerful border enemy, Clan Ghost Bear; the fabulously powerful Federated Commonwealth of House Steiner and House Davion collapses into five long years of bitter civil war.

JIHAD
(3067–3080)
Following the Federated Commonwealth Civil War, the leaders of the Great Houses meet and disband the new Star League, declaring it a sham. The pseudo-religious Word of Blake—a splinter group of ComStar, the protectors and controllers of interstellar communication—launch the Jihad: an interstellar war that pits every faction against each other and even against themselves, as weapons of mass destruction are used for the first time in centuries while new and frightening technologies are also unleashed.

DARK AGE
(3081-3150)
Under the guidance of Devlin Stone, the Republic of the Sphere is born at the heart of the Inner Sphere following the Jihad. One of the more extensive periods of peace begins to break out as the 32nd century dawns. The factions, to one degree or another, embrace disarmament, and the massive armies of the Succession Wars begin to fade. However, in 3132 eighty percent of interstellar communications collapses, throwing the universe into chaos. Wars erupt almost immediately, and the factions begin rebuilding their armies.

ILCLAN
(3151-present)
The once-invulnerable Republic of the Sphere lies in ruins, torn apart by the Great Houses and the Clans as they wage war against each other on a scale not seen in nearly a century. Mercenaries flourish once more, selling their might to the highest bidder. As Fortress Republic collapses, the Clans race toward Terra to claim their long-denied birthright and create a supreme authority that will fulfill the dream of Aleksandr Kerensky and rule the Inner Sphere by any means necessary: The ilClan.

CLAN HOMEWORLDS
(2786-present)
In 2784, General Aleksandr Kerensky launched Operation Exodus, and led most of the Star League Defense Force out of the Inner Sphere in a search for a new world, far away from the strife of the Great Houses. After more than two years and thousands of light years, they arrived at the Pentagon Worlds. Over the next two-and-a-half centuries, internal dissent and civil war led to the creation of a brutal new society—the Clans. And in 3049, they returned to the Inner Sphere with one goal—the complete conquest of the Great Houses.

SUBMISSION GUIDELINES

Shrapnel is the market for official short fiction set in the *BattleTech* universe.

WHAT WE WANT

We are looking for stories of **3,000–5,000 words** that are character-oriented, meaning the characters, rather than the technology, provide the main focus of the action. Stories can be set in any established *BattleTech* era, and although we prefer stories where BattleMechs are featured, this is by no means a mandatory element.

WHAT WE DON'T WANT

The following items are generally grounds for immediate disqualification:

- Stories not set in the *BattleTech* universe. There are other markets for these stories.

- Stories centering solely on romance, supernatural, fantasy, or horror elements. If your story isn't primarily military sci-fi, then it's probably not for us.

- Stories containing gratuitous sex, gore, or profanity. Keep it PG-13, and you should be fine.

- Stories under 3,000 words or over 5,000 words. We don't publish flash fiction, and although we do publish works longer than 5,000 words, these are reserved for established *BattleTech* authors.

- Vanity stories, which include personal units, author-as-character inserts, or tabletop game sessions retold in narrative form.

- Publicly available *BattleTech* fan-fiction. If your story has been posted in a forum or other public venue, then we will not accept it.

- Multi-part stories. Your story must be a self-contained stand-alone story with a clear ending, not Part 1 of a series

- Stories that go beyond the current timeline in published *BattleTech* products. As of this writing, any stories set after June 3152 will be automatically rejected.

MANUSCRIPT FORMAT

- .rtf, .doc, .docx formats ONLY
- 12-point Times New Roman, Cambria, or Palatino fonts ONLY
- 1" (2.54 cm) margins all around
- Double-spaced lines
- DO NOT put an extra space between each paragraph
- Filename: "Submission Title by Jane Q. Writer"

PAYMENT & RIGHTS

We pay $0.06 per word after publication. By submitting to *Shrapnel*, you acknowledge that your work is set in an owned universe and that you retain no rights to any of the characters, settings, or "ideas" detailed in your story. We purchase **all rights** to every published story; those rights are automatically transferred to The Topps Company, Inc.

SUBMISSIONS PORTAL

To send us a submission, visit our submissions portal here:
https://pulsepublishingsubmissions.moksha.io/publication/shrapnel-the-battletech-magazine-fiction

BATTLETECH™

SEIZE YOUR DESTINY!

As shockwaves from the Battle for Terra ripple across the Inner Sphere, new leaders stake their claim and forge their own destinies. Take command in this bold new era and begin your campaign with the *ilClan* sourcebook and *Tamar Rising*, *available now*, and *Empire Alone*, *coming soon*!

Printed in Great Britain
by Amazon

59675414R10126